Jozua Marius Willem van der Poorten Schwartz

**My Lady Nobody**

A novel

Jozua Marius Willem van der Poorten Schwartz

**My Lady Nobody**
*A novel*

ISBN/EAN: 9783337028251

Printed in Europe, USA, Canada, Australia, Japan

Cover: Foto ©Andreas Hilbeck / pixelio.de

More available books at **www.hansebooks.com**

# MY LADY NOBODY

A NOVEL

BY

## MAARTEN MAARTENS,

AUTHOR OF

"THE SIN OF JOOST AVELINGH," "GOD'S FOOL" ETC.

*COPYRIGHT EDITION.*

IN TWO VOLUMES.

VOL. II.

LEIPZIG

BERNHARD TAUCHNITZ

1895.

# CONTENTS

## OF VOLUME II.

---

### PART II.

#### (CONTINUED.)

### PART III.

# MY LADY NOBODY.

## PART II.

### CHAPTER XXV.

#### CORONETS AND CROSSES.

MEANWHILE, untouched by the bustle and slush of the market town, or the still greater turmoil and filth of its more distant metropolis, the little village and wide demesne of Horstwyk lay serene under their mantle of unsullied snow. Surely each additional myriad of inhabitants deepens the vulgarity of their place of abode, as when ink-drops fall measured into a glass of pure water. The country has its full share of vices—every anchorite's cave has that. The country has snobbishness, perhaps, more than the town. But it has not vulgarity.

Snobbishness, be it observed, is by no means a marked characteristic of the Dutch. There was little of that element in the heart-felt and healthy veneration which the surrounding country side offered as natural tribute to the lord of the manor. The lord was a legi-

timate and very actual centre of interest for miles
around, radiating wisely diversified influence to all parts
of the horizon. Can any thoughtful man dispute that
God had willed it so? The pursuit of rank is one
thing. Of that the Horstwykers knew very little. The
perception of proportion is another: it is still existent,
though moribund, because the masses confuse it with
humility, or, still more blunderingly, with humiliation.
The Horstwykers were not humble—the Dutch peasant
is not—but they were self-respecting. It is the man
who dearly loves a lord, and can't get near enough,
that wants to see him hung up on a lantern-post.

To many hundreds of simple souls the reigning
Baron van Helmont was the one visible manifestation of
human greatness.

The Divine is intangible and, at any rate, non-com-
parable. The gleam of the Horst through its ancestral
trees, was a daily reminder of Rule.

The change, therefore, in the King one feels—whom
we all have, even Emperors—convulsed the whole community, at first, with much more than curiosity. The
old Baron had lolled on the throne for so many easy
years. The old Baron had never lifted his sceptre. All
his influence—great as it was—had been automatic.

Everybody liked him, for he had never, by doing
anything, given cause for offence. And everybody liked
Gerard, destined, by the very *insouciance* of his open-
handed condescension, to conquer all simple hearts.
The new lord was an unknown quantity. Men lifted
their heads, expectant, not decided as yet, in what
direction to shake them.

Ursula, of course, they all knew from her infancy,

but as one, more or less, of themselves. She had lived rather a sequestered life, keeping much to herself, and to her father; yet they had always benignly approved of the parson's daughter, chiefly on account of her absolute freedom from all forms of assumption and self-assertion, such as clerical womankind too often affects. But, as Baroness van Helmont, her character seemed out of drawing. It must readjust itself to their ideas, if such a thing were ever possible. On the whole, the peasantry of the countryside did not approve of Baron Otto's choice; there was something incongruous in this too-human link between earth and heaven. Pharaoh should marry his sister, not his kitchen-maid.

Even the Dominé had felt this, though he knew himself to be a gentleman. Perhaps on that account.

Pharaoh, settling himself in his unaccustomed seat, might well have wished for a Joseph. His predecessor's years had been years of fatness, agricultural prosperity, but there had been no storing in granaries, to stint the full-bellied kine. There had been plenitude everywhere, and plenteous hunger. The hunger remained. Pharaoh resolved to be his own Joseph, but, face to face with famine, Joseph comes too late.

By the united assistance of the two old ladies Gerard's claim had been met. The Freule van Borck had been very particular about the legal part and the mortgage, holding long consultations with her notary. In all business matters women, starting from the conviction that their defencelessness is sure to be imposed upon, insist on driving bargains of granitic hardness. When four per cent. represents a fair rate of interest, a woman demands six, ultimately resigning herself to accepting five, because a woman, you know, can't hold out against men, as she querulously tells you ever afterwards. The notary was compelled to restrain the Freule's fervour of self-sacrificial money-getting. As the weeks crept on she became more and more resolved to assist her nephew advantageously. And, when everything had at last been arranged, the estate was left saddled with a heavy annual payment it could barely sustain.

"Never mind," said Otto, looking round on the costly treasures he mightn't sell and didn't want. That had become the brave refrain of his resolve. "Never mind," and then he set his teeth hard. It was very different from the *tout s'arrange* of his race.

He steeled himself, doggedly, and a little dogmatically, to "putting things right." That process, of course, annoys the numerous persons who don't care to be told that things were wrong before. Besides, no adjustment is possible—especially not a rectilinear one—without knocks and shoves in all directions.

First and foremost, Otto had to do battle with his mother. The widow resented as an insult the suggestion that anything could need alteration.

"Things have always been like that in your father's time," she said over and over again. "And, Otto, I cannot understand all this talk of yours about income and expenditure. Of course, people have income and expenditure. Surely, your father must have had them, too; but he never worried about them as you do."

Otto knew this. It had been a favourite maxim of his father's—not, perhaps, an altogether incorrect one—that only small incomes need balance to a hair. "Rich

men," the Baron used to say, "have other resources besides their revenues."

"But your father always told me that you were a
bad manager because over-anxious to be a good one,"
the Dowager would murmur, querulously. "The excel-
lence of management, he always said, was moderation,
and, dear me, Otto, you manage more in a month than
your father in all his lifetime. But you don't sell the
art collections, mind. They belong to me. Your father
always said you would sell them."

She even insisted on finishing the costly decoration
of the west room, to Otto's bitter annoyance. "Would
you leave it unfinished?" she asked, with a flash of her
old bright spirit. It was almost fortunate for Otto that
she had never completely recovered from the shock of
her husband's death. For hours she would sit, silent
and motionless, in the boudoir she had filled with his
portraits from all parts of the house. And when the
Baron entered, she would quote his father at him.

"I *will* spend less than my income," repeated Otto,
grinding his heel into the carpet. It sounds easy in a
big house, but, in fact, it is easier in a small one. He
retrenched, and made the whole family most increas-
ingly uncomfortable. When, at last, he extinguished
the great, wasteful fire in the hall, there was a palace
revolution. The butler gave notice. "For I'm too old,"
he informed Mynheer the Baron, letting him have a bit
of his mind, "to expose my life at my age in them
draughty passages."

"Very well, go," said Otto, fiercely. But he didn't
like it. The man had been with them for years. The
Dowager-Baroness cried at thought of his leaving. All

the servants looked sullen and demonstratively blue-
nosed. For weeks the new master had been causing
them successive annoyance. Some kind of chivalry
taught him to screen his young wife.

"Let me do it, dear," pleaded Ursula, when Otto
complained that he must speak to the cook. "Surely
that is my department."

"Oh yes, it is," he said, looking out of the window.
"Oh, yes."

"Well, then, what has she done? She seems to me
a nice, pleasant-spoken person."

"Oh, they are all that," cried Otto, facing round,
with sudden eloquence. "They are all nice, all pleasant-
spoken! My father's people always were. Imagine,
Ursula, that this woman, whom mamma has had in her
service for fifteen years, daily—mind you, daily—writes
down a pound of meat more than the butcher brings,
and divides the profits with him!"

"How can she?" objected Ursula, who had not yet
got accustomed to a household in which such things
were possible, and even proper.

"How? Don't ask me how. I suppose she calls it
'perquisites.' I met an English marquess once, who
told me that in his father's time the annual beer bill
had touched two thousand pounds. His was three
hundred. It's all a question of authorising theft by
silence. Keep your fingers off the tap. That's all." He
laughed.

"I'll weigh the meat to-morrow, myself," cried Ursula, rising already to do it. "That will stop them at
once. We weigh it at home; that's to say, Aunt Mopius
often does. And I've had to scold Oskamp's boy before.

I should never have thought it of Oskamp. I suppose, Otto, your mother never weighs the meat?"

Otto smiled.

"So that will be all right. Don't worry, dear, I'll see to it myself."

"No, I think you had better not," reasoned Otto gravely. "I—I think I had better do it. My mother, you see, Ursula, will take anything of that kind more easily from me."

He hurt her cruelly, for it was by no means the first time she had thus been checked in the well-meant endeavour to assume her legitimate duties. She turned away in silence, and took up some needle-work.

Somehow, he realised, helplessly, that things were again uncomfortable. "My dear child," he explained, "it is only because I am anxious to shield you."

But she stopped him.

"I don't want to be shielded," she said, quickly; "at least, not *always*."

And she beat back her emotion, looking away, with trembling lip.

He stood, uncertain, gazing at her, and his eyes grew half-reproachful.

"Oh, of course, you don't understand!" she exclaimed, unwillingly reading his thoughts. "You have married a plaything, Otto. You cannot comprehend my wanting to be a wife."

"My dear child——" he began.

He too constantly called her that. She detested the name. She knew well enough how much he was her elder.

"I am not a child," she cried, passionately. "I am a woman, and your wife."

"Yes," he replied, sternly, reading discontent in her pent-up vehemence, and perhaps a little assumption; "you are now the Baroness van Helmont."

"I am not. I am not!" she cried, recklessly, and dropped her work in her agitation. "I mean I am not that only. I am sick of merely being that. I am your wife, Otto. I have a right to be recognised as such."

Otto paced down the large room and up again.

"I am sorry," he said stiffly, "that you consider yourself slighted by anyone, but I cannot ask my mother to leave the house. There are difficulties, of course, in your position. I am the first to admit them. We all have difficulties. Often they are unavoidable. Yours seem so to me."

She looked at him, her brown eyes dilated with horror; then suddenly, very sweetly, her tenderness flowed across them.

"Oh, Otto," she said softly, "why do we so constantly misunderstand each other? It is you by whom I want to be recognised as your wife—nobody else!"

Then he caught her to his breast, and kissed her seriously, as they kiss who love deeply, but apart.

"I want to take my share of your work," she continued, caressingly, "and, especially, my share of your worry. I am so tired, Otto, of sitting in the big drawing-room. To you, at *least,* I want not to be 'My Lady Nobody.' I didn't marry you for that."

"What did you marry me for?" he questioned, playfully.

"Certainly not for that," she replied, gravely, and the answer fell cold on his heart, for all that it left unsaid. A moment afterwards she added, "Of course, because I love you." She thoughtfully spoke her conscientious verity; but love is quicker than thought.

He left her, with a kind little pat of encouragement, and she sank down beside the dog, hiding her sunny brown head in the softly responsive fur. She could feel Monk's great heart beating gravely. The room was very large and empty. The house was very large.

Yes, though he did not realise it, Otto van Helmont had married his wife for her face—a sweet apparition, bright and fresh among the home-flowers, a suggestion of the dear fatherland, a dream of wholesome Dutch girlhood. He had married for that most unsatisfactory of all reasons; "because he had fallen in love." Not even a fortnight—be it remembered—had elapsed between his first sight of Ursula and their engagement. A man must either know his wife before he learns to love her, or else he must never need to love her, or else he will certainly never learn to know her. That last eventuality, the rarest, is surely the most desirable, but only if the love be mutual, and exceedingly great.

Otto, then, had never penetrated into a character whose reserve was so like his own that he could not understand it. He loved his young wife, and kissed her; and he fancied, like so many men, that his consciousness of loving her was sufficient for all her wants. As for her position in the house, in the family, if it was uncomfortable, could he help that? Was not he himself

weighed down by his difficulties, his responsibilities, the
worry of universal deepening displeasure? What were
the pinpricks she complained of compared to his
wounds? Her mamma-in-law was inconsiderate; his
mother was unkind. Her dependents were not always
courteous, his own people hardened their countenances
against him. He could not help thinking that much of
her petulant soreness—well, she was young—was
provoked by mortification because of the scant dignity
or authority her sudden elevation had brought her.
Had she not said to him: "I will not be My Lady
Nobody; at least, let me not be it to you"?

She was annoyed, then, at being it to him, and to
all. The combination vexed her. She had hoped, as
My Lady, to be Somebody indeed.

He sighed from irritation. It was not his fault.
Yet he was a little disappointed in Ursula. He had
thought hers was an essentially gentle nature, unassuming,
unaspiring. Even not desiring to meddle and share in
her husband's affairs, because that, for a young girl, is
impossible. A thoroughly womanly woman, who cried
out in horror at thought of men's work, such as sheep-
slaughtering, or of men's play, such as a fox-hunt; a
woman who could be tacitly brave, on occasion, able
to endure though unable to act. Thus had she revealed
herself to him in the week of his swift immersion, his
model woman, in a word. That is the worst of tumbling
into love. You marry your model woman and have to
live with your wife. Now, Ursula was far superior to
Otto's ideal. There is nothing more hopeless in human
relationships.

He turned impatiently from himself and went down

to the room where his bailiff was waiting. All that morning he had been weighed down by the prospect of this interview. No, he was not the man, in his gentleness of heart, to "set things right."

"You can do as you like," he cried, starting up from the other's excuses and tergiversations. "You can go or you can stay. But never again, if I live——" His heart throbbed wildly as he bent that cruel, hated look of his on the sullen retainer: "Never again, by God, shall you charge one and eight for a labourer's wages while paying him one and five!"

---

## CHAPTER XXVI.

### FREULE LOUISA.

IN the grey loneliness of Ursula's married life there was, however, very little solitude. The house contained too many various elements for that. And county society, which was plentiful, took a great interest in her on account of the romance of her courtship. By the coincidence of the old Baron's immediately subsequent death, she had come face to face with her whole circle of acquaintance, during the days of her *début* at the Manor House, through the medium of that most trying of social functions, the visit of condolence. All these people knew her from her birth; many of them called her by her Christian name; it seemed to her, and to them, that she was masquerading. She was nobody's cousin.

And the Matres Familias who looked regretfully at Otto—there were many such—could hardly be expected to look benignly on Ursula. But they all patronised her most amiably, and patted her on the back, and showed that they were trying to "make her feel quite like one of us." And Ursula, who could not be unnatural, nevertheless strove hard to be natural—if anyone fathoms what is meant by that combination of miseries! The whole lot of them studied her attitude, and compared her with what she was before her marriage, and

endeavoured to accentuate a difference. One dear old
lady told her kindly "that she really did very well."
Another took her aside: "Do not be self-conscious, dear
Ursula," she said. "Just be yourself, my dear, just as
you were formerly. We like you best like that." Surely,
there was no cause for the historic Lady Burleigh to
"take on" so; before her marriage she had not resided
in Stamford-town.

The Dowager Baroness was far too well-bred to
mortify her young rival intentionally! she was far too
well-bred not to do so daily without intention. The
Dominé's daughter must now take precedence? Impossible. Mevrouw van Helmont retained her seat at
the head of her table. The servants came to Mevrouw
for orders; not that Ursula cared at all about this, or
wished in any way to domineer, but. her clear nature
shrank from the discomfort of hourly confusion. "Oh,
what does it matter!" thought Otto, harassed by the
real troubles of his own administration. His wife did
not complain to him. She retired to the big drawing-
room, with empty hands, and found solace, for hours,
at her beloved piano. It was a superb Steinway grand
of the old Baron's buying, very different from the little
cottage instrument at the Parsonage. For years it had
been the object of Ursula's secret envy, and now it was
the one acquisition she heartily rejoiced in among all
the grandeurs of the great house which were not even
hers.

"Does Ursula always play the piano?" asked the
Dowager, wearily, when her son came in to visit her.
"Did she never do *anything* else in her old home?"

"She is such a first-rate musician, mamma," apo-

2*

logised Otto. "That requires a great deal of constant practice."

"I suppose so. In my day nobody was a first-rate musician, except the professionals."

"So much has changed," said Otto, patiently.

"Perhaps." The Dowager was making a spring-coat for Plush, what the French call a *demi-saison;* she laid down the sky-blue scrap upon her heavy crape. "Still, Otto, I wish things could be arranged a little differently. Does it not strike you as rather incongruous, with an eye to the servants and the trades-people, that this house of mourning should resound with dance-music from daybreak to dark?"

Otto went to his wife. "I like the playing very much indeed," he said. "But a little solemn music would make a delightful change. Do you always prefer dances, Ursula?"

"This is a scherzo, Otto, out of one of Beethoven's symphonies."

"Is it? I wish it sounded a little less—gay."

Ursula struck the piano a violent crash, and then ostentatiously dragged, banging through the same composer's "Marche Funèbre." Towards the end she looked up defiantly at her husband standing in the embrasure of a window with folded arms. Suddenly she broke away from the music, and threw herself on his breast.

"I am sorry," she said.

The Freule van Borck was the member of the household—an unimportant member—who took most interest in the newcomer. Otto's fondness seemed devoid of investigation, like his mother's apathy, but

Aunt Louisa looked upon the fresh factor in her old maid's life of fuss-filled monotony as a worthy subject of scientific experiment. Was Ursula—or was she not —*quelqu'un?* That, said the Freule van Borck, is the question.

Louisa van Borck had created for herself a peculiar position in her sister's family. Some twenty years ago her tiresome existence with her old father in the Hague had come suddenly to an end through the conclusive collapse of Mynheer van Borck's financial operations. He was about seventy at the time, and she thirty-eight. She had never wanted to marry, nor had she ever had an opportunity of wanting. Her ambition had always been to live with herself, occupying, enlarging, and fully inhabiting her own little entity, as few of us find time to do. That nothing much came of it was hardly her fault. She had a lot of little fads and fancies with which she dressed up her soul for want of better furniture.

"We must go and live with the Van Helmonts," Louisa had said to her protesting parent. "It is unavoidable."

"But, Louisa, your money, your share of your mother's money——"

"Cannot support us both. Besides, I don't intend to die in a workhouse."

So the old gentleman had to turn his back upon the sweets of the "Residency," and die away into the wilderness. Of course, the Van Helmonts made room for their relatives. "So that's settled," said the lord of the Horst. "Tout s'arrange." But grandpapa's brain soon got clogged, in the still country atmosphere, from inertia and want of winding up. For many years his body vegetated in an upper room, with an attendant and a box full of toys. Nobody objected to him, nor was anyone ever unkind. Besides, he had still his pension of four hundred a year, which made a welcome addition to the family revenues. Yet it was he they regretted mildly when he died.

Freule Louisa could not honestly be accused of unthriftiness. "I know nothing about money matters," she was wont to exclaim, with pink-spotted agitation. "You mustn't talk to me about money. I haven't got any to spend." Nobody knew how much of her private fortune was still in her possession, or how much she had possibly lost by investments. "You will see," Baron Theodore had always prophesied, "Louisa will die a pauper." His wife doubted it.

She had insisted upon making an arrangement with her relations which was especially antipathetic to their temperament. She paid a "pension" price for herself and maid of so much per diem, with deduction of one-half for board during absences of at least a week. In addition to this, she paid for the use of the carriage each time she drove out, according to a scale of her own careful concocting. So much per hour, so much per horse, so much if nobody else went with her. The whole thing was just like a hotel bill, and she enjoyed it immensely. "I am not going to sacrifice my independence," she said. The Baron, of course, considered the business "disgusting"; but he never pushed his objections beyond a certain limit of opposing vehemence. He simply refused to have anything to do with the Freule's laborious computations, and the Ba-

roness was obliged to receive and receipt the monthly
payments, which would sometimes remain on a side-
table for days. Once or twice a dishonest servant took
a gold piece without anyone being the wiser.

The Freule did not approve of her sister's domestics.
Her own maid was perfection: angular (like herself),
middle-aged, cross-eyed, cross-grained, and crossed in
love (so she sometimes told Louisa), one of those bony
asperities whose every word, like their every contact,
cuts. The name this person gloried in was Hephzibah,
and she belonged to a religious sect which was supposed to embrace exclusively the elect, although these,
in the opinion of each individual member, were re-
presented by a minority numbering one.

Nobody in the house knew half as much about
himself or about any other member of the family as
Hephzibah. Her mind was a daily chronicle up to
date, with all the back numbers neatly filed. Fortunately, her exceeding taciturnity limited the circula-
tion.

"Hephzibah, I am watching my niece," the Freule
remarked from time to time. "She has an interesting
part to play in the comedy of life."

"Yes, Freule," replied Hephzibah, who thought life
was a tragedy.

"Will she rise to the height of her position? I love
my sister and I love Gerard, but I should like to see
Otto conquer them both, and Ursula conquer all
three."

"Yes, Freule," said Hephzibah. She hated the
young Baroness, for Ursula had attempted to show
kindness to Louisa, whose forlorn inanity called for

pity. The Freule's sharp eyes were far-sighted and weak; she liked being read to for hours together, and she frequently complained of her maid's incapacity for pronouncing or punctuating anything, even Dutch.

"*I* will read French to you with pleasure, Aunt Louisa," said Ursula.

"Oh, no, my dear, no." The Freule took her aside in great agitation. "I could not be so inconsiderate to Hephzibah, I could not. Oh, no."

Still, in a hundred small ways, too wearisome to relate, Ursula filled up her time with attentions to the little old maid. It was a relief to find someone she could do something for. She learnt a lot of Rossini's opera-airs on purpose because the Freule had stated that she "adored Rossini."

"Otto," said the Freule one morning, "I should like to speak to you."

He stopped, with his hand on the door-knob.

"Yes?" he answered, his thoughts intent on the morning's disagreeable work.

"Otto, I have considered, and"—the Freule fidgeted—"under present circumstances I should wish to—pay seven florins more per week for my board." The Freule gasped.

"Why?" asked the Dowager, sharply, from the top of the breakfast-table.

"Don't interfere, Cécile. I see in the paper that prices everywhere are being raised."

"Oh, nonsense," said Otto, turning away.

"Well, I intend to do it, so now you know. And, Cécile, you need not make any difference."

"Difference?"

"Yes, in the *menus.*"

"I should think not, indeed," exclaimed the Dowager.

How difficult is the path of virtue made for most of us by our relations. During the whole of the Freule van Borck's terrestrial pilgrimage she never committed another action worthy to rank with this voluntary conquest of her ruling passion. Yet nobody understood it.

"Van Helmont of the Horst," she said to herself, "shall remain Van Helmont of the Horst." And she deducted the thirty pounds from her already meagre charities.

No one at the Manor House had ever been prodigal in almsgiving. The old Baron had reckoned the poor a public nuisance; the Baroness provided them with systematically indiscriminate pennies; Gerard flung away an occasional hap-hazard shilling. And the new lord was by no means generally generous. He had very definite ideas on the subject. Charitable help must be strictly limited to the "deserving poor," whatever that may mean—*only* the deserving, and *all* the deserving. The word was his shibboleth. On paper it looks exceedingly well.

Also he never gave money where he could give work, and he never gave work where he could give advice as to work elsewhere. He was forty when enabled and called upon to put into practice his carefully·elaborated theories regarding pauperism. All the paupers of the neighbourhood, to a man, resented a charity which had lost the charm of the happy-go-lucky. But to no one came more bitter disappointment than to Ursula, o'er the sun of whose crescent bene-

volence her husband's theories spread in tranquil
clouds.

How often had she not pictured to her father the
wide use she would make of an expanded scope and
increasing opportunities! Shall we venture to say that
the constant thought had been a comfort, or at least an
encouragement, through the months of her love-making?
She had always worked fairly hard, with her limited
means, in her father's parish, nothing exaggerating, and
setting nobody down in malice.

"And you will find sympathetic support in your
husband," declared the Dominé. "I know that he
suffers greatly under his father's bright indifference"
—the Dominé, sighed—"for instance as regards the
Hemel."

The Hemel—so it is still inappropriately called;
the word means "Heaven"—was at that time a small
hamlet outside the Dominé's jurisdiction which had long
been notorious in the whole province for the wild and
profligate charater of its consanguineous population.
The people were mostly Roman Catholics, but, even
had this not been the case, their pastor would hardly
have paid them much attention. He was a very different man from Roderick Rovers. "The poor ye have
always with you," he repeated. And to his colleague
he would have said, "Hands off!" Ursula rejoiced to
realise her new position as lady of the Hemel as well
as of the Horst. Oh, the cruel disappointment of dis-
covering that the poor of the Hemel were not deserving.
They were everything and anything but that.

"Be just before you are generous," said Otto. "First,
we must pay our way, dear Ursula, and that, in a

landed proprietor's life, includes an immense amount of unconscious, and even unintentional, philanthropy. What we have left we will gladly give away, but let us be careful to confine ourselves to worthy recipients of our bounty."

Never mind, there is plenty of good to be done, as Ursula knew, without almsgiving.

"I wish you would not go to the Heinel," pleaded Otto in the face of her efforts; "you would do me a great favour, Ursula. Mother has so many causes of complaint against me already, and she is dreadfully afraid of infection. Besides, it is altogether useless. They only make a fool of you. Nothing good ever came, or can come, from that horrible place."

So life flowed on at the Horst, for its chatelaine, in a narrow little stream, over rocks, amid a vast splendour of scenery. The Baron, her husband, working day and night in the almost hopeless effort to make both ends meet, waxed sombre and careworn beneath the ever-increasing dislike of his numerous dependents. Towards his wife he was always affectionate, closing the door to his heart-chamber of torture and seeking relaxation as from a beautiful plaything. And Gerard, except for the briefest of visits, remained at Drum.

When the Stork, some twelve months after the old Baron's death, tapped at Ursula's window, her life was no longer empty. Suddenly the Baby filled it to over-flowing. Everyone manifested an absorbing interest in the Baby, as was his due. Even the Freule Louisa, for Babies, surely, are vast potentialities. Miss Mopius forgot her slumbering grievances and rubbed the Baby's back with fluid electricity. The Dominé christened his grand-child, wearing his Legion of Honour, as he had done at Ursula's wedding. But the Dowager Baroness very nearly refused to be present at the ceremony, for the heir of the house received the single name of Otto.

———

## CHAPTER XXVII.

### PEACE AND GOODWILL.

"How cross he looks!" said the Dominé, benignly, dangling his grandson on one awkward knee. "I believe he disapproves of existence. Do you know, children, it has struck me from the first, I can't understand why your son should have been born with such a look of chronic discontent. What do you mean, Ottochen?" He shook the morsel of pink-spotted apathy, and laughed innocently at its unconscious sneer.

Involuntarily the parents' eyes met. Otto walked to the window.

"Life is good, Ottochen," continued the Dominé, his eagle face alight with tenderness. "Life is very beautiful. People love each other, and the love falls like a rainbow across every background of cloud. Everything is beautiful, especially the storms." The baby puckered up its face into one of those sudden, apparently causeless fretfulnesses which the masculine mind resents. "Thou wilt grow up," said its grandfather, "into a brave soldier of the Cross"—the baby overflowed in slobbery, but agonising, sorrow. Ursula hastily took it from the Dominé's clumsy deprecations.

"It is strange," protested the Dominé, "that we weep most without a reason. When the reason comes we often forget to weep."

This time the elder Otto's eyes remained resolutely fixed on the snow-girt landscape.

"He was frightened," explained the young mother, reproachfully, as she hushed her screaming charge.

"Frightened! Ah, just so!" The Dominé rose, a warm flush on his face. "That is the cause of most of our sorrow. Frightened! If men were less afraid of trouble, they would see how little there is of it. Good-bye, children, I am going back to Aunt Josine." And the Dominé marched off, his armless sleeve swinging limp beside his elastic figure.

Otto turned round into the darkened room. It was true the whole atmosphere of the house had long been one of latent worry. He rested his hand silently on Ursula's shoulder, and a great feeling of assuagement spread over both their hearts. The baby's shrieks were dying down into an exhausted gurgle. Both parents gazed deeply at the child.

"Ursula," said the Baron presently, "if you feel strong enough, I should like to have one or two people here for Christmas. I should like to invite the Van Helmonts who were so kind to me during my period of hard work at Bois-le-Duc. Theodore van Helmont and his mother. They are our only relations of the name. And I think they have been kept too much out of the family."

"Are they really the only other Van Helmonts besides us?" questioned Ursula.

"Yes," he answered, recoiling hastily, as she had done, from the proximity of his brother's name, "but there is a brand-new Van Helmont now,—the heir!" He placed a soft finger against little Otto's bulgy cheek.

"True. How funny! Do you know, I had never thought of it." She coloured. "I never think," she added, "of what is so far away as that." She rose and kissed her husband, and held up the child to him.

"Otto," she added, "supposing—if—if there had been no baby, and——" she stopped.

"The Horst would have been sold by auction," he burst in, violently, "two months after my death. Do you think I have ever lost sight of that? All through this anxious year, Ursula, the thought has never let me rest."

The words frightened her. Could anything have brought home more clearly the separation of their lives?

"Theodore van Helmont is a good fellow," Otto went on, "hard-working and honest. I thoroughly respect him. I should like you to know him. But he isn't much to look at."

"Why have they never been here before? I don't remember hearing of them till you went to Bois-le-Duc."

"Well, as I tell you, young Theodore isn't much to look at. And my father greatly objected to his cousin's marriage at the time; he never would see him after."

"Whom did he marry?" asked Ursula, looking down into the cradle and readjusting its coverlet. "I mean— *what?*"

"She was a farmer's daughter from the other side of Drum. He picked her up when staying here, some thirty years ago. I remember it quite well. My father was furiously angry."

"And he never forgave the son," mused Ursula, with

one finger in her little Otto's clammy clasp. "Not even the son. I thought people always forgave *the son*."

"I assure you she is quite a nice, motherly person, and so unpretentious. That is what I like in her. It will be a pleasure to have her here, if only mamma consents to put up with her presence. Poor woman, she told me she had never even visited her own relations. I suppose she didn't dare."

"Her own relations," repeated Ursula. "Isn't that a difficulty?"

"I don't see why, if people would only take things simply! She can go to them from here. No one believes more firmly than I do in true nobility, but it is not dependent on surroundings."

She smiled up at him: "Ah, Otto, you say that on account of—me?"

But the suggestion annoyed him, with the pain of its voluntary abasement. "The two cases have nothing in common," he said, almost angrily. "If there is a possibility that you, or any one else, might draw absurd comparisons, I had better give up the idea at once."

"No, no. I shall be glad to have them. Baby must learn to know, and be good to, all his relations."

"Next year might do for that. But, Ursula, talking of Baby's relations, we might ask your Uncle Mopius and his wife."

"I consider Harriet has behaved disgracefully——" began Ursula.

"Just so; and your uncle enjoys the idea of our being angry about the money. That's why I want to ask him," he added proudly.

"Then, Otto, if it is to be a family reunion, should we not"—her voice dropped to a whisper; she fingered a button of his waistcoat—"ask Gerard too?"

"Yes, we will ask Gerard," he answered hurriedly, annoyed that she should utter what he had been making up his mind to say. And then he left the room without another word.

Ursula smiled to herself, and immediately began to apostrophise the helpless infant: "And we will have a Christmas tree, Baby," she said, "and a lot of beautiful lights, Baby. And warm socks and shoes for the babies that haven't got any, Baby. And you shall give blankets and coals to all the old women, Baby."

But even this appalling prospect did not move little Otto. He lay staring steadily, and that constant frown, which his grandfather said he had been born with, wrinkled the raw beefsteak of his unfinished little face.

Meanwhile Otto had gone to tell his mother of the coming festivities. The old Baroness did not seem to pay much attention, immersed as she was in a sort of memoir which she had been recently concocting to the glorification of her departed lord.

"What did you say young Helmont's name was?" she asked suddenly, peering over her heavy gold eye-glasses.

"A family name, mamma—Theodore."

"It is an insult," said the Dowager, and her gaze once more fell on the page in front of her.

A fortnight later the various guests had all arrived; the Dominé greatly approved of their coming. "Let

others less favoured share your happiness," he said to
his daughter. The good Dominé, while constantly
eloquent of the battles of life, rejoiced at the peace
which he dreamed round about him. Yet he still had
"Tante Josine." The light of his life had flitted away
to the Manor House.

Nobody could see Theodore van Helmont and contest the accuracy of Otto's statement that the young
post-office clerk wasn't much to look at. One thing
showed very plainly, and that was his peasant blood.
But he made no attempt to hide it; he had a quiet
and unassuming manner, like his lumbersome mother,
and would hardly have attracted attention but for his
peach-like colouring, which made him almost an Albino.
He was awkward in the unaccustomed vicinity of ladies,
and spoke little, dropping away into the shade, unless
somebody touched on his hobby. This no one ever did,
except indirectly, for that hobby was "social science,"
a number of "ologies" unconnected with life. His
mother often wondered that so good a man could also
be so clever; her own philosophy was of the simplest,
all condensed into one unconscious rule: never to remember an injury, while never letting slip an opportunity
of doing a kindness. Her only attitude towards the old
Baroness van Helmont was one of respectful sympathy.
Of Tante Louisa she felt afraid, for Tante Louisa had
asked her, on the evening of her arrival, whether she
believed in woman's suffrage, and she had not known
what "suffrage" was. The Freule Louisa, it need hardly
be noted, believed in no suffrage at all. "If only we
could stop the million asses' braying," she was wont to
remark, "perhaps we should hear the lion's voice at

last." This remark was not her own. She had got it out of "the Victory."

The quiet clerk, dull, with comparative content, over a merciful volume of engravings, had pricked up his ears when he heard the Freule start "a sensible subject." It was small talk that did for him, reducing his brain to chaos. "The principle of government by majority," he said, "being once universally accepted, there appears to be no logical reason for leaving that majority incomplete."

"Government by majority is a pleonasm," said the Freule, tatting away. She meant "an anachronism," whatever she may have meant by that. The young man hastily returned to his engravings.

"The majority is always wrong," interposed the Dowager Baroness, very decidedly, "and, therefore the larger it is, the more wrong it must be." She had remained in the drawing-room chiefly from disgusted curiosity, and now sat listless, her delicate face, like a sea-shell, among her heavy weeds.

"But, Mevrouw," began Theodore again, from a sense of duty.

"Hush, it is certainly so, young man; besides, my husband always said it was. I am so sorry to see a Van Helmont a Radical." Her face flushed impatiently, and, in the awkward silence, Ursula said it was a beautiful starlit night.

"The stars are so pleasant in winter-time, are they not?" remarked Theodore's mother, whose fat hands lay foolishly in her substantial lap, but the Freule van Borck was not going to stand such sentiments as these,

"Oh, yes," she said briskly, "Ursula always notices the weather. Some people do, and never talk of anything else. I wish you would tell me, Mynheer van Helmont—we were discussing the subject the other day—would you rather do wrong that right may ensue, or right for the sake of wrong?" The Freule was very fond of propounding these problems of the "Does-your-mother-like-cheese?" order. Some spinster ladies "affection" them just as *their* spinster aunts used to propose *Bouts Rimés.*

"You must leave me a few moments to consider my answer," replied Theodore, gravely.

This was quite a new experience for the Freule, and hugely delighted her.

"A very sensible young man," she thought. "And you, Gerard?" she asked, turning to her nephew meanwhile.

Gerard had arrived at the Manor House the day before; it was just about a year since he had last slept in the house, and his mother's heart yearned over him.

"I should do what I liked best," said Gerard, promptly, always pleased to exasperate his aunt.

"Gerard, you have no principle. What does your cousin conclude?"

"Right and wrong, as we refer to them, are such very vague terms, Freule," responded the young clerk, thoughtfully. "But, supposing the words to be used in their absolute sense"—the Freule nodded—"I should do the immediate right."

"Bravo," said Otto's deep voice from a distant sofa. "And now, Ursula, will you give us some music?"

"Oh, yes, music," assented Theodore's mother. "I

love music.    The loveliest organ comes past our house
on Fridays.    I quite long for Fridays to come round."

The last sentence was addressed to the Dowager,
who smiled graciously, for she was watching Gerard.

"My daughter-in-law plays a very great deal," said
the Dowager.

But the evening was long.    Everyone hoped for
diversion from the Mopiuses, who were expected on the
morrow, and a general yawn of relief hung heavy round
the bedroom candles.

"Theodore Helmont is straight right down to the
bottom," Otto said to his wife as soon as they were
alone, "You see how earnest he is, and how wise.    If
ever you stand in need of a counsellor, Ursula, I hope
you will turn to Theodore.    He is one of the few men
on whom I could fully rely."

"You are my counsellor," replied Ursula, wishing
the words were more widely true.

———————

## CHAPTER XXVIII.

### THE SECOND MRS. MOPIUS.

WHEN the Baronial invitation reached Villa Blanda, Uncle Mopius immediately said "No." He wanted so exceedingly to go that he revolted from himself, and then stuck to his assertion of independence. For, most of all, he wanted not to want to accept.

"We have no need of their patronage," he said, pompously, over his morning paper. "Villa Blanda will cook its own modest Christmas dinner. Ha, ha! I have no notion of sitting down to a coroneted dish containing one skinny fowl."

"What did you say?" asked Harriet, with an affectation of indifference. "Were you speaking to me?"

"My dear, I said we should not accept."

Harriet, who had been trying to make up her mind, was glad of this timely assistance.

"And why not?" she questioned, sharply. "Of course we shall go. What excuse would you give?" She did not wait for his answer. "I don't intend to have Ursula saying I'm afraid of her, or ashamed, because of the money and marrying you. No, indeed; we shall certainly go. Johan must hurry round to the dressmaker's immediately." She stroked her pretty morning-gown. Her dressmaker now was the one who had employed Mademoiselle Adeline.

"Dressmaker!" said Mopius, sharply. "Nonsense, Harriet; you have more dresses already than my first wife wore out in all her life."

"I am going to have two new evening frocks," replied Harriet, ignoring the reference. "I have no good dinner things. They will have to sit up all night to get them ready." She smiled pleasantly at her own importance.

"We're not going," said Mopius, settling his bull neck into his shiny collar.

She looked across at him quickly, and again she smiled.

"Yes, we are, because I want to," she said, cruelly, without a shadow of playfulness. Mopius by this time had resolved that wild horses should not drag him to the Horst.

A simple Dutchwoman, however, is not a wild horse. Alas, she is more commonly a jade. Occasionally she is a mule.

Harriet sat down, watching her husband's sullen face. Suddenly, from love of ease, she changed her tone.

"Did he want to stay at home with his own wife?" she said, "like two turtles in a nest. Did he want to have a Christmas-tree all to themselves, and buy her a lot of lovely presents? That was good of him, and his wifie will give him a kiss for it."

In the first months of their married life this tone had been fairly successful; it had obtained for her the numerous fineries, of which Jacóbus's soul now repented.

"Stop fooling, Harriet," he now said, most unexpectedly. "I'm going to remain where I am because I hate dancing attendance on lords and beggarly great people. I'm a rich man, I am. And besides, there's a meeting of the Town Council on Tuesday."

"Did you hear me suggest," continued Harriet sweetly, "that it was my intention to go?"

"Yes, hold your tongue and attend to your house-keeping. The beef was underdone yesterday. It never used to be in my dear departed's time."

"Jacóbus, that is your second allusion this morning to your dead wife. It marks a new departure, for till now you had wisely kept her in the background. But I must warn you, once for all, that I won't stand it. Besides, it's quite useless. Didn't I know the poor fool? Wasn't I present at her daily sacrifice? I am perfectly aware that she loved you in a different way from mine. She was like a faithful dog, poor creature, and you led her a dog's life."

A reproachful tear—not self-reproachful—stood in Mynheer Mopius's yellow eye.

"Mine is a more natural affection. I love you in a reasonable, matrimonial way. Not only for your gray hairs"—Jacóbus winced—"but also for the comforts of our mutual *entente*. So we shall order two nice new dresses and depart on Tuesday morning."

"Your aunt was a better woman than you, Harriet."

"She was not my aunt; don't call her so. Of course she was much better than I. Had she not been, you would have been a better man."

"I don't understand," said Mynheer Mopius, help-lessly, "but I am not going to the Horst."

"*Don't* want to see wheels go round," quoted Harriet, whose course of novel-reading in all languages was very extensive, "but you will, though."

She went over to her writing-table and carefully indited a little note. Jacóbus sat watching her nervously. She closed her envelope and got up without speaking.

"Written to Ursula?" asked her apprehensive lord.

"Oh dear, no; there's time enough for that. It's a note to Madame Javardy," and she rang the bell. "Take this at once," she said to the servant.

Mynheer Mopius rose on his spindle legs, protuberant and goggling.

"I am master of this house," he began, "and I forbid——"

"Leave the room, Johan," broke in Harriet, with suppressed vehemence, and, turning, as the man obeyed, "Jacóbus," she said, "listen to me for one moment. That man knows you ill-treated your first wife. Everybody in the house knows it, but Drum society doesn't, so you needn't mind. Poor thing, she never told; but I shall, mind you, Mynheer the Town Councillor. If you ill-treat me, I shall cry out—cry out as far as —as Mevrouw Pock, for instance, and leave the rest to her!"

"Ill-treat you, Harriet!" spluttered Mynheer Mopius.

"Yes, ill-treat me. Do you know what they call Mevrouw Pock in Drum? 'Sister Ann,' because she's always on the look out for tidings. Mind they don't call you 'Bluebeard' at the Club to-night."

"They'll say: what did you marry me for?" cried Jacóbus.

"Yes, they will—the women will; but the men will pity me, because I'm young and good-looking, and you're——old, Jacóbus. Oh, don't bother," she went on hastily; "I'm sure I make you comfortable enough, and you can have everything you want. Only, I'm not going to put up with being teased out of pure whim, as you used to do. If you've a reason for stopping, I'll stop, but as you've no reason, we go."

She swept to the door.

"Harriet," said Mopius, solemnly; "this is very wrong. You make scenes, Harriet; a thing I detest——"

She came back to him.

"Scenes," she repeated. "No, indeed. This is merely a conversation. If we were to have a scene"—her dark eyes flashed—"I think I should beat you, and if we were to have a second, I—I should kill you. But we love each other; pray don't let us have scenes."

She left her consort to preen his ruffled feathers.

Said Harriet on the night of her arrival at the Manor House:

"I want to speak to you for a moment, Ursula, where nobody can hear us. Come into my room."

Ursula followed, wondering.

Harriet stood by her dressing-table in Madame Javardy's wonderful white cashmere, all embroidery, with silken Edelweiss. She seemed uncertain how to begin.

"Ursula," she said at last, "I suppose you were very angry with me, weren't you, for marrying your Uncle Mopius?"

"I?" exclaimed Ursula, in amazement. "No, indeed; why should I——"

Then she reddened, suddenly understanding.

"Oh, of course, I remember," continued Harriet, "you don't care about money and all that kind of thing. Still, you married Baron van Helmont. Yes, I know; he's not as old as Mopius. Don't interrupt me. All I wanted to tell you was this. When I married, I looked to my marriage settlements. Your uncle has plenty of money, and I secured a handsome jointure, but, unless I should still have children, the bulk of his property goes to you and your heirs. I told him to make that arrangement, and saw to his doing it. *I* don't want money for money's sake, nor more than I'm entitled to. Good-night."

"Good-night," echoed Ursula, and drew hesitatingly nearer.

"Don't," said the bride, holding her aloof. "I'm all right, thanks. What a dear little boy you have! Good-night."

## CHAPTER XXIX.

### THE BLOT ON THE SNOW.

THE brothers got on very well at first; they sat silent or talked about things which interested neither. They were as little as possible alone.

Gradually, however, Gerard's persistent light-heartedness produced the opposite effect of a dead weight on the other man. His very laugh, so easy, so frequent, jarred on Otto's hearing.

"Debt is theft," thought Otto. "How can he find it in his heart to laugh with such debts as his?" And the Baron bent once more, with a resolute sigh, over his weary pile of accounts.

Gerard, meanwhile, was manfully making the best of his return to his old home. He rejoiced to be again among the familiar surroundings, and especially he rejoiced in his mother's company. He spent long hours in her boudoir every morning, helping her with the memoir, and, therefore, talking much about old times. It was a difficult diversion. He did his very best to laugh.

He also did his very best to make things pleasant with Otto. Towards Ursula he could not but feel differently; he avoided her as much as possible, and she, in her eagerness to conciliate, seemed almost to be laying herself out to please him. Their relations were strained, and everybody noticed it.

"And what do you say to the baby, Gerard?" demanded Aunt Louisa.

"Nothing, aunt. One has to say, 'Tiddie, iddie, too-tums, then,' to babies, or something of that kind, and I don't feel equal to it. I never say anything to babies."

"Ah, but this is *the* baby," retorted the old maid, annoyed. "However, I can understand your not caring much about him; he has definitely put your handsome nose out of joint."

Gerard did not answer, in his sudden distress. And then, that none might harbour such horrible thoughts with any show of reason, he set himself to heroically admiring his little nephew, and the forlornness of his affectionate nature soon facilitated the task. Ursula was delighted at this *rapprochement*, on neutral ground. She initiated her brother-in-law into many shades of infant development where the careless observer would merely have seen a blank.

They were together by the cradle, in the breakfast-room, on the morning of Christmas Eve. There was to be a small dinner party in the evening; the Christmas Tree for the villagers not taking place till the following day. The Van Trossarts were coming, and Helen Van Troyen with her husband. Helen had written to say that she must bring a German friend of Willie's.

"He is beginning to take notice," said Ursula for the twentieth time. "Don't you see how he opens and shuts his little fingers?"

"But he always did that," objected Gerard.

"He did it without any reason," exclaimed the young mother, sagely. "He does it now, *when he knows there's something near.*"

Gerard laughed, Ursula laughed also; she was happy in the possession of her husband, of her little son, all the warmth of a woman's home.

In another moment Gerard's face had clouded over.

"Ursula," he said, with a violent effort, "there's one thing I *must* ask you. I ought to have asked it a year ago. It's wickedness letting these things rankle. Why did you make trouble between Helen and me?"

A flood of scarlet poured over her drooping face. She tried to speak, but, for only answer, fresh waves came sweeping up across the dusky damask of her cheeks. She sank down beside the cradle, hiding away from him.

"Can you not guess?" she whispered—into the baby-clothes.

No; he could not guess. He had already sufficiently wronged Otto with regard to the Adeline business; all through the year he had striven to convince himself that Mademoiselle Papotier must have been mistaken. Spoilt darling of many women as he undoubtedly was, he had not enough of the coxcomb in him honestly to believe that this woman had acted solely from pique. Nor could he have uttered that explanation, though it still hovered round him.

"Gerard, I knew," said Ursula, so low that he had to bend over her half-hidden head. "I *knew*. Oh, Gerard, if only you had married the other one."

Then a long silence arose between them, for Gerard had understood. In the strange bluntness of our world-wide morality it had never entered into this honourable gentleman's head that anyone could deem Adeline's claim on him an obstacle to his proper settlement. And now that strange "cussedness," partly chivalric and modest, which always caused him to blow out the lights on his brighter side, checked the easy vindication that he had actually offered marriage to the foolish little dressmaker. He stood silent and ashamed. Ursula did not lift her face from the sheltering coverlet.

When at last he spoke it was to say: "In one thing I have long misjudged you, Ursula. I should like to confess that just now. I didn't believe you about that stupid rendezvous. I have admitted to myself since then, that you went, as you said, for another's sake." He understood that Ursula had somehow constituted herself Adeline's protectress. "I want to confess that just now," he repeated, contritely.

She did not thank him for telling her he no longer thought her a liar, and worse. "So you believe now," she simply said, lifting her head at last. "You believe in my honest acceptance of Otto." Then she rose from the floor, flushed and troubled, but with a proud curve of her neck.

"Ursula," said the young officer, as much troubled as herself, "I thank God for the lesson you have taught me. I—if more women thought as you do, we men would be better than we are." His young face was very solemn, he looked straight towards her. Unconsciously she laid one hand on the breast of her little sleeping child, and, with an upward flutter of her strong brave eyes, held out the other. He took it, hesitated, and then, stooping, touched it with his lips.

When he dropped it, there stood Otto, in the door-way, watching them.

He came forward into the room, pretending not to have seen.

"Well, Gerard," he said, with forced geniality, "so here is the heir. Some day I hope this young man will sit in my seat and look after the dear old place better than I do."

Gerard resented the palpable aim of the words.

"Who knows?" he replied, lightly. "He may never have money to keep it up. If he has brothers and sisters, the estate goes to pieces anyhow. What's the use of your struggling and wasting your life for an idea? Why not sell a couple of farms and have done?"

"That's what you would do," said Otto, grimly; "sell the whole thing."

"Yes, I should, if I really wanted the money."

"I know you would," shouted Otto, breaking loose, glad of the pretext. "I· know you would, you spend-thrift! Spendthrift and profligate, you would do any-thing—for pleasure."

His eye flashed from one to the other, and Ursula read the flash.

She remained standing quite still, her hand on the baby's coverlet. Gerard shrugged his shoulders. "My dear fellow, don't be so angry. I shall sell nothing," he said, and walked into the adjoining room. Otto, already ashamed of himself, went out by the passage-door.

The baby was fast asleep, breathing heavily. Ursula remained standing still.

The room was very silent. Presently a quick spasm of trembling shook her, and, with a frightened glance to right and left, she hurried away down the vestibule, out into the wintry morning.

She ran swiftly along the avenue and turned into the high road, · taking the longest route to the village because it had lain straight in front of her. The gaunt ice-rimmed trees in the pallid air swam round about her through a mist of her own creating; the desolate plain, stretching white and cold, seemed to mock her with its snow-bound loneliness. She shuddered as she ran.

Near the turnpike she stopped. She would meet a human being there, the turnpike man. He would touch his cap. Not that. She shrank back.

And in the pause she asked herself where she was going. To her father, of course, home to her father's consistent love—the one thing in this world she could for ever rely on. Home, to the old home, to weep out her agony upon one faithful breast.

And even as she pictured to herself for a moment what she would do when she reached the comfort of that embrace, she felt that she could not do it. There are valleys of the shadow through which a true-hearted woman must take her way alone.

She stood a black speck in the surrounding bleakness. The turnpike man, peeping through his little window by his cosy stove, wondered lazily why she did not come on.

At last she turned, and, slowly retracing her steps, branched off into the park. Her one aspiration now was to get away from all possible contact with sympathy.

She went stumbling, as fast as she could, over the uneven, snow-laden ground, deeper, only deeper into the
silence of the wood. Her foot caught in invisible roots,
she hurt herself without perceiving it. Her eyes were
dry and hard, despite the cloud behind them.

Gasping for breath, she sank down in the snow and
leant up against a tree. All around and beyond her
was the absolute desertion she had longed for, stretching away in an unending sameness of confused black
pillars, whose naked tracery bore the pellucid vault of
heaven. The dull glitter, all-pervading, lighted up her
forest "sanctuary"; not a sound was heard, except when,
once, a snapped twig came rustling to the ground.

Her husband had doubted her honour. Even supposing he had done so for one moment only, during
the briefest flash of thought. What did that matter?
He had doubted her. Other words and acts now came
falling into their places, deepening an impression never
before perceived. She brushed them away indignantly;
she wanted none of these. It was enough.

She could never go back to him. How could she
see him? How speak to him? How could daily contact be possible between a husband and the wife whom,
for one instant only, his thought had sullied? He who
thinks thus once may at any hour pollute his thoughts
anew. Priest and priestess cannot kneel again in the
temple one of them has desecrated; no repentance, no
forgiveness can wipe away the stain across the marble
god. She hung staring in front of her, and the soak-
ing snow crept upwards on her dress.

She had no wish to do anything tragic, to make
any scene or scandal. Only she felt that she *could* not

go back to her husband's welcoming smile. It was not
the insult to herself, although that drenched her cheek
with purple; it was the new horror that had arisen
between them as if a toad were seated in his heart.
Gerard's wickedness of loose living was not as bad as
this. Oh, men were horrible, horrible!

Something moved on the white ground in front of
her, so close that she could not but notice it. A red-
breast, half frozen, hopped near in a flutter of perky
contemplation, wondering, perhaps, if she was alive.
She pitied the poor little forsaken creature, and felt in
her pocket with a sudden movement that scared him,
for some morsel of bread which she knew could not
possibly be there.

And, as she sat, hopelessly waiting, she could not
tell for what, the distant boom of the village clock
came faintly trembling towards her in one long stroke,
the half-hour.

Half-past—what? Previous warnings must have
reached her unheard. She looked at her watch. Half-
past twelve. And at noon little Otto would have cried
out for her, dependent upon his mother for the very
flow of his life.

She started to her feet, and commenced running
as best she could among the trees. Constantly she
stumbled in her haste, once she fell prone into a yield-
ing snowdrift. She hurried on breathlessly—a clearing
showed her the house; she rejoiced to see it. How
long the time still seemed till she had reached the
steps! In the hall her husband crossed her path. She
shrank aside; the wailing of the child, above the nurse's
vain attempts at hushing, already fell upon her ear.

4 *

Otto remarked with astonishment the condition she was in, but he said nothing. Gerard's voice could be heard in the distance, amid the clash of billiard balls. He was teaching Harriet to play.

"Go," said Ursula, roughly, to the nurse. She flung-to the door of the nursery, and, violently, locked it. Then she took the screaming child to her breast. Her teeth were firm set; her whole face was hard and rigid, but her eyes were very tender.

Half an hour later she went down to lunch. Her guests were talking and laughing. Otto came forward immediately to speak about the afternoon's arrangements. The Van Trossarts must be fetched from the station. The Dowager beckoned her aside.

"My dear," said the Dowager, "the butcher has forgotten the cutlets."

## CHAPTER XXX.

### CHRISTMAS EVE.

THAT evening everyone was to help Ursula in the arrangement of her Christmas entertainment; but, as usual, a couple of willing spirits did the work, and the rest lounged about and talked. A big tree had to be decorated, and plenty of useful presents were awaiting assortment and assignment. This Christmas benefaction had been a long source of tranquil enjoyment to the young wife through the expectant autumn weeks; she had made many of the presents herself in the pauses from daintier work. She still endeavoured to-night to take an interest in it all.

Helena van Troyen was among the lookers-on. She frankly confessed that she had come to enjoy herself, and as an immediate step towards the attainment of her object, she drew the gentlemen away from the tree and around her. To her husband she said:

"*You* may help," and Willie walked away laughing. But the poor relations were Ursula's real adjuvants, delighted to be useful while finding some occupation for their hands. .The son stood on a ladder half the. evening, the mother's dumpy fingers fashioned innumerable little gold-paper chains. Willie started a conversation with Harriet Mopius and was getting on very well till he unfortunately asked where she lived.

"Why, in Drum!" said Harriet, whereupon Willie felt annoyed.

"Yes, Gerard is my cousin," cried Helen; "I am delighted to see him again! He is an old admirer of mine, an accepted lover before you were born, Herr Graf!"

She was all a-sparkle in palest pink and diamonds and her own pearly vivacity. The German beside her bowed solemnly. He was a very big German, five foot eleven by two, padded at the shoulders and pinched everywhere else so as to look twice his original size, like an enormous capital T. Mevrouw van Troyen called him her *cavaliere serviente,* and had naturally brought him to the Horst, with her maid, her King Charles, and her husband.

"You think me a child, Meine Gnädigste," said the German. "Well, so be it. Cupid was ever a child, yet Venus played with him."

"What nonsense," laughed Helen; "but you Germans are all so sentimental; to us it is delightful, by way of change. My cousin is not sentimental; he is charmingly opaque. Come here, Gerard, at once; I want you to make friends with Count Frechenfels."

There was an attempted challenge in her words and manner, as if she called upon her quondam lover to determine how completely the old wound was healed.

But Gerard had no intention of making friends with his belated rival. He disliked the man; he would have disliked him in any case, for, generally speaking, every Dutchman hates every German. The feeling is inborn, and very deeply regrettable, but it has little to do with the more recent annexation scare. Even the most ignorant Hollander must be aware that the near oppressors of his country have ever been, not Germans, but French. Racial discrepancies are at the bottom of the antipathy, accentuated by the irritating manner in which the overgrown young Teuton now often pats his dwarf of an elder brother on the head. The Count had been distributing pats all during dinner.

Gerard found it very hard work to be happy at the Horst. Even his mother had turned against him, worrying him about a subject he conscientiously avoided—his debts. And now Helen began bothering him with a sequel to Finis. He felt Ursula's eyes upon him, as he had felt them all day; they were full of a dumb appeal, he could not tell for what. The eyes did not answer his question.

Their hunted look grew all the more alarmed, if he approached. Did she already want him to leave the house? And if so, why? His thoughts of Ursula were growing more kindly, more like the old feeling of careless approval. That morning had revealed her to him in quite a new, and very beautiful, light.

"Count Frechenfels is most interesting, Gerard," said Helen. "He was in the Franco-German war, and he has been wounded—everywhere! There was room. My cousin, also, is a soldier—Herr Graf."

"Ah!" said the Count, through his eyeglass. "Is it you that the Baron was telling me of, who had served with the army of Africa?"

Gerard looked uncomfortable.

"But no, my dear Count," said Helen, laughing; "that was my cousin Ursula's father! Gerard has never killed anything but ladies."

"Ah!" said the German again, in a different tone, and dropped the eyeglass. "La campagne des dames. Well, it is that in which the worst wounds are received."

"My cousin does not think so," murmured Helen, cruel in her coquetry. Gerard's eyes blazed with a quick flash of resentment. His sister-in-law had drawn near, from a helpless feeling that she must amuse her guests.

"Ah, yours is a splendid army," continued Helen, provokingly. "I don't think I should care to be an officer unless I could be a Prussian. Victorious, irresistible, bronzed, scarred, the cross on your breast— that's a soldier! What's the use of a sword that you never can draw?"

"Come, come, you are too hard on your cousin," said Count Frechenfels, with patronising complacency. "After all, he cannot help himself. We Germans, also, we do not kill men in times of peace."

"At least not officers!" exclaimed Gerard, breaking loose.

The big Prussian replaced his eyeglass, with silently insolent interrogation.

"You know as well as I, Herr Graf," continued the young Dutchman, hotly, maddened by the other's contempt, "how many privates commit suicide in German barracks, driven to despair by ill-treatment and blows. This year's official statement"—he turned first to Ursula, then to Helen—"gives the number at nearly three thousand. Half the truth, as Von Grietz assured me, not counting those who are killed outright."

"That is not true," said the Count, coldly.

"What?"

"Your authorities are wrong. It is what the Liberals and Socialists say, and that kind of people. And, supposing it *were* true! Meine Gnädigste, I had not expected to find a Radical among your friends."

"You are quarrelling," replied Helen, brusquely. "That is very stupid, and very bad form. Of course you Prussians are brutal, Count; we all know that, but it is what we like in you—at least, we women. In our effete civilisation you are deliciously fresh."

"All I ask is to please," said the Count, with an unpleasant grin. "I will appear in a wolf's skin, at your command."

"Hush, you will make Gerard jealous! But imagine, Ursula, in the West of Europe, an officer daring to flog his recalcitrant men! It only bears out what I was maintaining. These are warriors: what say you?"

"The Frau Baronin's opinion has weight," smirked the German, bowing low. "She is the daughter of a hero," and, perhaps unconsciously, his half-closed eyes stole round to Gerard.

"I suppose if a man is a soldier, he ought to enjoy fighting," admitted Ursula, coming forward. "It seems a strange occupation for a Christian, but my father doesn't agree to that. You know, Gerard, he always declares: if he had two arms, he would be off to Acheen."

"Ah, Acheen!" cried Helen. "Just so; that's where you ought to be, Gerard! and every Dutch officer! That's what I can never understand. The whole lot of you dawdle about here in cafés and ball-rooms, and the flag over yonder sustains defeat after defeat."

"Tell Willie to go," retorted Gerard.

"So I do. And he asks, 'What! go and get killed?' And I say, Exactly."

"Meanwhile, it is we who are doing our best to defend your flag," interposed Count Frechenfels. "Your colonial army consists very largely of Germans."

"Then why do you not defend it better?" said Gerard.

The Count shrugged his shoulders. "What will you have? It is not our own."

Gerard turned mutely to Ursula. Her eyes were flashing. "There are brave Dutchmen enough over yonder, Herr Graf!" she exclaimed, "and brave Dutchmen enough here at home, willing and eager to go! All cannot exchange into Indian regiments. Helen, why do you speak so of our soldiers? There is not a nation in Europe has been braver than ours!"

"Ah, bah!" said Helen. "Then why doesn't Gerard go? You, yourself, said your father would, and he is a clergyman!"

Ursula looked at Gerard. Again that strange alarm came into her eyes, which still shone with indignation.

"I shall not go for your ordering, Helen," answered Gerard, in a burst of almost ill-mannered spite. "Honestly, I attach more importance to Ursula's opinion."

Helen laughed.

"Quite right," she said. "So do I. Only, unfortunately, Ursula agrees with me. Ursula, you shouldn't be afraid to say what you think."

"I?" asked Ursula, proudly. "Yes, I agree with you in one point. I am my father's child. I think every Dutch soldier who can"—she looked steadily away from Gerard—"should help to blot out the disgrace in Acheen."

They were standing in a circle; the German twirled his moustache.

"When I go," said Gerard, softly, "you will have to be very good to the one loving heart I leave behind." And he turned on his heel.

"Ursula," exclaimed Helen, "your evening is decidedly dull. Your relations from Bois-le-Duc are estimable people, but your evening is dull. I think I shall go and help the estimable young man on the ladder. Make him take *me* for the top device of his tree, Herr Graf. Challenge him if he says I am not enough of an angel!"


But other challenges had to be seen to first. Gerard waylaid his antagonist ten minutes later.

"Count Frechenfels," he said, "you have twice called me a coward in the course of this evening."

The Prussian drew himself up.

"And once a liar," continued Gerard.

"I said nothing of the kind," began the Count.

"And twice a liar," amended Gerard. "And I hope you will give me an opportunity of proving that I am neither."

"I am at your service," said the Count, stiffly. "You are quite unintelligible to me, but I am fully at your service. I shall ask Mynheer van Troyen to act for me."

He was passing on with another bow.

"Oh, no nonsense about seconds," cried Gerard.

"That'll stop the whole business. I'll arrange with you whatever you want arranged."

The Prussian noble's eyebrows rose in undisguised dismay.

"Mynheer," he cried, "must I teach you the alphabet of honour? A duel without seconds? Am I speaking to an officer and a gentleman? It would be murder. Of course I refuse."

Gerard barred his way, white to the lips.

"Count Frechenfels," he said, gently, "allow *me* to call *you* a coward."

The Prussian stopped, suddenly frozen into bronze. The Iron Cross gleamed, alive, on his breast.

"What do you want of me?" he asked, huskily. "I will shoot you with pleasure whenever and wherever you like."

"Come out to-morrow morning at seven," replied Gerard. "It won't be light sooner. I shall expect you outside. What will you have? Pistols? Swords? Rapiers?"

"Swords," said the German, walking off.

He hurriedly hunted up Willie van Troyen.

"Your younger cousin," he said, "he is—peculiar, is he not? There is a suspicion of mental derangement?"

Willie roared with laughter.

"Gerard?" he cried. "No, indeed! Why, he very nearly married my wife."

"A—ah!" said the German, suddenly thoughtful.

Gerard went upstairs immediately, after a specially tender good-night to "the one loving heart" that would care. He threw open his window, and stood looking out into the frosty night. The Christmas bells came pealing through the stillness. True, it was Christmas Eve.

The bells were ringing their message of peace and goodwill. Gerard closed the window again. He had never fought a duel before. He had never been present at one. Duels are as rare in the Netherlands as in England. He wondered how many "encounters" the German had had.

He sat down to make a few farewell arrangements, as is best in such cases. He wrote a long letter to his mother and a short one to Otto. That was all. What did it matter? Even supposing——

. He was furious with the weight of his dejection. He hoped that he would kill the Prussian.

At her dressing-room window also, late, stood Ursula, listening to the bells. They had long since ceased to ring, yet still she heard them on the starlit air. "Peace and goodwill. Peace and goodwill."

Through the open door came the slow rhythm of Otto's breathing. She quailed, as it fell on her ear. Nothing could change.

"Glory to God in the Highest," she said tremulously. And she passed into the other room.

## CHAPTER XXXI.

### "WHOSOEVER SHALL SMITE THEE——"

BEFORE the house, next morning, in the dull grey dawn, the two antagonists met. It was bitterly cold and misty, with that wet frost, all shadow and shiver, that precedes the late wintry sun. Gerard drew his cloak around him as he saluted the Count. Under his arm he held a long green-baize bag.

"You still wish it to be swords?" he asked.

Count Frechenfels waved his hand in haughty acknowledgment.

"Permit me to precede you," said Gerard, gravely.

They walked away into the park with quick, ringing steps. Only once Gerard broke the silence. "Excuse me," he began, looking round, "but I think we had better go some distance. The clash, you know." The German repeated his gesture.

In silence, then, they reached the little clearing which Gerard had selected. Here he paused. As it happened, the place was the same where Ursula had fought her battle the day before. It was a natural halting-place for those who wandered in the wood.

The robin lay stiff and stark with upturned legs. Gerard kicked it aside.

Count Frechenfels looked to right and left. "Your

doctor?" he said at last. "Where is your doctor? At least you have arranged for a medical man?"

"No, indeed; he would have warned the police," replied Gerard. "What do we want a doctor for?"

The German hesitated. "But it is murder," he said, half to himself. "No one does such things. Supposing one of us is badly wounded. Mynheer van Helmont, you know that not one man in ten would consent to meet you like this?"

"I don't care about the other nine," replied Gerard, inconsequentially. He threw down his bag. "Count Frechenfels," he said, "you insulted the Dutch army in my person last night. There is nothing more to be said."

The Count began to get ready. "So be it," he answered. He took up one of the swords. "It is the Dutch army we fight on," he said, significantly. "However this mad affair ends, that is clearly understood!"

"Of course," replied Gerard, with some slight wonderment.

"Very well. I am ready, Mynheer. This is not a duel, but a fight!"

In another moment they were clashing at each other amid the surrounding stillness, their swords ringing in the constant concussion of the parry. The morning as yet was almost too dark for their object, especially here, under the white-rimmed trees; but as the metal shone and flashed in the haze, high over the combatants' heads the intensity of the moment's expectation seemed to clear away the mist. A sword-duel, even when well ordered, is always disconcerting because of the noise;

in this case, as the German had remarked, the combat, when it deepened, without umpire or timekeeper, was not a duel but a fight.

"I shall kill him," thought Gerard, but at the same moment he felt that this would not be an easy thing to accomplish. It required the utmost vigilance on his part to ward off his enemy's blows; he found but little opportunity for independent attack; he began uncomfortably to realise that the Count was the better swordsman. Also the Count was the taller of the two—a very great advantage. Gerard set his teeth hard in the continuous crash of the other's onslaught. The whole wood seemed listening, holding its already bated breath.

Suddenly—in a flash of lightning, quicker than thought—the young Dutchman realised that his guard was gone, that his opponent's sword was upon him, bearing straight down upon his unprotected head, with the certainty of terrible wounding, the possibility of death! With unthinkable swiftness he understood it and even found time—in that hundredth of a second —to await the inevitable end. In that hundredth of a second, also, he saw his antagonist swerve aside under the very force of sweeping downwards, swerve with a sudden slip of his footing, just enough to cause the aim to diverge, while exposing himself in his turn. In that hundredth of a second Gerard knew, as it passed, that he had the German in his power, that he, not the German, was become, by a twist of the wheel, the irresistible victor, that his sword, once more curling aloft, could descend where he chose. And he *did* choose—still in that immeasurable atom of existence— and struck his foeman, not through the skull, but, with a quick revulsion from murder, in a hideous long gash across the cheek.

It was over. The Count reeled and recovered himself as Gerard ran forward to support him. Then, his long passion grown suddenly cool, with his profusely bleeding victim beside him, Gerard felt there was nothing left but to avow himself tardily "an idiot." He looked round desperately for the indispensable assistance he had previously scouted. He would have called out, but what was the use of calling? Even as he told himself that it would be utterly useless, he became aware that his sylvan solitude was not deserted. The figure of a woman, making towards him, became visible through the trees.

He recognised her with immense relief—only Hephzibah, his Aunt Louisa's maid. Angular in every fold of her dark stuff gown and shawl, that cross-grained female approached the little group in the clearing.

"Help the gentleman to sit down, Jonker," she said, without looking at Gerard. And she began deftly arranging a bandage with two spotless pocket handkerchiefs which she produced from inner recesses. They were her Sunday handkerchiefs (ready for the morning's devotional exercises). No cry of anguish broke from her as she calmly tore them into strips.

Count Frechenfels watched her skill with evident satisfaction. After all, why should he let himself be comfortably killed in contradiction to all the correct rules of carving? He was contented with himself: he had behaved with great magnanimity, like the "grand seigneur" he was.

"I will go fetch a carriage from the stables," said Gerard.

The woman nodded, engrossed in her work; when she had finished, she stood waiting, erect by the wounded man, like a soldier on guard.

It seemed a long time before Gerard returned with the brougham which he had got ready unaided. As Hephzibah established the Count in the carriage, the Jonker turned for one last look at the scene of the combat, wondering whether he could account for that sudden slip of his adversary's to which he felt that he owed his life. Something black in the hard snow caught his eye. He stooped quickly and took up a woman's dark glove, half imbedded and trodden down. The Count's foot must have slid on the soft kid. Gerard thrust the glove into his pocket. One of Hephzibah's squint eyes, at any rate, was fixed on the Count.

A few minutes later the little brougham stopped before the doctor's house in the village street. The village street was empty, blinded and asleep, yet Gerard, on the box, as he sat amid the jingle of the harness, felt that the dead walls were Argus-eyed, and that his secret was become the world's.

"Good gracious!" squeaked the doctor from his window, in a red nightcap. "Good gracious, Jonker, what has occurred?"

"Nothing of importance," replied the Jonker's loudest tones. "Come down, and I'll tell you."

Curiosity accelerated Dr. Lapperpap's enrobing. Soon he was examining the patient by the light of hastily raised blinds.

"And how did this happen?" asked Dr. Lapperpap.

"I did it," replied Gerard, promptly. "Sword-exercise."

The doctor cast a quick glance from his twinkly black eyes. "H'm," he said; "an accident. *Of course.*"

His tone rendered further discussion superfluous. It was arranged that, for the present, the Prussian should remain where he was. Gerard drove Hephzibah back to the Manor House: the good woman despised all pomps and vanities, yet she was by no means insensible to the honours of her position. The Count had presented her with one florin.

Near the avenue she applied the carriage-whistle.

"I will get out here, Jonker, please," she cried, and then, standing in the early snow: "On Christmas morning!" she said, while her whole figure grew heavy with reproach.

"Hephzibah, however did you come to be out in the wood?" asked the Jonker, hastily.

"In their affliction they shall seek me early," replied Hephzibah.

The quotation was inappropriate, for her omnifulgent eyes had watched the gentlemen leave the house, but the sacredness of the words staggered Gerard. He held out a gold piece.

"No, Jonker," said the waiting-woman. "Not from you. Not for this. It would be blood-money." And she marched away, gaunt and grim, down the lines of grim, gaunt elms.

As Gerard came up from the stables to the house he caught sight of Ursula walking on the carriage sweep. For one moment a great impulse came over

5*

him to go and ask her why she, as well as Helen, seemed so anxious to have him out of the way. He could understand Helen's feelings—or, at any rate, he thought he could. Well, he had spoilt the German's fine countenance for the remainder of his stay. Count Frechenfels would carry away with him a memento of his visit to the Lowlands.

But what would be the use of worrying Ursula? Gerard hated to make a woman uncomfortable. He had done it already, yesterday—after a full year's hesitation. And she had taught him a lesson he would never forget. How greatly he had wronged this purest among women! Generous natures always own an immense debt of gratitude to those they have wronged.

"Gerard," cried Ursula, "I have dropped a glove. I feel sure I came out with a pair." She held up one for him to see. Gerard had a disastrous weakness for blurting out the very thing he wanted to keep back.

"Not unless you have been in the wood already," he said, producing the missing article, which Ursula, of course, had dropped, not now, but the day before. Then he put it back. "I want you to let me keep this," he added.

Her eyes grew troubled. "Oh, no—no," she protested. "Give it back to me at once!"

"But it can have no real value for you. Whereas, for me"—his voice trembled with the memory of his terrible escape—"let me keep it," he said.

Ursula knew not what to say or think. Slowly she dropped the remaining glove on the ground at her brother-in-law's feet; slowly she raised her faithful eyes to the level of his own. In that moment, quite un-

expectedly, as by a revelation, he saw how very beautiful she was. He stood before her dismayed, his heart
full of yesterday's conversation, of this morning's ex-
periences. "Ursula," he stammered, "I—I am going
to Acheen—at once!"

"I thank God," she said, with solemn bitterness,
and left him.

Meanwhile the wretched husband shrank back behind his dressing-room curtains. It was true that he
had begun to spy on his wife. He hated himself for
doing it. He despised himself for believing the clear
testimony of his eyes.

He went down to breakfast; somebody said he was
looking ill. "It is the worry at the close of the year,"
he told his mother; "this time I can certainly not make
both ends meet." Mopius had a business-man's suspicion of financial complications. Under the influence of
the sacred season and the baronial splendour around
him, he offered his "nephew Otto," just before going to
church, a considerable loan, free of interest. The Baron
courteously declined it. "If Mopius were but a gentleman!" he reflected, with a sigh.

So the Dominé preached his festival sermon to
various inattentive ears. Gerard had disappeared, suddenly recalled to Drum; Helen was wondering what had
become of Count Frechenfels. Willie would have been
fast asleep but for Aunt Louisa's persistent pokes; the
Dowager was trying to remember whether it was in
'42 or '43 that her husband had broken his arm out
shooting three days before Christmas. "Note," said
the Dominé, "that the message of peace is brought by

the hosts, that is, armies, of heaven. It is always so in the history of the Church, as of each individual Christian. Nowhere is this truth made more consistently manifest: *Si vis pacem, para bellum.*" That was what the peasants of Horstwyk admired most in their pastor. He quoted the New Testament at them in the original Hebrew.

When the service was over, Otto remained behind to speak to his father-in-law. The preacher's last words still hovered about the deserted pulpit: "Not till the city has surrendered, does Emmanuel issue his proclamation of peace and goodwill." Otto went into the vestry, where the Dominé was resting in his armchair, the Cross showing bright on his ample black gown.

"I can't bear it any longer!" exclaimed Otto. "I must speak of it to someone. I must speak of it to *you.*"

"What is your trouble, my son?" said the Dominé gently. "If we confess our sins to each other, it often helps us to confess them to God."

Otto started back. "How do you know that it is a sin?" he asked.

"Our troubles usually are, are they not?" said the Dominé simply.

"It is a sin, and it is not a sin. I cannot resist it. It is stronger than I."

"I will help you all I can." The Dominé's face grew very pitiful. "In most of our troubles men can help, God in all."

"But I have proof," cried Otto, hastily. "So much proof—too much proof. Only listen, father."

He began speaking of his doubts, and the old man shrouded his face with one hand—his only one—white and transparent.

When Otto ceased speaking, a long silence ensued. At last the Dominé removed his hand, and Otto stared in horrified amazement. The minister's clear face had become dark purple; veins stood out on his forehead which Otto had never perceived before. He began speaking, in a very low voice, but that voice also was new to the hearer:

"Go," he said, "I have nothing to answer you."

"But, father," cried Otto, "speak to me. Pity me! For pity's sake, don't let me lose the only friend I have!"

The Dominé rose to his full height, in his long robes, pointing to the door.

"Go," he repeated. "God forgive you. I cannot. Not at this moment. *My Ursula!* Go!"

And Otto, stalwart and sunburnt, crouched to slink away.

## CHAPTER XXXII.

### THE GREAT PEACE.

THE Christmas party at the Manor House broke up not over pleasantly. Everybody seemed to realise the vague clouds that hung over the dark end of the year. Some particulars regarding the German visitor's sudden indisposition had, of course, oozed forth into the half-light, bewilderingly indistinct. Helen departed in high dudgeon, frequently repeating to her husband that whatever had happened—and she didn't want to know—was undoubtedly Ursula's fault. Mynheer Mopius said that "the higher classes of this country were hopelessly depraved."

Count Frechenfels slipped away to his native land in silence, and the military authorities took no cognisance of the affray. Of his own free will, therefore, Gerard asked to be transferred to a fighting regiment in the Indies, and very quietly and quickly he got ready to embark. He was eager to go, to escape from duns and the narrowness of his present hampered existence. And also to fly from a vague new sensation which, whenever he turned to it, caused his heart to leap up with dismay.

"I cannot understand why," said the poor Dowager, feebly; "but, somehow, I seem not to be able to understand anything any more. It all used to be so different. Gerard, the whole *world* cannot have altered because your father died?" She gazed at him as if half expecting to hear that it had. "And I wanted you to help me with the Memoir," she continued. *"You* remember about the old, bright days. Otto doesn't know. And now you also are going away."

She began to cry, looking so white and fragile, with the snoring dog upon her lap.

"I couldn't sell your father's collections, Gerard, could I?" she complained. "He wanted me not to. Still"—a long·pause: her face lighted up—"if that would keep you from going to that horrible place, I—I think I could venture. I think he would understand if I explained, when we meet again."

"No, no, let me go," said the young man, in a choked voice. "I shall come back to you, mother, with a 'position.' You will be proud of me."

The Baroness shook her head.

"I am that already," she said. "It is so uncomfortable here, I do not wonder you have enough of it. Otto is always 'busy' with 'business,' like a shopkeeper, and Ursula doesn't even love him."

"Mother!" cried Gerard.

"Not as I understand love—not as I loved your father. But, as I admitted, I no longer know. Sometimes I think I shall end like poor grandpapa, my head gets so tired; only I am still so much younger than he was, Gerard—oh, Gerard, your father died·too soon. God has been very hard on me. I never say any clever things now, as I used to do."

In the hall, Gerard, still stunned and heart-sore, was waylaid by Tante Louisa.

"I have got a little present for you," began that

lady, in her most nervous falsetto. "It has cost me a great deal of privation, Gerard. What with the increase of expenses everywhere—I have twice already felt obliged to raise my 'pension," although Otto pretends to object—I really can hardly afford it. But, then, it is a farewell gift."

Gerard took the envelope she proffered him, gratefully, wondering whether it contained . ten florins or twenty-five.

"And I should like to say, Gerard," subjoined the Freule in a flutter, "that I highly approve of your conduct in going, and also of your fighting the German. He was insufferable. Hephzibah has told nobody but me."

"Hephzibah," said the Freule in her own room. "In my youth I could have married a Prussian. We met him at Schlangenbad. But I loved my country."

Gerard, opening his envelope, extracted a banknote for one thousand florins.

When the younger son had sailed away with his strange new uniform, to the land of falling cocoanuts and cannon-balls, the waves of emotion at the Manor House settled down into a disagreeable ground-swell. Otto had made up his mind to "forgive and forget," a combination foredoomed to failure; Ursula walked straight on by her husband's side, with a gloved hand in his. It was useless to talk about forgetting. She would never do that. Not as long as a proud woman's heart beat under her wifely bosom. With scrupulous tenderness she smoothed the daily deepening furrows upon the Baron's careworn brow.

And the months passed on, exceedingly like each other, excepting that Baron Otto made himself fresh enemies with every fresh act of justice. He was stern and, necessarily, stingy. It was true that his honest impulse to discuss his suspicions with Ursula's father had cost him the last friend he possessed in Horstwyk. He clung the more tenaciously to his life's object. And he idolised his child.

On this point, at least, there could be sympathy between husband and wife. Little Otto was querulous over his infantine troubles. He disliked teething, and going to sleep, and cold water, and hot water, and eczema. He did not take kindly to existence. It is that class of children which, universally forsaken, hang on, by the nails, to their parents' hearts. There was no danger of Ursula's heart becoming atrophied. In one thing she did not obey her husband; she slipped in and out among the poor a great deal more than Otto knew.

But, having no money, she came with empty hands, and her visits were rarely appreciated, except by the purely imaginary poor person, who thought a glimpse of her bonnie face was better than a sixpence any day.

Winter was coming round again when Otto one morning received a letter from a person who signed herself "Adeline Skiff." The person spoke of great wrongs she had suffered from Gerard, of present distress, and of possible assistance. Otto had never heard of Adeline Skiff, but, with his usual thoroughness he took the next train to Drum, and unexpectedly called upon the lady. He knew her again when he saw her, although she was very much changed.

Adeline lived in a blind alley, amongst odds and

ends. She was the only inhabitant who wore a fringe, and this fact afforded her daily satisfaction. Otherwise, her reputation was dubious, and her slovenliness undoubted.

She received the Baron in a small front room, filled by a sewing-machine and two children. She hastened to explain that her husband, who was not over-kind to her, had lost his last place in a lawyer's office on account of his stubborn integrity; she got a little dressmaking, not much; she had hoped that Mynheer the Baron might be moved to do something for her or her children. She pushed forward two dirty-faced boys; Otto started, involuntarily, at sight of the elder. Adeline smiled knowingly.

"I cannot verify your story," said Otto.

Adeline looked up quickly. "Can't you really, Mynheer the Baron?" she retorted.

"And my brother, did he not give you money?"

"Yes, he gave me three thousand florins," replied Adeline frankly, "and my husband spent them."

"I cannot help that," said Otto.

No, he was not willing to assist her. She appealed but little to his sympathy.

He could not believe she belonged to the "deserving poor," and he told her so. How had she got hold of her worthless husband?

"By advertisement," replied Adeline, offended. "The same way your worthy lady tried to get hers."

"What do you mean? You are insolent," said Otto, haughtily.

"Oh, of course, Mynheer the Baron; poor people always are, when they speak the truth. But when the

Baroness was advertising for a husband she couldn't be sure that she'd get such a good one as you."

"If you mean anything except insult," said Otto, frowning, "tell me the truth and I will pay you."

Whereupon Adeline told, with slight embellishment. Ursula had answered advertisements, Gerard's among the number. She had "wanted" a husband. So, of course, she had accepted Otto's proffered hand.

"A *mésalliance* is a mistake after all. There is something in blood," thought Otto, in the train. He went home quite quietly. But that evening, to Ursula's wonderment, he dropped, for the first time, his good-night kiss.

That year's winter opened dully. Otto had let the shooting; it was a sacrifice of which he could not trust himself to speak. No one came to the house in the absence of battues. Gerard wrote home regular letters to his mother, bright letters, but the Baroness, bored to death, was growing somnolent and slow.

Bad accounts of Gerard—mostly false—occasionally reached the Manor House. People said he was exceedingly wild and devil-may-care. Rumour told, moreover, that he had got himself entangled, on the journey out, with the governess of an English family.

"Thank God, we have the boy," said Otto.

One evening, late in October, the father came into the nursery where Ursula was trying to make "Otto-chen" balance himself against a chair.

"Ursula," began the Baron, hurriedly, "where have you been this afternoon?"

Ursula slowly lifted her eyes to his excited face.

"At the 'Hemel,'" she said, firmly. "Vrouw Zaniksen
was ill again. And her baby, too. They were absolutely
destitute. So I went."

"The baby is dead," burst out Otto. "It is a case
of malignant diphtheria. I met the doctor just now.
He warned me." The father sprang forward, placing
himself between wife and child. "Leave the room!"
he cried. "Don't come back to-day. Leave the child
to me!" He caught the boy so violently to his breast,
that Ottochen began to cry. Ursula hurried away, un-
resisting, with that wail in her ears.

A few hours later, when they were alone together,
she said very meekly: "Forgive me, Otto."

He looked up wearily.

"I forgive you this," he answered. Then with an
effort as of one who breaks through a hedge. "But
not," he added, "the having married me when you did
not love me."

She was a very proud woman, yet in this moment
of his misery she knelt down by his side. "Dear husband," she said, "if I wronged you it was in innocence.
How, except by loving, can a woman's heart learn
love?"

Otto sighed, crushing down the accusation that she
had learned the lesson since, but from another teacher.

"Ursula," he said, "there is a foreboding in my
heart to-night of coming trouble. God grant it prove
only a foolish fancy. But, if not, then let us at least
lighten each other's load. Ursula, look into my eyes.
Tell me, dearest, that it is not true, this story of your
hunting for a husband, of your marrying me because
others had drawn back!"

"It is not true," she said, bitterly, still kneeling, but with scornfully averted glance.

"Tell me it is not true that you have ever loved any one else."

This time she faced him fully. "It is not true," she repeated.

"Ursula, God knows I have never wronged you by a word."

"I have never wronged you by a thought," she answered, rising to her feet, and he felt that, whatever time might alter, one shadow must remain.

"I love you," he said. "I have loved you from the first. I shall always love you through all my weakness and all my wrong."

She put her arm round his neck and kissed him.


Twice during the night Ursula slipped away from her room to listen at the nursery door. She crept back gratefully amid the perfect silence. The slight irritation in her own throat was what people always feel, she told herself, at the bare mention of diphtheria. Yet all next day she kept away from little Otto.

She was sitting at the piano, when her husband came in to her, with a white scare on his bronzed face.

"The child is not well," he said, hoarsely. "I have sent for the doctor."

Ursula started up. "Oh, Otto," she cried, "is it the throat?" Otto nodded. "Then I can go to him," she said, "now," and ran from the room.

The white spots were there; she saw them despite the little creature's struggles, and her heart sank. But

she also had a few white spots. There was so much
false diphtheria.

The doctor, however, looked grave, and muttered
"Angina pellicularis." He was angry with Ursula. "I
shall stay," he said, and she cowered down by the
little bed.

Then followed an evening of unbroken anxiety.
The child grew rapidly worse, and the parents could
do nothing but watch its gaspings. Towards midnight
the doctor performed the horrible, unavoidable opera-
tion which gave it a little more air.

In the lull of suspense Ursula's gaze fell upon Otto.
"And you!" she said, suddenly, "you are ill! You, too!
Doctor!"

Otto sank back in responsive collapse.

"It's no use holding out any longer," he panted.
"Doctor, I'm afraid there's something wrong with me
too."

"Let me look at your throat," said the doctor,
harshly. "Here's a pretty bit of business," he added,
turning to Ursula.

Very shortly after there were two sick rooms opening out of each other, and the whole household trod
softly under the near terror of Death. All through the
silent morning Ursula passed from bed to bed, her own
pain gone, feeling nothing but the dull agony of useless
nursing. Hephzibah had quietly installed herself as as-
sistant. The child's usual attendant was too full of
personal alarm. Tante Louisa came to the door with
persistent whisper. Miss Mopius left a bottle of fluid
electricity and ten globules of *Sympathetico Lob.*

The doctor, who had been away for his rounds,

came back in the afternoon and inserted a tube in the
father's throat also. Ursula did not dare to question
his solemnly sullen face.

One thought seemed chiefly to occupy Otto as· he
lay choking. He had written on a piece of paper—
finding no rest till they gave it him—the following
words:—"I must die before the child. Tell the doctor
to *make* him live so long. Or kill me. Never Gerard,
Ursula. Never, never. You first. For another Helmont!"

She had read the message in her deep distress, and
understood it. Dutch law no longer admits entail. If
Otto died childless, his mother and brother were his
legal heirs. But Ursula would be heir to her *father-
less* son.

She clasped her husband's hand in response to the
hunger of his eyes, and when the doctor came she put
the question which was straining through them.

"Doctor, he. wants me to ask it. If—if this were
to be fatal"—she went on bravely—"which do you
think—first?"

"How do I know?" replied Dr. Lapperpap, roughly.
"Pray to God for both. Both of them need your
prayers."

Once again Otto signified his wish to write, in the
short-lived winter day—

"Never Gerard," he scrawled. "You will help. By
every means. Only not Gerard. Promise."

She bowed her head, but he pressed his finger on
the final word. In his dying eyes there. was a passion
of eagerness she could not resist. Promise! promise!

"I promise," she said. And it grew slowly. dark.

Presently Ursula came through the intervening door into the nursery. Hephzibah looked up.

"Mevrouw," she said, "it's no use trying to deceive you. The baby is dying. It can't last many minutes. It's the Lord's doing. Blessed be the terrible name of the Lord!"

Ursula knelt down and calmly kissed the little congested forehead. What did the danger matter? Perhaps she was courting death.

Then she went back to her husband, and gazed deeply upon his terrible struggle. She could do nothing to help him. But she felt that this agony, also, was approaching its end.

Hephzibah knocked gently. "Mevrouw," she whispered, "Mevrouw, it is over. The poor little thing is at rest."

Some moments elapsed before Ursula appeared. Then her face stood out, in the dusk, hard and set.

"Go downstairs," she said. "Go away, and leave me alone with my dead." She pushed forth the waiting-woman, and locked the nursery-door behind her. For a moment she waited by the cot; then she returned to the inner room. It was now quite dark. A quick shuffling made itself heard in the passage. Somebody tried the lock. Ursula took no notice.

Half an hour later she opened the door and passed out into the hall. An oil-lamp was burning there. She shaded her eyes from its glare.

On the staircase she met Aunt Louisa. "Come into the dining-room, aunt," she said. "There is something I must tell you." She sank down on the nearest chair, by the glitter of the untouched dinner-table. "Dearest

Aunt Louisa," she said, "you mustn't mind too much. God has taken Otto to Himself. And—and He has taken baby also."

Aunt Louisa began to cry.

"Don't cry," said Ursula, almost impatiently; "*I* don't cry."

"Otto and baby!" sobbed the Freule—"oh, Ursula, Otto and baby!"

"Yes, doesn't it seem strange?" said Ursula, staring in front of her.

After a moment's pause she added, "Aunt Louisa, somebody must go at once, I suppose, for the doctor, and also for the notary. Mustn't they?" She went across and rang the bell.

"Anton," she said, "two messengers must be off instantly, one to the doctor, one to the notary. No time must be lost. Anton, your master is dead. And the Jonker is dead also."

The man's face grew white, and his eyes overflowed. Ursula turned hastily away.


The notary was the first to arrive. The widow received him alone. After the usual preliminaries of condolence he told her that Otto had left no will.

"I am sure of it," said the notary, "for he talked the matter over with me. Before the child's birth he was anxious to disinherit the old Baroness, his mother. When I told him that this would be quite impossible he said there was no use in his making a will."

"The Baroness has no claim on the property now,"

said Ursula. "She is very nearly childish, as you are aware." The Baroness would mean Gerard.

"If Mynheer, the Baron, died after your little boy," said the notary, as gently as he could, "then his mother and brother are his heirs. But, Mevrouw, if the Baron died first, then your little boy inherited the property *at that moment,* and you, being a widow, are the only person entitled to any estate left by your child."

"My husband died first," said Ursula.

Notary Noks rose in his agitation. "Then, Madam," he said, "you are the owner of the Manor House. Henceforth you are the Lady of Horstwyk and the Horst."

Ursula looked into the lawyer's face. "It is an inheritance of debt," she said.

———

# PART III.

## CHAPTER XXXIII.

### INTRIGUE.

"Ursula van Helmont is better," announced Willie, dawdling into his wife's boudoir; "they say she will live."

Helen glanced up from her book, not without a slight shade of impatience.

"Who told you?" she asked. "Will you have some tea? It's quite cold."

"Much obliged. Oh, everybody told me—they were talking it over at the Club."

"And supposing she had died," continued Helen, carelessly, "of this diphtheria or brain fever, or whatever she had, then I suppose Dominé Rovers would have reigned at the Horst?"

"I suppose so," replied Willie, eating a great hunch of plumcake, "but you mustn't ask me, because I don't understand. However, it's so idiotic that I dare say it's law."

Helen smiled.

"Really, Willie," she said, "you are growing quite intelligent."

"Oh, it's not me," confessed honest Willie. "Everybody was saying it."

A tinge of disappointment stole over Helen's mobile face.

"And doesn't it seem utterly ridiculous and unjust that, if Ursula Rovers marries again, all the Helmont property will go to that Smith or Jones, or whatever his name may be. It's shamefully hard on Gerard."

"Of course Ursula will marry again," said Helen. "People who have been married like that always do."

"Like what?"

"Willie, you are insufferable. Surely, 'le secret d'ennuyer, c'est de tout demander.' Like that. Neither happily nor unhappily. They have had a glimpse of possibilities. It is like gambling without a decisive turn of luck either way; one goes on. *I* should marry again."

"If I give you a chance," grinned Willie, who understood *that*.

"Which you are not gallant enough to do. Unless you seriously object, Willie, I should like to go on with my book."

He walked across and took it out of her hand.

"'La Terre'!" he said. "Really, Nellie, your tastes are catholic."

"Have you read it?" she asked, with a faint blush.

"Yes. Somebody told me it was Zola's dirtiest, so I looked at it once in a way."

"Ah, there, you see, lies the difference. You read it for the dirt. Yes, undeniably Zola is dirty, but he is not immoral. However, I think he is dull. He photographs caricatures, and that is in itself absurd. One photographs realities; caricatures should be drawn. No, I am not speaking to you, Willie; I am speaking to somebody as an audience: one has to sometimes. I'll throw away this book, if you like." She looked up at her husband almost entreatingly.

Willie hesitated, standing in the middle of the room. "Oh, no," he said. "After all, it's your business, not mine."

"All right. Don't eat too much cake."

Helen returned to her volume, but not to her reading. Between her eyes and the printed page there settled, immovable, a vision of a handsome, animated angry face, and once more she saw a blue-paper novel flying into a corner of the room. "No man that really loves a woman would like to think of her as reading such as book as that."

She turned away, on her couch, and stared hard at the pink-embroidered rosebuds on the wall.

"What! Crying?" exclaimed Willie, in great distress, coming round from the window. "Why, Nellie, what's the matter? Is your toothache bad again?"

"Yes, very bad," she sobbed, breaking down. "Do go, Willie, and send me Mademoiselle Papotier with the little bottle of laudanum."

Mademoiselle Papotier had remained at the Van Trossarts', but she frequently came to spend a few days with Helen. She now duly appeared, summoned by loud cries from her host.

"Papotier," said Helen, thoughtfully, "if ever I have a daughter I shall not educate her as you educated me."

"That is a reproach, my dear," replied the French governess, serenely, knitting on steadily with mittened hands.

"No, it is a compliment. You developed the heart. You did right. But I should kill it."

"My child, I could not have killed your heart; it was too large." The little old doll laid down her work, to gaze affectionately at her former pupil.

"Why has God sold us to men that we must live with them?" cried Helen, passionately. "He should have given us to angels or to brutes. We could have been happy with either of those."

"Fi, donc, ma chérie," said Mademoiselle. "The good God knows his business better than you."

"Ah, my dear Papotier, you are an orthodox Christian. You enjoy all the consolations of religion and neglect all its duties. It is a very advantageous arrangement to be an orthodox Christian."

"It is," replied the Frenchwoman, with a quick gleam of malice. "For we Christians, although we do wrong like other people, at least occasionally have the grace to leave off." She dropped her eyelids, and her needles clicked.

"Yes, when you are tired of it," retorted Helen, who perfectly understood the allusion to her penchant for her cousin. "And then your priest gives you absolution. I would not buy off the flames of hell at the rate of a florin per fagot." She paused, meditatively. "And feel them burning just the same," she added. Then she laughed. "Papot," she said. "You do not know that I have got a new admirer? No, I do not mean Willie, though he certainly is more considerate than he used to be. My admirer is old, and fat, and yellow; his name is Mopius, and he is uncle to the

Queen of the Horst. I met him there the Christmas before last. Him and his—charming young wife."

"Yes?" assented Mademoiselle, listlessly. "My dear, you have many admirers. Fortunately they are platonic" —she sighed a little sigh—"As were mine."

"This one is obstreperous," persisted Helen, glancing at the clock. "He presented me with a big bouquet last night at the Casino ball, making a fool of me before everybody. And he asked permission to call without his wife. Such things should be done without asking. I am expecting him even now."

"My dear, what will you do with him?"

"I don't know. Be revenged on him, some time, for last night's *Jocrissiade.*"

Mevrouw van Troyen shut down her teapot with a vigorous snap.

"There he is," she said, as the bell rang.

"My dear, your tea is not drinkable."

"What does that matter? Is it not for an admirer?"

Mynheer Mopius entered, looking as smart as a blue-speckled yellow waistcoat could make him. His thin hair was observably neat; he bowed off the retreating Papotier with a grace which bespoke his familiarity with the saloons of the aristocracy.

"I am come, Mevrouw," he said to the mistress of the mansion, "to express my condolence. I assure you I felt for you last night."

"Really? You surprise me," said Helen, meaningly. "Certainly, I deserved your pity. And everyone else's. But these mixed entertainments are always a bore."

"I was alluding," replied Mynheer Mopius, solemnly; "to the tragic death of our cousin Otto."

"Oh, were you? But that's several weeks ago. I don't think I can claim much sympathy on account of the death of my cousins. Please don't, Mynheer Mopius. Besides, he was your nephew—wasn't he?—so you can condole with yourself."

"He was." Mynheer Mopius thoughtfully stroked his hat. "We are a—kind of connections, Mevrouw."

"Ursula and you? So I understood," retorted Helen, hastily. "I hope Mevrouw Mopius is well? It was very kind of her to send me those flowers last night."

"How delicate! How high-bred!" reflected Mopius. "Oh, Mevrouw," he stammered, "it was nothing. The merest trifle——"

"But she must never do it, or anything like it, again."

Mynheer Mopius was doubly charmed. Whenever he made a fool of himself, he was tempted thereto by the belief that ladies found him irresistible. Some few men develop that fancy. Surely, in Mynheer Mopius's case, his first wife was more to blame than he himself.

"The unfading roses are yours," he said, simpering and bowing.

"Have another cup of tea," interrupted Helen, sharply. The old Indian, as we know, was a great connoisseur; he had gulped down two bowls of hot water already, imagining that it would not be proper to refuse. He meekly accepted a third, but its tepid unsavouriness aroused his native assumption.

"If I may make so free," he said, "I should like to ask where you get—ahem!—*this,* Mevrouw"—he tapped his cup—"and what you pay for it?"

"Two and ninepence, I believe," replied the lady, sweetly. "If you wish, I'll ring and ask the cook. I'm glad you like it. There's plenty more."

"Only two and ninepence!" exclaimed Mopius, horror-stricken. "That's the worst of it; you Europeans fancy you can get things without paying for them. I was in the East myself for twenty years; *I* know what good tea is, nobody better. I was famous for my tea at Batavia, Mevrouw, as Mevrouw Steelenaar told me, the Viceroy's wife. "Mynheer Mopius," she said to me, "where do you get this delicious mixture?" But I wouldn't tell her. However, I'll send you some. 'Pon my soul I shall. You shall know what tea is. I'll send you a pound to-morrow. I'll send you ten pounds."

Helen bent forward from her listless couch; a lily of the valley dropped away among the laces of her gown, and Mynheer Mopius caught at it with eager fat fingers.

"Mynheer, you will send me nothing," said Helen gravely. "Did I not make my meaning plain enough just now?" Then, not wishing to go too far, "I cannot receive presents, thank you." And, unconsciously, the twinkle in her angry eyes wandered away to a big portrait of her florid Willie.

"Ah!" said Mopius, and put the lily in his button-hole. He did it fondly, lingeringly. He understood that young husbands are jealous, however unreasonably, of experienced, intelligent men of the world. His manner exasperated her. "I am sorry," he said, flicking the flower. "I should have been only too glad, had there been *anything* I could have done for Mevrouw van Troyen."

Mevrouw van Troyen burst out laughing. "Really?" she cried, "even leaving me when I must go and dress for dinner? Mynheer van Trossart dines with us to-night; he is going to take me to the theatre." She rose.

Mopius rose also, but hung back. "Ah, the Baron van Trossart," he said. "Just so! I am very anxious to make his acquaintance. Some day, perhaps, I hope——" He hesitated, looking wistfully at Helen.

Suddenly his manner, his tone, his expression explained the whole thing to her. It was not her young beauty that had attracted this poor creature. She remembered having heard someone speak of the town councillor's ambition. There was a vacancy in Parliament——

"You can stay and meet him now, if you like," she said, ungraciously, but grasping at vengeance swift and sure. "Oh, yes, he is well enough, thanks; only rather worried about this approaching election for Horstwyk. They can't find, I am told, a desirable candidate."

She paused by the door. One look at Mopius's face was sufficient. "I don't take much interest in politics," she continued, "but, of course, my godfather does. He has so much influence. And he tells me that at Horstwyk they want a moderate man, one that would go down with many of the clericals—a Conservative, in fact. Such people are so difficult to find nowadays. Everybody is extreme."

"But—but—excuse me," stammered Mopius. "One

moment, I beg. I had always understood that the Baron van Trossart was a Liberal———"

"A Liberal? Oh, dear no. He would be a Conservative if there were any Conservatives left. As it is, he would never espouse the cause of an extremist. He sympathises with the Clericals in many things. And now I must really go upstairs. I will send my husband in to amuse you. Don't talk politics to him, Mynheer Mopius. He knows no more about them than I." *

Mynheer Mopius, left alone, wiped his blotchy, perspiring forehead. It was a master-stroke to have insinuated himself thus into the graces of this great lady whom he had been lucky enough to meet at the Horst. He felt very friendly towards Ursula.

"Ah, Jacóbus," he said to himself in the glass, "you will be 'high and mighty' ** yet." And he smiled at the vanity of women.

Willie came lounging in obediently and carried off the worshipful town-councillor to the smoking-room.

"A fine house, Mynheer van Troyen," said the conciliatory Mopius. "Exceedingly tasteful."

"Oh, it's well enough," assented loose-tongued Willie. "But the money's my wife's, you know. And, by Jove! don't she keep it under lock and key!"

Having reached the tether of his conversation, the

---

* There are three political parties in the Dutch Parliament—the Roman Catholics, the permanent Liberal majority (who are aggressively anti-religious), and a small, much-persecuted Protestant remnant. All issues of any interest are religious. There is no longer a Conservative party.

** Title of Dutch Members of Parliament.

young officer fell a-yawning, and soon suggested a little quiet *écarté.*

"There's half an hour more, at least," he said.

Did Mynheer Mopius know the game? Yes, Mynheer Mopius had played it twenty years ago in India. Ah, indeed: they play for high stakes there! Willie suggested fifty florins. He played better than Mynheer Mopius. Twenty years is a long time. When Baron van Trossart joined the two gentlemen, Mynheer Mopius had lost five hundred florins, but he found himself on quite familiar terms with Willie, and in the same room with Baron van Trossart. He bowed pompously, patronising the man who had just plucked him. "His wife would have accompanied him," he said, "but that interesting circumstances——" and he smiled knowingly to the great noble before him, on whose haughty features the look of chronic moroseness sat so well.

A little preliminary awkwardness was deepened by his praising, all astray, the amiability of the Baron's "charming daughter," but presently the tide flowed swiftly into its preconcerted channel, Helen herself having entered, resplendent with a couple of diamond stars, to direct its course.

"No, Mynheer van Trossart," said Mopius, nervously hurried, "I should never feel in sympathy with extremists. What we need nowadays, as I take it, is moderation, pacification, the old Conservative spirit, in fact."

"Ah, yes, ah!" said the Baron. He was rather interested in Mopius, having heard of him as one of those men who are willing and able to spend money in a good cause, if thereby they can further their own.

"Just the person, perhaps, for a candidate," he said to himself.

"Only," continued Mopius, ingenuously, "such people are so difficult to find. Everybody is extreme, and that frightens off the undecided voters. Now, I cannot help sympathising with the Clericals in many points. We have wronged them. Undoubtedly, we have wronged them. Each man, Mynheer van Trossart, ought to be permitted to serve God in his own way."

"Oh, undoubtedly," said the Baron, a little uneasily nevertheless.

"Personally, for instance, I take a great interest in the movement on behalf of confessional schools. I am speaking, of course, of private initiative." He hesitated; Helen nodded encouragement across the Baron's meditative study of his cigar. "I would go even a little farther. I consider that some well-proportioned concessions—— The development of Atheism, Mynheer van Trossart, is not one that I contemplate with satisfaction."

The Government functionary turned in dismay. "Why, Mynheer," he exclaimed, "I had been quite given to understand you were a Liberal?"

Helen's voice broke the ensuing silence. "We really must go in to dinner, papa. We shall be late for the theatre. Good-bye, Mr. Mopius; my compliments to Mevrouw!" She took the Baron's arm and drew him away. "I like a fat fool," she said on the stairs, "your lean fool is only half a fool. He can't look the part."

## CHAPTER XXXIV.

### THE NEW LIFE.

URSULA awoke from a long dream of suffering. The world was very dark all around her, and she strove to lie still. But even while she did so, she knew by the steady pulse once more swelling in her brain, that the endeavour would prove fruitless. Alive again, she must live.

Her husband and her child were dead. It was she who, despising Otto's fears of infection, had brought death into the house. Something told her that Otto, had he survived, would tacitly have laid the loss of the child at her door. And yet it was impossible to say for certain. Death changes all our perspectives. Ursula's was not a nature to sink away into maudlin self-disparagement. She did not dash the tears from her cheek, but she resolutely lifted her head.

Nothing however, makes us so tender towards those who loved us as the thought that we have done them irreparable wrong. When Ursula arose from her sickbed, it was with the firm resolve to honour her husband's memory by the daily sacrifice of her whole self to that which, but for her, might still have been his own life-task. She took up his cross exactly where he had laid it down. That was all she thought of—neither right nor wrong—neither God's providence, nor her own unfitness — only to do exactly as Otto would have wished.

"I understand perfectly," she said, sitting, cold, with the blackness of her mourning about her. "I told you at the time, Notary, exactly how it was. There is no ready money—not even enough to pay the death duties. There is nothing except mortgages, the interest on which only hard work can meet."

"You will have to sell some of the land," replied the lawyer, hopelessly. "You had better sell the whole place. You can't keep it up, anyhow. Not that present prices will ever pay off the mortgage."

The widow remained silent for a moment; there was little of the "nut-brown" colour left in the stately face against the oaken chair. "I shall never sell an inch," she said, at last. "Never as long as I live."

"That is a long time," retorted the matter-of-fact man of business. "A great deal may happen"—he glanced at his beautiful, beautified client—"Meanwhile, everything of value in the house belongs, I understand, to the Dowager Baroness?"

"It does."

"The Dowager Baroness, it appears to me, if I may venture to say so, is lapsing into second childhood."

No answer. The room was very lofty and empty. The far stretch of naked country was very chill and bleak. The Notary got up to go.

"If I were you," he said, "I should rid myself of the whole thing. I should decline to inherit. It's a hopeless thing from the outset. Gerard will have his mother's fortune to himself now, some day. He is all the better off for having missed the dead weight which has fallen on to your shoulders. It was a narrow squeak."

She came up to him, quite suddenly, close. "You think that," she said, with thick utterance. "You understand that. Always remember it. Do you hear?" A clear passion had overflowed the dull dark of her eyes. Violently, she mastered the trembling which shook her from head to foot.

"Of course, my dear lady; it is evident. Your brother-in-law could hardly have sold the property as you will. Yes, yes, as you will. Never mind; take your time. It is an experiment."

"No," she said, "it is not an experiment. Good day."

Notary Noks considered himself a very shrewd man. He perfectly comprehended the young Baroness's resolution to play the fine lady as long as she was able. "She's been dem lucky," reflected the lawyer as he drove away; "but she'll have to marry again and marry money if she wants to keep on. It's a queer end of the Van Helmonts." He had known the pastor's girl ever since she was a baby; his opinion of the proud, pale woman from whom he had just come away was distinctly unfavourable.

Ursula passed through the long, grey library, and, drawing a curtain, softly entered the old Baroness's rose-garlanded sanctum.

Through the south turret window the sunlight lay in an amber bar. And, encased in the clear gold, like a fly, sat the little black Dowager, surrounded by her papers, writing with the serene concentration of a well-defined literary task. She looked up across her glasses, pen in hand.

"I am busy," she said, her tone full of mild annoyance. She was always busy, the more so when Ursula disturbed her, endlessly busy with the "Memoir," noting down the same trifles over and over again.

"I know," replied Ursula, meekly, "but I thought you would like to have this, so I brought it you out of the hall."

It was a letter from Gerard away in Acheen, the first response to the more explicit account of their common bereavement, coming back to them across the wide void of five months' illness and solitude.

The Dowager tore open the envelope. Ursula waited, uncertain how to give least offence.

"There is a message for you," said the Dowager when she had finished reading, "but I shall not give it you. It is an absurd message. It is an absurd letter in many ways. Poor Gerard, his sorrows have turned his brain. Like mine. Like mine. Like mine."

She gathered together her papers, aimlessly, scattering them as she took them up.

"Stay with me, Ursula," she said, querulously. "I have nobody to help me with these important documents. There must be a letter somewhere dated August the 5th, 1854. Or is it April—April, '45? It is a letter from a friend of your father-in-law, I forget his name. I had it a moment ago. Or was it yesterday I had it? I was reading it to cook. *She* remembers things. She has been with me a long time. She remembers my dear husband quite well."

"I will look for it," said Ursula, taking care not to

disturb Plush, who always made a bed for herself in the very midst of the crackly confusion on the table. "Is this it?"

"No, indeed," replied the Baroness without glancing up to verify her verdict. "You don't know, Ursula. You are a newcomer. Cook is right, though I told her some things are best left unsaid."

She went on folding and sorting, muttering to herself with a quiet little ladylike laugh.

"Gerard is ridiculous," she presently broke out with angry energy. "He says he would have had to sell the place as well as you must now, so where's the difference? He is a fool. He would not have had to sell it, no more than Otto. Did Otto want to sell it, Ursula?"

She sat back in her chair, glowering with her light-blue eyes at her daughter-in-law.

"No," said Ursula, bending low over the writing-table.

"Aha! I thought you would try to deceive me. I forget a good many things, but I remember this. Do you hear me, daughter-in-law? I have never loved you; I had little reason to."

Her voice rose shrill with quavery passion; she tried to steady her feeble little frame with blue-veined hands on the massive arms of her chair.

"But what does Gerard mean when he says—what does he say?—I forget—he says I must be kind to you. What does he mean? I have always been kind to you. But what right had you—better have plain-speaking—to come and steal away my house from my son? Eh?" She started to her feet; the dog, disturbed by her cry, sprang up, barking furiously. "What right?" she repeated. "It is Gerard's—I told him so. I told him to come and take it away from you. He writes back 'No.' He is a coward—a coward as they all are, for a woman's face."

She sank back whispering the final sentences, and began to cry, with noiseless, unrestrained tears.

"Dear mamma, we will not sell it," pleaded Ursula, though she knew how uselessly. "You see Gerard says again he would have done so. Let us be glad, then, that he has not got it yet. Perhaps, some day, when he thinks differently—meanwhile—in—trust——"

She stopped, not daring, nor caring, to proceed. But the Dowager had only caught at one sentence.

"No, we will not sell it," she repeated; "no, indeed. Attempt such a thing and I appeal to the police! *You* sell what belongs to another. You! Listen, Ursula. I am not as strong as I was. I forget things. I daresay you imagine I am growing childish. But be sure of this: that however stupid I may seem to become, I shall always know about the Horst. I shall watch over it for Gerard. I have written to him to come back, and he will come. You alter nothing—do you understand? Nothing. Oh, my God, I am a poor defenceless old woman. Have pity upon me, and make my head keep strong. Oh, if Theodore had only not died—not died! Oh, my God, my God!"

She shrank together, like a lace shawl thrown aside, and the tears trickled down among the trinkets of her watch-chain.

Ursula rose and went out into the deserted corridor. From one of the stands by the distant hall-door

a brown-tinged "Maréchal Niel" fell to pieces with a
heavy thud on the marble pavement.

"Monk!" cried the Mistress of the mansion;
"Monk!"

With great yelps of greeting the St. Bernard came
bounding towards her.

———

## CHAPTER XXXV.

### "MRS. GERARD."

EVER since Otto's sudden death the Freule Louisa had felt stirred to practical philanthropy. Something about "redeeming the time" had got wedged in one of her ears. With her own fair hand she had concocted during Ursula's long illness uneatable messes for the invalid, and, mindful of the poor thing's former overtures to herself, she had very nearly brought on a recurrence of delirium by insisting on reading Carlyle's "French Revolution" at the bedside. Routed by the doctor, she had extended her uncertain assistance to the village; but her efforts were much hampered by the steadfast resolution that neither personally, nor through the medium of her maid, she would incur any risk of infection. When the turnpike-woman's little boy went up to the Manor House for a promised bottle of wine the Freule rolled it across to him, her smelling-bottle held tight to her nostrils, over the broad slab before the open door. And, somehow, the little boy was awkward or frightened, and the bottle rolled away down the steps in crimson splashes and a puddle. All the village heard the story with a burst of derisive reproach. "Which seeing it was after *confinement,*" said the bottle-nosed turnpike-man, "a thing about which the Freule couldn't be expected to know."

"You can never be quite sure with these people, Hephzibah," explained Freule Louisa, anxiously. "There is always a possibility of your catching something they haven't got."

"What you catch soonest is what you can't catch afterwards," replied Hephzibah, who meant fleas. Personally, the handmaid had a weakness for domiciliary visits which afforded her an agreeable opportunity of telling the people of her own class—her inferiors, as she called them—how entirely they themselves were to blame for any misfortunes they might happen to have had.

On the gusty day which brought Gerard's letter the Freule, accompanied by her faithful attendant, had departed to the Parsonage. Every Wednesday afternoon through the silent winter months the "ladies" of the village met in Josine's drawing-room, and sewed innumerable nondescript garments for tropical converts from nudity to the inspiring strains of long-drawn letters monotonous with sickness and privation. Of this little Horstwyk Society the Freule from the Manor House was Honorary President. It had taken to itself the appellation "Tryphena, Rom. XVI. 12," and had gloriously fought and conquered the opposition "Tryphosa" which the doctor's wife had rashly started without Honorary President, but with a mission-field that could boast two genuine murders. Some of the Tryphena people rather regretted the annihilation of Tryphosa. It had formed such a fruitful theme when the missionary letters gave out.

"My dear Josine, I have got a most interesting report," said the Freule, eagerly, taking off her heavy boots in the little Parsonage passage. The President and Secretary hated each other like poison. "The man at Palempilibang has lost two more children from dysentery—isn't it dreadful?—and his wife has been so very bad they will have to take her up to a hill station for change of air."

"I cannot understand it," argued Josine, as they advanced to join the others; "I packed plenty of medicine in the box we sent out last Christmas. I wrote to Leipsic on purpose so as to make sure it should be genuine. And with me, when I have symptoms, Sympathetico——"

"My dear, I should not imagine it of any use in actual disease," replied the Freule, hurriedly taking refuge from her own temerity in the bosom of "Tryphena."

"Ladies, I have a most interesting report for this day's meeting," she began, with the common eagerness to promulgate calamity. "I shall not spoil it by picking out the best bits beforehand, but I must just tell you, because you will be so sorry to hear it, that Jobson, of Palempilibang, has lost two of his remaining seven children from dysentery, and his wife is so exceedingly weak the doctor says she cannot remain at the station. Isn't it very, very sad? Ah, Juffrouw Pink, I am glad to see your cold is better."

All the ladies looked at each other, and nodded sympathetically. The Freule's news was quite in keeping with the ancient order of things. "Out yonder" was very far away, and people always died there. When they died you had a vague conception that you were getting your money's worth. Juffrouw Pink, the very fat wife of a churchwarden, and a recent member, sat helplessly entangling the fateful disease, in her woolly mind, with the crime of Nonconformity. Mevrouw Noks, the notary's angular consort, laid down the little garment she had been engaged on.

"So *that* will no longer be necessary," she said, deliberately.  Josine, who liked to be noticeably sentimental, murmured "Fie!"

Meanwhile, Hephzibah, in the kitchen, was overawing the little Parsonage-maid.  But the thing was easy, soon-effected, oft-repeated, and she yearned for bolder game.  Presently, the drawing-room bell rang, and Hephzibah rose, aware that her weekly deliverance was come.

Every Wednesday afternoon the Freule Louisa would check the Secretary's report-droning to remark: "My dear secretary, I am sure you will excuse me, but might I ring just one moment for my maid?"  Somebody would, of course, hasten to comply with the noble President's request—the interruption was far from unwelcome to the gossip-loving community—and the Freule Louisa would compliment herself on again having invented a pretext to make sure of Hephzibah's obedience to orders.  Practically, the pretexts were but three: a handkerchief from the winter-mantle, a forgotten letter for the post, and the drying of the Freule's boots.  And Hephzibah, having made her cross-grained appearance, immediately sallied out on errands of her own.  For the Freule never rang twice—lest she should make the discovery she dreaded.

Hephzibah was not afraid of dirt or disease.  Both she knew to be the outcome of human wickedness, and with human wickedness Hephzibah Botster had little to do. She feared only one thing in this world, or the other world, the Intangible, consolidated and incorporated for her in a great overshadowing conception, the Devil. Hephzibah believed overwhelmingly in the Devil. Her existence was full of him. And therefore, strong-minded saint though she was, she did not like to find herself alone in the dark.

As a rule, she spent her Wednesday afternoons with Klomp, the lazy proprietor of the tumble-down cottage in Horstwyk wood. Klomp was what she chose to call "a sort of a distant connection of hers," he being disreputable, and a cousin-german. This disreputable man she had, however, made up her mind to marry, for her chances were infinitesimal, and she felt that the tidying him up would be a glory and a joy.

As she now went zig-zagging along the road, crooked in feature and movement, through the sloppy haze of dull-brown bareness, she came across a shy urchin who was gathering forbidden firewood. Him she immediately accosted, like the Bumble she was.

"Do you know, you boy, who comes for children that steal?"

"Jesus," stammered the frightened culprit, giving the invariable answer of all Dutch children to any question that savours of the Sunday-school.

"The Devil! The Devil! The Devil!" reiterated Hephzibah, with impressive vociferation. "Do you understand me? The Devil." She attempted, ignoring physical impossibilities, to fix both her eyes in one soul-searching stare. But the little boy lifted his own pale-blue orbs in saucer-sized reproach.

"It's very wrong to swear," he said gravely.

So Hephzibah continued her way, for "Answer not a fool," she reflected, "according to his folly." She saw, through the gaunt glitter of the trees, Klomp's half-detached shutters hanging forlorn. She wondered who had opened them on this usually deserted side. Certainly not Klomp. She smiled grimly. She would put things to rights, as was her custom, and scold him.

She heard voices inside the house, an unknown woman's voice, and laughter—actually laughter from Klomp, whose utmost exertion, in her presence, hardly attained to a smile. She pushed open the door and entered, indignant. Some chipped crockery was spread over the crippled table, and behind an odorous paraffin-stove and coffee-pot sat a frowsy female of spurious pretensions to elegance—a female with whom Hephzibah was not acquainted, but whose name was Adeline Skiff. The virtuous Abigail immediately wrote down the stranger "a bad lot," and less virtue would have sufficed thus correctly to apprise her.

"Company! Dearie me!" cried Hephzibah, in a whole gamut of spinsterly suspicion. "And where, pray, are Pietje and Mietje, John?"

Klomp yawned.

"Wednesday, is it?" he said. "So much the worse." After which uncourteous allusion he subsided.

"Let me introduce myself to the lady," interposed Adeline, all mince and simper. "I am a cousin of Mynheer Klomp's, and I have come to stay with him for a week or two."

"Cousin!" repeated Hephzibah in a tone of flat denial. She stalked to the table, and sat down square.

"Now, John, I'm a distant connection of yours, and I know all about your family. And what cousin may you be, mum, pray, and on which side?"

"Oh, I never can remember those genesises!" cried Adeline, with a charming laugh, as she hastened to arrange her fringe.

"Dirty hands!" reflected Hephzibah.

"My name is Botster," she said aloud, "and one thing I know for certain, Madam, that you never were a cousin of mine."

Adeline looked surprised at this open aggression, but Adeline had never liked disagreeables of any kind.

"Have some coffee?" she asked. "There is a little —a little taste from the coating of the coffee-pot, whatever it may be, that gives quite a peculiar flavour, as I was just telling Klomp."

She laughed again, and the sluggard smiled contentedly.

"Oh, nobody ever rinses it out," he said. "I boiled some rat's-bane in it the other day."

Adeline shrieked.

"Of course, you are a stickler for neatness, Juffrouw —Juffrouw?"—cried Hephzibah furiously, letting one of her eyes travel down the soiled ribbons of the visitor's tawdry dress, "I like people to be tidy, not like you, Cousin John. Cleanliness is a great virtue, Juffrouw. Perhaps you know it is placed next to godliness."

"Yes, I see it is," replied Adeline, with a gesture of sudden malice, "sitting side by side."

To such levity Hephzibah could allow no recognition. She was burning to find out the intruder's name, and, after some futile strategy, which deepened the mystery, she boldly demanded it.

"Why, Klomp," replied Adeline, "Klomp, of course, isn't it, Cousin John?" She winked at Hephzibah's relation impudently.

"I don't believe it," said Hephzibah.

"Well, if it isn't, I'll make it so. Some day, perhaps, I'll tell you more, and some day, perhaps, I shan't. If you were going to have a new white dress, what colour would you have it trimmed?"

"If I, or any other decent person of our class, were going to have a white dress, it would be a night-dress," retorted Hephzibah, "and she wouldn't have it trimmed at all."

At this Adeline giggled and Hephzibah glared.

"Any one can see," said Juffrouw Skiff, "that you're a thrifty body and don't waste your money on personal adornment. Married, I dare say, eh?—ah? and a large family to look after."

Both Klomp and Adeline roared.

"I'm maid at the Manor House," said honest Hephzibah proudly; "own maid to the Freule van Borck."

"You don't say so!" Adeline's manner had grown suddenly serious. "Now, that's a remarkable coincidence. I'm very much interested in your Manor House, Juffrouw Potster. I know your people."

"Really?" replied Hephzibah politely. "I don't remember seeing you at any of our dinners. Did you come alone or did you bring your cousin Klomp?"

This time Adeline flushed scarlet, but she was resolved to avoid a quarrel with a servant from the Horst. Deserted, for the time at least by her husband, she had heard of Ursula's great good fortune, and had made up her mind to come and find out some means of extorting money from the Helmonts. Her plan of campaign was as yet undetermined; meanwhile she had taken the cheapest of lodgings with Klomp, who was, of course, in no wise a relation. "It will look better to say we are connected," she had suggested, intent upon "keeping dark" at first. "You can have the room for nine-pence," had been Klomp's only reply. "No attendance, mind."

She now got up and walked to the window, with a glance at her reflection against the greasy pane. "There are your girls, Klomp," she said, "with the child. The poor darling can never have enough of that dear little porker. Hear him shriek with delight. Are *you* fond of children, Juffrouw Boster?"

Klomp sauntered out to his affectionate Pietje and Mietje, now strapping young women both. Immediately Hephzibah came up behind the smiling stranger by the open door. She had not much time to lose.

"Look here, you," she said, hoarsely. "What have you come here for? After no good, I'll be bound. But you leave this man, mind you. Cousin or no cousin, he's my man, not yours." She was desperate at the thought of her lessening only chance.

The other turned tauntingly in the doorway.

"Your man?" she repeated. "What d'ye mean? Can't you take a joke, you fool? You don't imagine, do you, that I want to marry Klomp?"

Hephzibah shivered with horror and spite. Visions of King Solomon's impudent-faced fair ones rose up be-

fore her. "Jezebel," she said inconsistently, but with
commendable candour.

"Tut, tut," answered Adeline, looking away. "Your
dress is a shocking bad fit. I'll alter it for you. I had
no idea you came here courting, Juffrouw Boster—and
in such a dress as that!"

Hephzibah longed to strike the woman, but she only
stupidly repeated, "What did you come for?" amid the
laughter and cries of the others close by. Then suddenly she stamped her foot.

"Go away or I'll make you."

"You!" retorted Adeline, fairly roused. "What next,
you Poster! Know that you are speaking to your betters.
Imagine the insolence of it! I and Klomp! I! The insolence of it! Klomp and you; yes, that is another
matter. Here, Baby! Baby!" A sudden resolve seemed
to seize upon her. Her little boy of some three or
four raw summers came unwillingly towards the house,
diverted from his course by continual grabs at the
porker's wispy tail. "Do you see this child?" asked
Adeline, catching hold of a faded blue mantle, and
turning up a pretty though mealy little face. "This is
my child, my only one." She had shrewdly left the
infant at Drum.

Hephzibah started, and vainly pretended to have
slipped. "Well?" she said.

"His name is Gerard."

Slowly the faithful servant lifted her crossed eyes to
the other's better-favoured face. "Hussy!" she said,
deliberately, with all an honest woman's slow pressure
on the term.

Adeline burned with the immediate umbrage of a

girl who feels her ears boxed. At a leap, she resolved to rejoice in the *rôle* which had long allured her.

"Menial," she said loftily, "know your place. You are speaking to Mevrouw van Helmont."

"Well," reflected Hephzibah, pausing for breath on her hurried walk back to the Parsonage, "I am glad that I *tola* her she was a liar. Still——"

Queer stories about the Jonker Gerard had been rife in the servants' hall. The domestics of the Trossart household had added their occasional items. It was pretty well known that Helen would have married her cousin but for some sudden impediment. Judging by appearances and gossip, there was nothing absolutely improbable in Adeline's story. In fact, Adeline very nearly believed it herself. Hephzibah wished that vigorous denial could prove it untrue.

And, then, the child! Hephzibah screwed her wrinkled face up till it looked like an enormous spider. That woman Lady of the Manor! *That* woman! Hephzibah shook her head as she hurried along. "Who is thine handmaid," she said aloud, "that she should do this thing?"

She was late, and she found the Freule waiting, shawled and gaitered and exceedingly nervous, in the dim drawing-room amid driblets of unwilling conversation with Juffrouw Josine. Louisa looked vehement reproaches and longed for courage to speak them; but Hephzibah was too violently excited by her afternoon's adventure to notice such trifles as these. The pair marched off through the damp twilight.

"Red Ridinghood and the Wolf," said Josine.

"Hephzibah," began the Freule presently, in a trembling voice, "I wish you would walk on the other side of the road. One can't tell where you may have been."

Hephzibah obeyed with silent protest.

"Hephzibah," hazarded the Freule a few minutes later, unable to bear any longer the gray atmosphere of disapproval, "what is this terrible secret you said you would tell me the other day? You have alluded to it several times lately, and always declared you dared not mention it in the house. Well, we are alone now, on the road."

"Oh, it's of no account," muttered Hephzibah. "And I couldn't shout it across, besides," she added, in a lower key.

"Well, come a little nearer, if you like, but not nearer, mind you, than the middle."

"It's nothing," said the maid, gruffly.

"Oh, but it is. Coming out, you told me it was most important. Now, Hephzibah, you are in a bad temper, because your conscience reproves you."

"My conscience!" exclaimed the immaculate maid. "My conscience reproves me a hundred times a day!"

"So much the better. Then tell me your secret."

A struggle was going on in the handmaid's bosom. She prolonged it for some distance, perhaps unnecessarily, but then she rather enjoyed a moral struggle. At last she said, in a dull, dissembling voice;

"I'm sure now, Freule, that Anne Mary steals cook's perquisites. I can prove it."

"Pooh! Is that all?" cried the disappointed Freule. "You've talked about that before, and I don't care a brass farthing, Hephzibah. A nice secret to make secrets of. Go along to the other side of the road, do."

Hephzibah obeyed, looking very wise.

———

## CHAPTER XXXVI.

### THE DEAD-AWAKE.

"Supposing I had told my secret," reflected Hephzibah, peeping through the keyhole. "Supposing I had
told my secret. If I hadn't met that woman at Klomp's
I believe I really should have told the Freule this time.
Wonderful are the ways of Providence! Imagine the
slatternly creature established here at the Manor House
playing the mistress over—*me!*" Hephzibah peeped
down again. "She in there's bad enough, the parson's
daughter. But, at least, she leaves a body alone." Then
Hephzibah shuffled away on velvet slippers, the only
soft thing about her.

The keyhole which had attracted her was Ursula's.
My Lady sat at her nightly task by the lamp. Her
forefinger was inked, her earnest forehead was puckered,
yet the figures would not add up right. She was learning book-keeping by double entry; twice a week a master
came from Drum.

She sighed, and pushed in her hand among her
rumpled hair. Romance is romance; alas, that in real
life it should so seldom be romantic! There was less
money, even, than in Otto's time. Therefore, things
went even worse with everybody than they had gone
in Otto's time. She sighed, returning to her distasteful task.

All the villagers disliked her, and she knew it. They considered it a slight upon themselves that their parson's daughter should usurp, by a fluke, the ancient throne of the Van Helmonts.

Ursula would not have minded this, however, had she known how to pay her succession duty and make both ends meet.

As she sat thus, working and worrying, the door was suddenly thrown wide open, and, without any warning, Hephzibah walked in.

Her face shone white, her whole manner and expression were as of one sick with alarm.

"Come upstairs, Mevrouw," she said in a shrill whisper, and when Ursula hesitated, she caught her by the sleeve. "Come upstairs," she reiterated, leading the way, but refusing any further explanation. Ursula mechanically followed. Gasping for breath, the woman ran along a dim corridor, and then stopped in the dark of an unused room.

"Hark!" she said, with uplifted finger.

"What?" answered Ursula, impatiently. "I hear nothing. Do you?"

For only answer Hephzibah passed behind her and closed the door, through which a faint glimmer of light had come stealing. They were then in absolute darkness.

"Well, what now? What is the matter?" repeated the young Baroness, with some anxiety in her tone. In the obscurity she yet perceived that Hephzibah had uplifted a finger.

"Hush!" said the maid. "You will hear it presently. There! There it is!" She bent forward, clutching at her companion. "There it is! What do you say now?"

Ursula fell back and tore open the door again, but the light thus admitted only showed looming shapes.

"I hear nothing," she said faintly, dazed, alone with this mad-woman. She had always had an undefined dread of the crooked-eyed maid.

"Oh, my God, I had an idea that if you came it would stop!" cried Hephzibah. "Oh, never mind the door. Door or no door, it won't stop now. I've heard it before, several times. It's like a man gasping. In there." She pointed to the closed entrance leading to an inner chamber. "Mevrouw, dare you really say you hear nothing at all?"

Ursula shuddered. They were standing in the deserted nursery; the room adjoining was that in which Otto had died. Both were now disused.

"Come, Hephzibah," she said, soothingly. "There is nothing here; you are mistaken. Come downstairs. You are distressed, poor thing, by the terrible memory of your nursing, in this very room. Do not think of it. I cannot trust my own thoughts to dwell on those days."

But the waiting-woman took no heed. She had fallen on her knees, and remained thus, her face averted towards the closed door of the inner chamber.

"O God, have mercy!" she wailed. "*She* doesn't hear it! What have *I* done? If I have done wrong, my fault is as nothing compared to her sin! She must hear it. Surely she must hear it." She paused a moment, and in a calmer tone: "It isn't fair," she said.

Ursula had clutched her by the shoulder.

"What do you mean? What do you know?" asked Ursula, resolutely.

Still the woman did not seem to hear her.

"Hush!" said Hephzibah, falling, with uplifted finger, into her earlier attitude of intentness. "Listen. A sobbing, choking noise, as of a man gasping for breath. I often hear it there. Not always. If I always heard it it might be fancy."

"What do you know?" repeated Ursula, with persistent stress.

Hephzibah hesitated. Before her rose the image of Adeline, fringe and all, giving orders in the store-room. She turned suddenly.

"Know, Mevrouw?" she said, "what should I know? A great deal less than you, anyway. I'm only a poor servant. I suppose it's some of Satan's doing. Ah, he's mighty strong · is Satan—mighty strong." She slipped away towards the glimmer from the passage, muttering, "Mighty, mighty strong," and so stole from the room.

Ursula made no effort to retain her. The door fell to, and the black silence seemed to thicken. Ursula stood quite still. Involuntarily she listened, scornful of herself. Something creaked in the next room, or near her —her heart leaped into her throat. With an exclamation of impatience she threw open the intervening door.

She had not entered these two death chambers since her illness. The inner one was empty and damply chill. Here the shutters were thrown back, and through the gaunt window a bluish greyness fell across the deeper dark. Ursula's figure struck against the dim twilight in a great black bar.

After a moment's hesitation she walked to the window, and gazed up into the night. Amid a confusion of tumbled clouds an occasional star lay peeping, like a diamond through black lace. One of them, close above her, seemed to be watching, steadily.

"Otto," said Ursula, in a firm whisper, "I am doing my best. I am trying to keep my promise. I don't know how God judges me. I don't know. Otto, I am doing my best."

She stood for some time thinking. Then she shivered, as if suddenly realising the clammy cold all about her, and hurried away.

In the corridor, just as the cheerful lamplight was broadening to greet her, she met Aunt Louisa, who emerged in a great hurry from her own private sitting-room. Aunt Louisa was evidently in one of her "sinful fits," as Hephzibah called them (Hephzibah called "sinful" whatever was distasteful to herself). The Freule's left hand held a letter, and her right hand an envelope. She cried out as soon as she caught sight of Ursula:

"Ursula, I *must* have my interest! I didn't ask you back for the capital—not even when Otto died. But, Ursula, I must have my interest."

Ursula paused. The Freule's whole face quivered with pink excitement. Both her extended hands shook.

"I don't understand, Aunt Louisa!" said Ursula, dizzily. "What is it?"

"Now, Ursula, don't say that. You know how nervous money matters make me. And I'm afraid it was very foolish of me to give my money to Otto, and I didn't ask it back, not even when you got it all."

"It's a good mortgage," interrupted Ursula, "and, besides, you couldn't ask it back."

"Now, don't throw those law terms at my head," cried the Freule, in a tremulous screech, "for I don't know what they mean. But I do know that it's very ungrateful of you to speak like that, Ursula, after what I've done for you all. And I left the money in your hands because I think you are strong, and, altogether, it is a very interesting experiment. But I must have my interest. I can't do without my interest. Here's my man of business writes that Noks has prepared him" —the Freule referred to the paper which crackled between her fingers—"for the possibility of there being some delay in the payment of the next instalment. Now, Ursula, I pay my board and wages punctually, and I can't have that."

"When is the next payment due?" asked Ursula.

"On the first of next month. Now, Ursula, don't look like that. It is you who are to blame, not I. Never have I been twenty-four hours too late, though poor Theodore used to leave the money lying about for days. But your mother-in-law once truly said that, at any rate, you had this of royalty about you—you could do no wrong! Well, *that* is strong, and I have no objection. By the bye, your mother-in-law meant it ironically. But strong people should, above all, be honest, Ursula, and it's dishonest to take advantage of the helplessness of a poor ignorant spinster like me."

"You will have your interest," said Ursula, by the stair-head, under the full glare of the lamp. "Noks was wrong." And she went slowly down into the vestibule. She felt that she must get away, for the moment, from this suffocating house.

She took a hat and passed forth into the night. A cold little wind was curling in and out among the trees. Everywhere spread the grimness, the bare, black hardness of March, shrouded in darkness and indistinctly threatening. Ursula's yearning went out, in this absolute solitude, to the husband whose strong love had lifted her up and placed her thus terribly high. Even a servant still heard his voice in its dying agony. Had she then, the wife, already forgotten him? No, indeed, more closely than during his lifetime their existences were interwoven, in her faithful fulfilment of his charge. She was possessed with a sudden foolish desire to hear that kind voice, that earnest voice again—ay, even the last gasp, as did Hephzibah! She hurried in the direction of the churchyard, of the vault where *he* lay. He had loved her, loved her, lifted her up—the simple village girl—to be my Lady Nobody. She wanted him again. She wanted him.

All at once, as she was hastening on, the memory struck her, like a new thought, of how he had doubted her honour. She stopped, stock still, in the middle of the road. Then, like a smitten flower from the stem, she dropped by the side of a broad elm tree, and for the first time since her widowhood, gave way to a passion of tears.

"What's this?" said a rough voice, close in front, and a dark lantern flashed out its hideous wide circle. "What are you doing here? Now then, look sharp."

The Baroness staggered to her feet.

"It is I," she stammered, "Mevrouw van Helmont," and then, recognising the local policeman, "I am not well, Juffers; help me home."

The man escorted her in amazed, if deferential, silence. He could understand even a Baroness being suddenly taken ill, but he could not understand a Baroness being out there alone at this time of night. It was not difficult for her to read his thoughts as he tramped on, lantern in hand; she gladly dismissed him, with an unwisely large gratuity, as soon as the lights of the house came in sight.

"Well!" he mused, standing, clumsily respectable, with the broad silver piece on his open palm, "she isn't too ill to walk, anyway. Straight as a dart. Blest if I didn't think it was Tipsy Liza. I wish that *she'd* march as easy when I takes her to the lock-up."

Hephzibah came forward as the young Baroness entered the house. With unusual politeness, but with averted eyes, she took that lady's hat. And Ursula, returning to her room, where her copy-books lay patiently, painfully waiting, felt that henceforth she was, more or less, in this silent servant's power.

"I will go on," she said, doggedly, settling down to "debtor" and "creditor," "with God's help or without."

## CHAPTER XXXVII.

### POLITICS.

NEXT day, the spring weather being mild and claw-
less, like a couchant cat, Mynheer Mopius arrived at
Horstwyk station.   He wore a silk neckerchief and new
goloshes, for Harriet was a careful wife to him in a way.
He had not felt in good health of late, and his leathery
cheek had deepened to gamboge.

"Be very cautious what you eat, Jacóbus," Harriet
had said as he was preparing to depart.   "If you par-
take of anything greasy, you are sure to be ill again."

"I don't care," replied Jacóbus recklessly.    "I'd
rather die than not eat.   What's the use of living if
there's nothing left to live for?  I'd rather die at once
than vegetate for thirty years on slops.   Pass me the
pickles.   I could wager that you make believe I'm the
baby that hasn't come!"

Harriet smiled thinly.   The greatest disappointment
which can befall a woman lay upon her.   Stowed away
upstairs were a pink berceaunette and a quantity of
little garments that had never been used.

"'There's not much chance of my getting rich food
at the Horst," continued Mopius.   "Ha! See? I should
think they weigh out their butter there."

"Poor Ursula," said Harriet, softly.   After a few

moments of silence, she added: "It was such a pretty little boy."

"Huh?"

"Jacóbus, how late will you want the carriage?"

"I shan't want the carriage."

"Not want the carriage?" Harriet well knew how he enjoyed driving away from the railway station amid an admiring crowd of acquaintances who walked.

"No, I shall come home on foot. Go you for a drive, Harriet; it's rather a nice day. It'll put some colour in your pale cheeks."

She looked across at him gratefully.

"Law," he said, "to think how you've gone off of late. Who'd have thought it? You were a deuced fine woman, Harriet, in days gone by."

"Oh, I'm a fine woman yet," she answered. "You must leave me a little time." She got up and walked to the window. "Willem is waiting," she said. "Goodbye. Mind you don't sit in a draught."

Upon arriving at Horstwyk, Mopius went straight to the Parsonage, whence he could most conveniently order a fly for the Horst. The Dominé came out into the garden, and gave his brother-in-law a hearty greeting. Nevertheless, he hastened to cut off any risk of a *tête-à-tête*.

"Josine will be delighted," he said. "Let us go in to her. We have not seen you for a long time, Jacóbus. Not since——" The Dominé threw open the sitting-room door.

"Not since the funeral," supplemented Jacóbus, standing in the middle of the floor. "Ah, that was a very sad business. Good-morning, Josine." He shook his head mournfully. Jacóbus was of opinion that social events should be made to yield their full meed of emotional enjoyment.

"Ah me!" replied Miss Mopius, heaving an enormous sigh. The whole apartment was littered with vari-coloured tissue-paper in sheets and strips and snippets. Miss Mopius was fabricating artificial flowers. Her whole face assumed an expression of deeply dejected resignation.

"How do you do, Jacóbus," she said, "I am glad to see you. I hope you are better. Sad, indeed. Did you say 'sad'?"

"I did," responded her brother, sitting down.

"Some people say 'sad,'" explained Josine, in the same tone of aggrieved acquiescence, "and some people say 'bad.' I say 'bad.'"

The Dominé, who had remained standing near, emitted what sounded like a slight grunt of impatience.

"Yes, Roderigue, you may object," continued Miss Mopius, carefully studying the pink paper frill between her delicate fingers, "but nothing will deter me from doing my duty. And it is my duty to point out distinctly, that our dear Ursula has committed what I do not hesitate to qualify as a *crime*. It may be painful to you as a father——"

"Oh, no, not any longer," interrupted the Dominé.

"I am inexpressibly grieved to hear you say so. But it is all the more incumbent upon me to show that I, at least, am not blinded by affection—or let me openly declare, by prejudice. I am devotedly attached to my niece, but, as I regretfully confessed to Mevrouw

Noks, and—and one or two other people, with tears,
ay, with tears I said it"—Miss Mopius selected a wire
and planted it in the heart of—her flower, "dear Otto
was murdered, inadvertently, of course, yet none the
less wilfully murdered." She shut her thin lips with
a snap, and twirled a wisp of green paper round the
wire.

"The weather is nice and mild," said Mopius, "and
for the time of year I should call it seasonable."

"I notice an occasional crocus," said the Dominé.

"He deserved a better fate," said Josine.

She shook her red ringlets and put up a thin hand
to her head. "My heart aches," she said, "to think
how easily it might all have been avoided. Ursula
was a child. Poor Otto; he wanted a woman of more
experience—not a plaything, but a helpmate. He
might have lived forty years longer. Ah, he deserved———"

"You," interrupted Jacóbus, fiercely, with a sneer,
his habitual form of humour. She bored him.

Miss Mopius rose to the occasion. Slowly she
smoothed out her crimson-figured wrapper. "Yes," she
said. "Me, if you like, or any other woman past thirty.
Jacóbus, you are unkind. Now you are here, you might
as well give me some money for 'Tryphena.' We
are sending out a box. I am making these flowers
for it."

"Flowers!" growled Mopius. "What?—to sell?"

"No—no, to send. Freule Louisa has knitted
seventy-three little tippets for the school children—
that's the useful part, Jacóbus. And I make these
flowers for their Christmas treat—that's the ornamental.

I must admit," cried Josine, with a simper, "that I *always* prefer the ornamental!"

"Where's your missions?" queried Mopius. "I daresay they've got flowers enough out there. Better than those." He contemptuously pointed a fat finger at a whole cluster of bright-coloured balls.

"In Borneo, Jacóbus, among the wild Dajaks, the head-hunters, Jacóbus." She rested her work in her lap. "So you despise my poor flowers? They will have, I feel confident, their message to those savage hearts."

"Bosh," said Jacóbus.

"What, do you not believe in the civilising influences of refinement?" Josine spoke with sudden asperity. "What are you but a Dajak?"—Jacóbus lifted his big bald head indignantly—"as the President of the Missionary Conference so beautifully said——"

"I? What does he mean? Who talked about me?" burst in Jacóbus, furiously. "If my candidature for Parliament exposes me——"

"You, I, everybody. What are we but Dajaks clothed and in our right minds? I feel confident that when the innocent children hang up my roses on the rude walls of their dwellings, their fathers will take down the hideous heads of victims which now form their only decoration. Jacóbus, could *you* leave a rosebud lying next to a skull?"

"Josine, you're a fool," answered Jacóbus. "I wonder how Roderick can find patience to live with you."

The Dominé sighed, then coughed hastily, blushing.

"What do the city missionaries say?" persisted Miss Mopius, who was accustomed to having the last word.

"'Beautify the home,' 'Put up a picture in your room.' Mine is the same principle. Jacóbus, after thus rudely abusing me, you might give me a contribution."

"Oh, well—there!" replied Jacóbus, fingering out a gold piece from his waistcoat-pocket. "But I don't believe in missionaries. They're all dashed nonsense and lies."

The Dominé started by the window, like a war-horse that hears the bugle-call. "Don't say that, Jacóbus," he interposed. "You shouldn't say that."

"Shouldn't? Shouldn't? I know more about missionaries than you do. A set of guzzling do-nothings, living on the money of silly spinsters like her." He pointed to his sister, who immediately put her hand to her head.

"You forget that I also have seen something of heathen countries," replied the Dominé, with somewhat heightened intonation; "and I, who was then a soldier of the sword, I delight to pay my tribute of humblest admiration to the soldiers of the Cross. Theirs is a certain daily sacrifice without possibility of fame or reward; and you, Jacóbus—forgive me that I say it— you people who have gone in search of money, where they go in search of souls, you, on your return, should at least have the grace to be silent about their occasional delinquencies, as they are about your continuous atrocities. Of course I am speaking collectively. I have not the slightest intention to insinuate——"

"Abuse Josine," cried Jacóbus, floundering to his feet; "I see my cab has come. Begad, why don't you pitch into Josine?"

"Josine is a woman," replied the Dominé shame-facedly, following his retreating brother-in-law down the passage. "I always feel that we are at a great dis-advantage with regard to the gentler sex, though I freely admit that Josine——"

"Well, you needn't work your steam off on me, and that when I so seldom come to see you! By Jove, it's too bad. Look here, Rovers, I am going on to Ursula. I wanted to have spoken to you about serious matters, instead of wasting my time on missionaries. You know I'm the Radical candidate for Horstwyk. Of course you'll support me, and Ursula will take her cue from you."

"I have no politics," replied the Dominé, resting his armless sleeve on the gate-post; "and Ursula will judge for herself."

"You mean to oppose me?" cried Jacóbus, sud-denly filling the fly-window with his big orange face.

"No; I never vote—I do not consider it a part of a pastor's work, but I certainly shall not influence Ursula."

"Oh, be hanged to you!" retorted Mopius, im-mensely put out; "but I'll undertake to manage Ursula without any influence of yours. Drive on, coachman—to the Horst."

The Dominé crept away to his sanctum with slow shakes of the head. He reflected that Mopius might have been right about "letting off the steam." But what can one do? Has Pericles not said that, "He who knows a thing to be right, but does not clearly explain it, is no better than he who does not know." Again the Dominé shook his head, and, with a mechanical glance at the foxed engraving of Havelock, he hurried to his easy-chair and his Bible.

Mopius meanwhile was hastening to his second and far more important interview. Gradually his ruffled feathers smoothed down, and he smiled with a certain complacence. Rovers had always been a wrong-headed fellow, and, therefore, obstinate. "Head-strong and head-wrong," was a favourite formula with Mopius, who, of course, considered himself to be neither. He had disapproved of Mary's marriage, although not knowing Captain Rovers at the time. Mary was handsome, he said, and might have done better. Besides, some exceptionally important people disapprove of all their relations' marriages on principle.

Mopius was now the official candidate of the Radical party. He had explained that he was uncle to the Baroness van Helmont of the Horst, and everybody had immediately understood his fitness for the post he coveted. For the influence of the Lady of the Manor must be all-decisive. It wanted but a word passed round to the tenants, and the election was secure. Was Mynheer Mopius assured of his niece's support? So many of these high-born ladies had a weakness for religion. It was old-fashioned, of course, and the worse for wear, but they inherited it like the family jewels, or gout.

Mynheer Mopius shrewdly closed his eyelids. The movement was eloquent of quiet strength. If that was all they wanted, he could set them at rest. He had his little plan.

Well, that was all they wanted. He need only bring

them a signed declaration from Ursula, and they would
recognise him.   So he started for the Horst to fetch it.
Meanwhile—such things leak out—he was practically
their candidate already.

Only the Baron van Trossart had been disagreeable
and exacting.   But he was notoriously an ill-tempered
man.  He had muttered stupid insinuations about wolves
in sheep's clothing.   And he had finally insisted upon
a written obligation from Mopius—"quite between you
and me, of course"—that the latter would always and
unconditionally vote with the Liberal party.

"Why, of course, Mynheer the Baron," Jacóbus had
said, eagerly.   "You must have misunderstood me when
we met in Mynheer van Tróyen's smoking-room.   'Always and unconditionally vote with the Liberal party.'
Where shall I sign it?   I have not the slightest objection.   You will support me, I hope?"

"Yes, and be d—— to you," said the Baron van
Trossart.

When Mopius arrived at the Manor House Ursula
was again closeted with the notary.   She rose with a
swift impulse of relief as soon as her uncle's name
reached her ear.   She looked harassed.   "You must
excuse me, Mynheer Noks," she said, going to the door.
"We can talk it over again another time."

"When?" said the notary.

"One of these days.   To-morrow, perhaps.   No, the
day after."

The notary followed her, inflexible.

"Mevrouw," he said, "we can't put off quarter-day.
There is the interest, and there is that bill I spoke of.

Three thousand florins are still wanting to make up the sum. In ten days' time you *must* have them."

"Must!" repeated Ursula haughtily, drawing herself up.

"Yes. Must. It's not my 'must,' but the law's. The law knows nothing of great ladies. High or low, must is must." Ah, thought the irritated notary, Mejuffrouw Rovers, I had you there.

"Mynheer Noks, I cannot keep my uncle waiting."

Mopius was standing in the small drawing-room with the Guicciardi ceiling, his fishy eyes unappreciatively fixed on a Florentine inlaid cabinet full of cameos and signets.

"A lot of money here," he said, by way of greeting, as Ursula entered. "And what rubbish outside a museum! Why, my terra-cottas at Blanda are ten times as effective."

"The things belong to the Dowager Baroness," replied Ursula.

"Why, you're the Dowager Baroness now, ain't you?" objected Mopius. "Harriet said so when we sent our cards. Who'd have thought it of Mary's child? Not that I care a brass farthing for barons or princes of any kind. You couldn't make a greater mistake, Ursula, than to imagine that I felt in any way proud about your elevation, so don't ever come offering to do *me* any service of any kind."

"It is the last thing I should wish to do," replied Ursula. "Won't you sit down?"

"Quite right, though I can't say you put it very prettily. However, in this family, it's I that confer benefits. I've come here with that object now. You're a mighty fine lady, Ursula; but you may be glad of a burgher uncle with a well-filled purse."

Ursula waited, wondering.

"I'm going to offer you money," said her uncle bluntly.

Ursula dropped her eyes to the floor. "You are doubly mistaken, Uncle Jacóbus," she answered in her coldest manner. "I am not a fine lady, nor am I a beggar."

"Hoity-toity! Not a beggar? H'm. No money wanted? Ha!" Mopius got up in all the splendour of his well-clothed portliness. "How about that bill which falls due on the first? Ah, you see I know. How about that, my Lady of the Horst?"

Ursula rose also. She was not too proud to accept assistance. But of some of our friends we know at once that their seeming favours cannot really be to our advantage. It is only a question of finding out.

"Does everybody in Drum know all about my affairs?" asked Ursula, her pale face turning very red.

"Everybody? Fie, am I everybody? Ursula, I can never forget that you are my own sister Mary's only child."

"No," replied Ursula, "I suppose not."

"But a good many people do know, undeniably. And that must end. It hurts my feelings. I am not a windbag of a noble. I am a simple gentleman, a hater of shams. I like money to ring clear on the counter, full weight." Jacóbus patted his waistcoat pocket. "So, Ursula, this is what I have to propose. Things can't go on in the present manner, nor can I have my niece sold up. I offer to make you an annual payment of five thousand florins——"

"Uncle Jacóbus!"

Mynheer Mopius smiled with contented deprecation.

"That is your side of the matter. As long as I represent the district of Horstwyk in Parliament. That is mine."

"But you may never represent Horstwyk in Parliament?"

Mynheer Mopius sat down again.

"That depends upon my Lady of the Horst," he said. "So you see it is very simple. You intimate to your tenants that you wish them to vote for Mopius, and I pay in to your bankers the sum I have just named."

Ursula remained silent, thoughtful.

"It is pure generosity on my part," continued her uncle, "for, anyway, you surely wouldn't have instructed them to vote on the other side. But that's my way. I don't mind. And I'm glad to help my sister Mary's child."

Ursula seemed slowly to have understood the very simple transaction. Her uncle watched her with a trace of anxiety in his unhealthy eyes. Surely there was nothing in his offer dishonest or dishonourable?

"There is one little objection to the arrangement you propose," said Ursula, at last.

"Of course," replied Mopius; "women always have one little objection to every arrangement—it is their way of getting the last word."

"I mean one objection which renders all others superfluous. You are the Liberal candidate and my sympathies are with the Clericals."

Mynheer Mopius sat back, puffing and snorting.

"Nonsense," he said, "Ursula, nonsense. What do women know about politics? Your father confessed he knew nothing, so he can't have taught you. And Otto, I was given to understand——"

"Let us leave Otto out of the question, please," interrupted Ursula, with some asperity. "In this matter, at least, I am my own mistress."

"But the traditions of the Van Helmont family——"

"The traditions of the Van Helmont family are, of course, Conservative, and Conservatism is dead. At this moment I, a woman, have to choose, according to my feeble lights, between State-atheism and a persecuted sect."

"And lose," said Mopius, "the five thousand florins."

But that was a stupid move. Ursula's eye kindled in the silence which ensued.

"Ursula!" exclaimed Jacóbus in despair, for he saw his chances fading, "you are utterly unreasonable! How dare you suggest that I am an atheist, that I have any objection to religion? I distinctly approve of religion. It is a praiseworthy and highly respectable thing, and I always allow the servants to go to church. Your Aunt Josine is right, you are nothing but a foolish child. What do you know about politics?"

"Very little," replied Ursula, calmly, "but it seems to me that the less one knows about politics the better one can choose between principles. And I choose the principle of liberty to worship God."

Jacóbus flourished his big hand till he almost touched her face. "Hang your quiet way," he cried. "There's no talking to a woman like you. So you mean to tell me your mind's made up, you fool? Instead of living here in luxury and splendour, all settled and comfortable, as I suggest, you'll let this over-mortgaged place come under the hammer and go home to your old father, without clothes to your back?"

Ursula stood, black and tall, by the desolate hearth. "Uncle Mopius, I don't want the money, but I'm very sorry not to be able to do as you wish. This is my sole opportunity, my single bit of influence, so to say, in my new position, and I must use it as I think best."

Tears of spite swam across Mynheer Mopius's vision. "Ursula," he said, "you—you idiot, why didn't you tell me you had political opinions *before?*"

"I didn't know you cared—but what difference would that have made?" she answered, innocently.

He caught up· his hat with an indignant swoop. "Never again," he said, "shall you touch a penny of mine. You are ruining my prospects and your own, from sheer caprice. I shall never, now, be a member of Parliament. But I'll pay you out. And to think that *you* have done this—you, who are my own sister Mary's child."

"Yes," replied Ursula, grimly. "I always was."

## CHAPTER XXXVIII.

### THE OLD PLOT.

"What now?" exclaimed Ursula, still standing where Mopius had left her, by the great unused fireplace. "I cannot even trust Noks, who chatters. Poor father knows nothing about business. I am quite alone."

Even as she spoke there flashed across her mind a memory of her husband's words: "Not Gerard. Never Gerard. If ever you want a counsellor turn to Theodore Helmont."

Hardly knowing what she did—certainly not knowing why she did it—she sat down and wrote a telegram, then and there, to this cousin she barely knew.

"Can you come here for two days? I greatly desire it."

As soon as the boy had ridden away, she wished she had worded her message quite differently. An hour later she wished she had not sent it at all.

"Mamma," she said at luncheon, speaking very loudly and distinctly, as people had to do nowadays with the old lady, "I have asked Theodore van Helmont to come and stay here for a day or two."

"Whom?" asked the Baroness.

"Theodore van Helmont."

"The house is yours, Ursula, now to do what you

like with, but"—the Dowager began to cry—"you might have asked somebody with another name."

"It is on business," replied Ursula, curtly.

"Business again," said the old lady, in an aggrieved tone, "since my poor Theodore died one would think we kept a shop. Oh, ask him by all means. He is the plebeian young man. I have nothing to say. It is the invasion of the—the—what, Louisa?"

"I suppose you mean the Goths and Vandals," replied Louisa, very busy with her meal, which she always treated seriously. "Well, the Goths and Vandals were a strong new element: they were just what an effete society wanted. The great misfortune of our modern civilisation is that all the Goths and Vandals have been used up."

"Invasion of the Goths and Vandals," repeated the Dowager. "But I don't mind. All I ask is to be allowed to finish my 'Memoir.' Then I shall go and sleep with Theodore and the children. You won't put me in the big vault, will you, Ursula? Do the graves belong to Ursula, too?"

"No, no," said Ursula, hastily.

"Who did you say was coming to stay here?"

"Theodore van Helmont, mamma, from Bois-le-Duc."

"Theodore," repeated the Dowager, reflectively. "That was Henry's son. I'm glad he's coming. He will be able to tell me in what year his father made that ridiculous marriage—the first *mésalliance* in the Helmont family."

"I could have told you that," declared Louisa, brightly. "'54 or '55."

"I want to be exact," replied the Dowager, in her uncertain drawl. "I've got it somewhere among my documents, but I couldn't find it again."

Two days passed without any answer. Ursula's heart burned within her: at the thought of this neglect she turned suddenly hot and cold. In her quietly imperious necessity she had never doubted but that her summons would be obeyed.

Several times during the twenty-four hours the old Baroness would ask when the guest was expected.

"We are in mourning, Ursula," she said. "I hope you will not forget that we are in mourning. I think you went out of it too soon for your father-in-law. But perhaps your customs are different." (This was a standing, oft-repeated grievance.) "However, it is barely nine months since your husband died."

"It is six," replied Ursula, "I shall not forget."

"The young man does not seem too anxious, certainly," interposed Aunt Louisa, over her crochet. "You ask him, and he doesn't reply. I preferred the days of chivalry."

"But you don't remember the age of chivalry, Aunt Louisa," said Ursula, whose patience was distinctly overwrought. She objected to hearing her own innermost thought thus clearly stated by the Freule.

"No, I was born fifty-seven years ago; I am in no way ashamed of it," replied Aunt Louisa, coolly. "But what has that to do with the subject? You must be very unimaginative, Ursula, or have read very little. If you weren't so careless about your books and didn't let them get dog-eared (as you do), I should lend you

Madame Roncevalles' book on 'The Decline of European Manners.' It is wonderfully interesting. It proves
from the fossil remains that the cave-dwellers, at their
cannibal banquets, always ate the women first."

"Louisa, it is time I had my piquet," objected the
Dowager, who never forgot her game. She had taken
the old Baron's place as Louisa's partner, and somehow
considered the continuation of this time-honoured insti-
tution as an almost religious tribute to her lord.

Under the reproachful wonder of her two com-
panions, Ursula began to remember with increasing
clearness that her impression of Theodore van Helmont
had been decidedly unfavourable. She had not been
able to understand her husband's admiration; but then,
Otto and she so seldom sympathised. She remembered
a grave young man, an awkward man, one of those
irritating people who were always judging themselves,
and had a logical reason for everything they did. There
are people who constantly seem to be standing aside to
look themselves down, superciliously, from head to foot.
She wished more than ever that she had not sent her
telegram. But, unfortunately for most of us, it is easy
to say, "Come," and impossible to say "Don't."

The only time she had met this cousin was on the
occasion of those Christmas festivities when the house
was full of guests. It was a time on which she could
not bear to dwell. For it was then that Gerard——

She stopped suddenly when the thought of all this
first rushed back upon her. Since her illness it seemed
as if the past had been locked away in a cupboard with
many partitions where its several incidents lay, not forgotten, but unrecalled. One by one, at the touch of

Chance, the various doors flew open, and some memory, sweet or painful, would leap forth from a seeming nowhere into the light.

She was out in the wood, on the windy March day, with Monk by her side, and all around her the black tree-trunks streaked the sullen sky. She realised that she was close to the spot where, on that Christmas Eve two years ago, she had sunk to the ground in the snow, the spot where Gerard had afterwards found her glove.

Why had Gerard fought that frantic duel? Otto had said that nobody fought duels but desperadoes. And certainly, as far as Holland was concerned, Otto must be accounted right.

Still, in this matter he had judged his brother harshly. Ursula believed that the duel had been fought in defence of the national flag, and she felt that, had she been a soldier, she would have done the same.

Not in this matter only had Otto wronged a nature he could not understand. Gerard, as their mother had said, was a sunbeam, genially playing from flower to flower. He was a firebrand newly lighted, that fizzes and crackles in its youth, before settling down to a steady glow. Now that he was away in Acheen his good qualities seemed all to stand out against the background of the home that had lost him. She had known him all her life, and during her long childhood, her long girlhood, he had been her playmate, her companion—more than that, the bright Phœbus of her modest horizon, her Prince—in his uniqueness—of Cavaliers. Everything around her, in the Manor House, in the neighbourhood, was connected with memories of joint pastimes and pranks. Ever since she could toddle she had been very fond of Gerard, with the tranquil affection of practised chums. But now he had fairly forgotten her. In his frequent letters to his mother, letters full of tenderness and rose-colour, he never even sent a token of remembrance. Stop—there had been that message the Baroness had declined to give in the first letter after their common bereavement. Perhaps there had been more. Ursula did not think so, for the Dowager gradually communicated her darling's epistles to everyone, repeating and re-reading them in scraps. Had she not immediately let slip the very message in question? "Gerard says he would have sold the place in any case, so where's the difference?"

Ursula sighed. Yes, after all, Otto was right. It couldn't be helped. Gerard's letters never spoke of danger, but, through others, news had reached Horstwyk that the Jonker had, on several occasions greatly distinguished himself. By and by he would come back, "rangé," and marry—marry a little money, and then——

Then her task would be done.

Meditating thus she reached the very spot which she had determined to avoid. A blackbird broke in, almost fiercely, upon her reverie, and she looked around. In an instant there rose up before her the meeting by the Manor House on that Christmas morning, and again she heard Gerard's voice saying, as he bent over an old brown glove, "I want you to let me keep this. It will be the most precious thing I shall ever possess."

The whistling wind struck her hot cheeks; the great

dog beside her leaped up, nose foremost, with vague, mute sympathy. She rushed away from the horrible place, tearing her crape in unmindful haste, hurrying to the open, the boundless heath, where the whole air was in a ferment of conflicting currents, that caught her and buffeted her, and flung her hither and thither amid a chorus of moans and sobbings, barks, laughter, and shrieks.

When at last she paused for breath, in a lull, she saw that she was not far from Klomp's cottage. So she got under cover of the trees again and directed her footsteps to the little tumble-down house. She had a weakness for Klomp. He was so signally "undeserving."

By the door leant Adeline, and, at a glance, each woman understood that the other had recognised her.

"Klomp, here's the Baroness!" cried Mejuffrouw Skiff, retreating a little before the suddenness of an encounter she had hitherto vainly sought.

"Wish her Nobleness a very good day for me," replied an uncertain voice from dingy depths unknown.

"Poor man, he's asleep," said Adeline, boldly. "Was it anything particular you wanted with him, Mevrouw?"

Ursula smiled. "No, indeed," she said. "On no account would I disturb his well-earned rest."

"Well-earned it is," retorted Adeline pertly. "His younger daughter's ill, and he's been sitting up with her all night."

Ursula's manner changed. "Mietje? I am sorry to hear that. Can I see her? What is the matter?"

"Oh, I don't know. Nothing much I fancy. You needn't know what, I suppose, as long as you send the regulation broth."

Ursula turned away almost eagerly. That she should meet this woman now! She had lost sight of her and her story, gladly, for years.

"I suppose you don't remember me, madam," said Adeline acidly. She had noticed the quick movement of aversion.

"Oh, yes, I remember you," replied Ursula, standing still. "But certainly I did not expect to find you here."

"Yet what is more natural, Mevrouw the Baroness van Helmont, than that I should come to have a look at my relations."

"I did not know the Klomps were any relations of yours."

"I did not mean the Klomps."

The two women looked at each other.

"Well," said Ursula in measured tones, "I hope you are doing better than you were. Good morning."

But again Adeline stopped her. "I am not doing well at all. As your Nobleness so kindly takes an interest in my career, I should like to explain my position if your Nobleness would deign to listen."

Suddenly the dog, Monk, who had been suspiciously watching the frowsy stranger, broke into a fury of disparagement which no commands from his mistress could quell. Adeline was horribly frightened. With a very cowed manner she retreated behind the door, but she shrieked from that place of safety that the matter was one of the greatest importance.

Ursula, having compelled the growling dog's obedience, with one firm hand on his collar, called to the
poor soul to come forth again.

"Say your say," she decreed, "and have done."

"It's only this," whined Adeline on the doorstep;
"I'm destitute, deserted with my child, not knowing
where to turn, and I'm Gerard Helmont's wife."

She had calculated her foolish "coup"; she was
aware that a wide gulf yawned between Ursula and
denial from Gerard.

"So it's I," she added, quickly, "who am the Baroness van Helmont, though not of the Horst, *you* know
why; and all I ask is a few hundred florins and to let
me go in peace."

"Do you mean to say," queried Ursula, "that you
claim to be Gerard von Helmont's legal wife."

"Yes, and it was you that wanted him to marry me,
so, in part, the fault is yours," responded Adeline, who
enjoyed mere lies for the telling, even when there was
nothing to be gained.   "Therefore, give me a generous
sum for Gerard's child, and let me go.  Why *everything* ought to be his, the young Baron's—all the wealth
and magnificence that you've got hold of, nobody knows
how."

And Adeline began to cry real drops.  Men cannot
yet manufacture genuine diamonds.  Women can.

But, notwithstanding her weeping, there was much
spite, and even a little menace, in her tone.

"Down, Monk, down," said Ursula.  "I shall not
ask you for further proof of your story, simply because
I know it is not true.  I wish it were.  I am fully
conscious that you have a claim to be what you say

you are and are not. Could I help you to obtain its recognition I would do so; but otherwise I can do nothing for you. I have no money, and, therefore, can give you none. In a couple of years, perhaps, there will be more at my disposal, and then, if things remain unchanged, you may write to me and I will do what I can for your boy. That is all. Now you had better go away from here. Have you understood me?"

• "Give me twenty-five florins," said Adeline.

Ursula drew the straining dog towards her, and passed down the narrow path. Half-way she hesitated.

"Oh, keep straight!" she burst out, pleadingly; "keep straight, for the child's sake. I'll send you the twenty-five florins, if you want them. Let me have your address in Drum, and I'll try to find you decent work. Oh, be an honest girl, for the love of God!"

"Send me the twenty-five florins," said Adeline.

Ursula crept back into the wood; her eyes were full of tears.

"Oh, Gerard, Gerard!" she said; "this is *your* work. God forgive you for deserting her. No pure-hearted woman can."

## CHAPTER XXXIX.

### THE COUNSELLOR.

As she emerged into the Avenue Ursula noticed a figure in front of her which she immediately recognised. It was walking at a deliberate pace, a valise and an overcoat thrown over one arm. The dog gave the alarm, and the figure looked round.

"Why ever did you not telegraph for the carriage?" thought Ursula.

The young man waited; his fresh-coloured face shone out in the all-pervading gloom.

Ursula wondered, as she drew nearer, what deliverance she expected from this pink-eyed little innocent. He looked like a solemn peach. How could she broach her unusual subject? Visible shyness was not one of her qualities; but she smiled rather foolishly as she walked, thought Theodore Helmont, and, for so recent a widow, improperly.

"You have come up on foot from the station?" she cried. "I wish we had known. Why didn't you telegraph?"

"Telegrams are expensive," replied the young man.

This sounded promising.

"I only got my leave this morning," he continued. "I couldn't let you know, so I simply came."

"Ah, you had to get leave?" said Ursula, her conscience smiting her.

"Yes: Government officials always must. Most people must who work for their bread. I am a Post-office clerk."

"I know, I know," answered Ursula, hastily. "Of course, I know, *Cousin* Helmont. Please put down your bag; it will be quite safe. I will send one of the labourers to fetch it."

"I can easily carry it myself," he said, more courteously; "I always do." And, although this time he said nothing about expenditure, she felt that he considered the tip.

After that the conversation lagged. Presently the young man said, with much timidity:—

"There is one thing I should greatly like, if you would be so very kind. My mother is exceedingly anxious about railway travelling of any sort, and she made me promise to let her know at once of my safe arrival. They couldn't telegraph at the station. Would there be a possibility, perhaps, of forwarding a message?"

"Oh, certainly," replied Ursula, demurely. "But— you know—telegrams are expensive."

Theodore's pure eyes grew troubled.

"The matter is altogether different," he said. "Perhaps, if you will allow me to explain——"

Ursula burst out laughing.

"Certainly not," she exclaimed. "What do you take me for? Of course, I perfectly understand. The boy shall get ready at once."

Theodore looked straight in front of him.

"I only wanted to say," he went on doggedly, "that my mother's anxiety is not irrational. She is quite unaccustomed to travelling herself, and we have never been parted before."

Ursula stood still on the Manor House steps. "Never been parted before!" she exclaimed. "Woe is me, what have I done?"

Theodore blushed in fresh waves of crimson. "Now you are laughing at me," he said, and his tone was distinctly annoyed. "You mustn't laugh at me. I am not at all accustomed to the society of ladies, and if you laugh at me we shall not be able to get on."

"No—no, I really meant it," Ursula hastened to say. "I honestly fear I have been exceedingly inconsiderate. I wish that your mother had accompanied you (oh, dear, no," she reflected, "there the expense comes in again!). But *you* must not say you are unaccustomed to the society of ladies——"

"My mother is not a lady like you," he remarked quickly.

"I am Ursula Rovers," she replied—"the pastor's daughter. I remember Mevrouw van Helmont very well."


In the solitude of her dressing-room she wondered what would be the next development of her devotion to Otto's memory, and chid herself for the ungracious thought. Then she went down to luncheon, expecting to find her guest in a corner of the library turning over picture books. That was the only pose in which his former visit had left him photographed on her brain.

To her astonishment, she heard him in earnest discussion with Aunt Louisa. "My dear Ursula," cried the latter lady, running forward, "your cousin Van Helmont is a most interesting young man. I have been telling him about European manners, and he most sagaciously remarks that the best of manners is to have none. How delightfully true!"

The subject of this outspoken eulogy did not seem at all abashed by it; probably he was accustomed to his mother's estimation of her only son.

"Pardon me," he calmly protested, "I was saying that I had read that observation somewhere. I am not prepared to maintain that it is absolutely correct."

"Oh, what does it matter whose it is," cried the Freule. "Everything we say must have had its origin with someone, so everything is really original. Now, that never struck me before. How new!"

"Yes," replied Ursula. "Will you have a rissole?"

"Thank you, my dear. One more, please. Thank you. Personally, what I most reprobate is the walking in line, like ducks. 'Do as others do.' The Bible says, 'Do as you would be done by,' a very different thing. I hope Mynheer Helmont, that you are unconventional, as I know your father was."

"I do not remember my father well," answered Theodore, pondering whether he could not get away that night.

"Oh, I never *met* him," said Louisa just as the old Baroness entered. The poor old lady, who would have said "J'ai failli attendre" in palmier days, now accorded all precedence to her literary labours.

"My dear," continued the Freule, addressing her, "this young man is exceedingly interesting. I had forgotten him, but now I remember I thought so the last time he was here. The best thing is to have no manners. Now, doesn't he put that well?"

"I daresay he finds it convenient," responded the Dowager. "How do you do, Mynheer Helmont? I am very glad to see you, I wish you would tell me when your father died?"

"It is seventeen years ago," replied Helmont, wonder-ingly.

"Quite impossible. I feel sure you are more than sixteen."

"I am twenty-four, but——"

"Mamma means 'married,' I believe," suggested Ursula, gently.

"'Married,' that was what I said," declared the Dowager, sharply. "Ursula, my soup is cold again. Manners or no manners, young man, you shouldn't make fun of a woman old enough to be your grandmother."

"I disapprove of such early marriages!" exclaimed the Freule. Ursula's eyes and Theodore's met. She burst out laughing, but he looked uncomfortably grave. "After luncheon," she said, "I must take you round, Mynheer Helmont. It is no use showing you the stables; we have only three horses left, and they are of the kind that would better do their work unseen."

He followed her obediently when they rose from table, and she pretended to take an interest in the small sights she had to offer her guest. The same can hardly be asserted of Theodore. He was painfully silent while she "made conversation," wondering all the time in what way she should broach the one subject she cared to speak about.

In this, however, he hastened to her assistance, for his patience came to an end, while hers still hung on a thread. They were standing in the palm-house, when he suddenly looked up at her—he had some little height to look up—and asked:

"What did you want me for, please?"

She had been laughing about some of the gardener's queer names for the roses; her voice suddenly changed, and everything but pain died out of it.

"I believe we are ruined," she said, facing him, "and Otto made me promise, if ever I wanted advice, I would appeal to you."

He seemed still to listen, plucking at the nearest leaves, for a moment after she had finished. Then he said, as if speaking to himself:

"Well, I'm very glad, at any rate, that I didn't ask a holiday for nothing at all." He glanced up at her anxious face. "Holidays are very rare with us, you know," he added apologetically, "I couldn't soon get leave again."

"Yet, I don't suppose you can help us," continued Ursula, relentlessly. "Nobody can."

"When people get down as low as that," replied the young clerk, frigidly, "they can usually help themselves. I presume that, however much money you may happen to possess, you want more. That, I believe, is what people of your class call 'being ruined.'"

She felt that he wronged her the more, by this constant distinction, after what she had said on the Manor House steps. "I possess no money at all," she said, wroth with herself for the helpless confession. "And

in about a week's time I must have three thousand
florins."

"In other words," he answered, with an angry wave
of his short arm round the greenhouse, "you *must* spend
thirty thousand florins with an income of twenty-seven.
Other people have an income of one thousand, and
spend *that*."

"No," she replied, "it is not that. We will say no
more about it. Come, let us walk on."

"Pardon me. It takes one person to start a subject,
but two to drop it. Will you permit me to express
myself plainly?"

"Oh, certainly. Dear me, Mynheer van Helmont, I
had understood you to say you were shy?"

"Again I beg your pardon. I can understand fun
and I can understand earnest, but which is it to be?"

"I apprehend you. You do not recognise humour
outside the comic papers. You are like my father.
*I* laugh most at the dentist's. It is to be earnest,
please."

"The house is crowded with treasures. Sell one
or two."

"I cannot: they belong to my mother-in-law."

"Do away with a carriage you can't pay for, and go
on foot."

"I cannot. I keep a sort of boarding-house, and my
two boarders pay for the carriage, not I."

"Eat dry bread instead of hot lunch."

"And drive away the boarders! There, you see I
answer plainly, too. Do you really imagine, that if I
could have solved my difficulties by merely eating dry

bread, I would have troubled you, a comparative stranger, to come all the way from Bois-le-Duc?"

"I don't know. The women of '93 could be guillotined, and willing, but they couldn't eat dry bread."

However, his tone was gentler, and his manner less assured.

"Now, will you let me, as we return to the house, explain how matters really stand?" she said. He nodded silently, and, under the bare, sky-piercing oaks, she softly told him the long story of her father-in-law's slow purchase and last testament, of Otto's life-work and dying charge, of her struggle to continue what they had begun in expectation of better times. He listened solemnly, his boy-face puckered up.

"It is your name, too," she said, in conclusion, "your race, your blood." And she measured the little plebeian beside her.

"Yes," he said.

"There it lies. And each rood that belonged to a Van Helmont four hundred years ago belongs to a Van Helmont now."

"It belongs to *you*," he replied, quickly. "And afterwards?"

She faltered.

"It will never pass from my keeping till it pass to a Van Helmont," she said, "so help me God."

In that moment even he could not press the point.

"You must give me time," he said; "I have three days' leave. Do not let us mention the subject again till the day after to-morrow. Meantime, I will have a look round and try to discover, if you can keep on, supposing the three thousand are found."

"Thank you. But, do you know about land?" She was just a little bit piqued. "I assure you I am very slowly learning."

"Oh, I know. My mother is a farmer's daughter. I have always been about with my uncle. If mother had given me my choice, I should have been a common farmer myself."

"A Van Helmont!"

"Pooh! That's what mother said!"

———

## CHAPTER XL.

### THE NEW BAILIFF.

As ill-luck would have it, Helen wrote to announce her visit for the last evening of Theodore's stay at the Manor House. She arrived before dinner, bringing the unwilling Willie along with her.

An almost oppressive quiet had reigned in the mansion, only rarely disturbed by the deep voice of Monk. The guest had spent most of his time out of doors, returning occasionally to closet himself with great memoranda and account-books. Tante Louisa complained bitterly that she got · next to nothing of his interesting conversation; Ursula anxiously fought shy of him; the Dowager, unexpectedly meeting him in the hall, asked her *confidante,* the cook, who he was.

"I shall stir them all up a bit," said Helen to her husband in the carriage. "I have seen them already once or twice since the event, and you can't go on looking lugubrious for ever. Besides, I don't believe Ursula is inconsolable. I shall ask her."

"No you won't," said Willie.

"Willie, don't 'put my back up,' or you'll make me do an unlady-like thing."

"You won't ask her, because you can't. I'd bet you a gold piece that you wouldn't dare."

"You wouldn't like me to dare." Helen's eyes strayed away through the carriage window.

"Indeed I should. I like pluck of any kind. In a horse, or a woman, or a dog."

"Only not in a man!" exclaimed Helen, a little bitterly."

"In a man it goes without saying. By-the-bye, what atrocious brutes these horses of Ursula's are. I've an idea, Nellie, that she's very badly off."

"All the more reason for her to console herself. A poor widow remarries much sooner than a rich one, and with far less opportunity."

"'Tisn't said that she'd better herself. If she marries she ought to marry Gerard. It would be her bounden duty."

"Thank you, for Gerard's sake," retorted Helen, now very bitterly indeed. And they lapsed into silence. Was there really any prospect of Ursula's marrying Gerard? It was this question which had long held Nellie van Troyen's heart as in a vice, pinching it and torturing it, and refusing to let it rest. It was this question which now hunted her to the Horst. She was determined to see with her own eyes how matters stood. "I shall find out," she told herself. "I must, even if I have to *ask* her. To think of Willie's trumpery gold-piece! It is horrible, all the suffering. But my life is a beautiful romance." She smiled, and reflectively arranged her dress. "You like me, you know, Willie," she said, "in pink."

"Yes," he replied, "though I don't know why. Blue suits your fair complexion better. But, somehow, I can't bear to see you in blue."

"I know why. Shall I tell you? It is because you have some delightful memories connected with a creature in blue."

"You are wrong," he said quite coolly. "It is because I have some detestable memories connected with a creature in blue."

"Oh, 'delightful,' 'detestable,' that is all one in such cases. So you see I was right. Here we are."

"Well, shall we wager?" he asked, as he helped her to alight.

"If you like. But you are pretty sure of your gold-piece, for I certainly shall not trouble her unless she drives me to it."

"So much the better. Don't dare, and pay me."

"Willie, I believe you would sell your soul for money," she cried.

He laughed.

"No, no, not his soul," she said to herself, half aloud, as she climbed the great stone steps. "Only his body, only all he's got to sell!"

The Dowager came forward to meet her niece, who had always been a favourite with the old lady, and the only possible successor she could consider with equanimity. "My dear, I am so glad you are come," she said, with a return of her vanished sprightliness. "Your visits are like those of the angels. And the house is so dull. Though certainly, at this moment, we have a guest."

"A guest?"

"Oh, he is Ursula's guest. One of the—the other Helmonts, that nobody ever used to see. But these are the days of the bend sinister. We have fallen on evil times."

Helen stood taking off her wraps, the little old lady helping her. "My dear," began the latter, somewhat tremulously, "I wish you would do me a kindness I want you to come and stay with us for a few days, and I will read you what I have written about the good old past. I read it to Ursula, but she does not know what it is all about. She is not one of us; it will interest *you*. There is a great deal in it about your mother."

"Yes?" said Helen. "Is it ready, aunt?"

"Ready, my dear? Oh dear no, how could it be ready? But I can show you what I have done. Do you know, I begin to fear it will never be ready?"— the Dowager's voice nearly failed her. "To give me plenty of time to write the memoir, your uncle ought to have died a great many years ago." Then, vaguely realising that she had incorrectly expressed her meaning, she began to cry with unmistakable persistence.

"Hush, hush!" exclaimed Helen, in her most impulsive tones. "Auntie, I shall be delighted to come; we will talk over the old days, as you say, and all the fun I used to have with Gerard. But would you not rather pay us a visit?" She drew the little lady's arm through her own. "I am so sorry. This is very hard for you—and for Gerard—this about Ursula."

"My dear, I thank you, but I cannot."

The Dowager nestled confidentially against the silver-pink sleeve of the fair creature beside her. They cooed over each other like a pair of high-bred doves. "I dare not leave the house for a single night. I have

an idea that something would happen if I did. I
am the last of us all, and I am set here to watch.
When Gerard comes back—Helen, you do not think,
do you, that they will really leave it to her for ever?"

"Poor auntie," said Helen, softly stroking the transparent cheek. "Poor auntie."

"What I cannot understand, is that *he* doesn't come
and take it away from her!" cried the Dowager, with
sudden energy. "I wrote to him to do so; Gerard never
was a coward. But I fear that Louisa's explanation is
correct."

"What is Freule Louisa's explanation?" questioned
Helen, quickly.

"She says that Gerard is in love with Ursula, and
always has been. She says that *that* is why he went
to India. If what she says is true, then Ursula has
robbed me of both my sons." And again the poor,
forlorn old woman began gently to whimper.

"Perhaps it is not true," replied Helen, pensively.
"Come, auntie, let us sit in the window-seat and talk
of Gerard. I suppose he will be coming back before
long."

"I don't know. I forget. Oh, Nellie, you don't
know how dreadful it is to grow old and forget. I can't
find my words sometimes, though I take care that nobody notices it. I feel that it would never do for
Ursula to discover that I have not all my wits about
me. Who knows what she might not do? *Sell the
place, perhaps!*"—her voice dropped to a whisper.
"Imagine that. Or sell some of your uncle's dear art
treasures that he bade me keep. She doesn't care for
them, I know, for she never seems to see them even.

I've watched her constantly. Oh, Nellie, I'm set here as sentinel, and—my strength is failing."

Helen felt that, irrational as she knew the feeling to be, she *could* not but think ill of Ursula. '

"I forgot one of the poor children's birthdays last week," wailed the Baroness; she alluded to her dead infants that slept beneath "The Devil's Doll"--"and Ursula didn't remind me to take any flowers. I have never forgotten before."

Ursula entered at the moment, tall and straight in her heavy gown. To both the gracefully drooping women whose soft clothes and figures intermingled against the darkening window, her presence at that moment seemed more than ever an insult.

"Shall we have lights?" she said in her clear voice.

"Oh, in the drawing-room, pray," replied her mother-in-law, pettishly. "Mynheer van Helmont is gone in there. He was looking for you."

Ursula withdrew into the adjoining apartment. It was very large and lofty, and the figures on its tapes-tried walls, half hidden under the great masses of sha-dow now clouding around them, peered forth in vaguely distorted gloom. Theodore was pacing the parqueted floor with moody tramp. He came forward at once.

"I want you," he said, hurriedly. "I must leave to-night. So we may as well have our talk at once."

"I am quite ready," she answered. "I did not wish to press you. Will half an hour suffice?"

"Ten minutes. Everything worth saying in this world by one human being to another can be said in ten minutes. But I should like you to sit down."

"Very well," she said. "No, not an easy chair. Thanks."

"I have looked into everything, superficially," he began, resuming his march in the dusk. "I must, in the first place, beg your pardon for misjudging you all. I came here with false impressions. When a man grows up, as I have done, in the bourgeois daily fight with poverty he is apt to form erroneous impressions of the life which his 'grand' relations lead, especially when his impressions are gained by hearsay. I beg your pardon."

He paused for a moment, then as she did not answer, he continued:

"In the second place I want to express my—my ad-mi—my *recognition* of the way in which you have carried on your husband's work. Few women, I imagine, would have taken up such a load or borne it so bravely. I didn't like your sudden telegram. I thought of the people who jump into the water and then call out to strangers to save them. There, that's off my mind. I am not good at compliments or excuses. I've no man-ners, as Freule Louisa says. Now to business." His tone, which had been agitated, immediately dropped to the habitual growl that partially masked his shyness.

"He reminds you," Helen had said when they met by the Christmas tree, "of a peach with a wasp inside."

"The truth is as you stated," he resumed; "nothing but hard work can keep the whole thing going. A forced sale would mean ruin. On the other hand, barring such extra expenses as death duties, you ought, with rigid economy, to pay your way." He paused for a moment. "With rigid economy," he repeated.

"I know," said Ursula, softly.

"There is nothing so hopeless as farming without capital—you know that better than I do. But the cherry orchards pay, and so, especially, do the osier plantations. Without these latter you could hardly get on. You have good tenants on the whole. One of them, however, will have to go."

"I know," said Ursula again, in the same tone, through the darkness; "but he can't."

"He must. I see we understand each other—the home-farm man—your sort of agent. I don't say he is dishonest. Otto seems pretty well to have stopped that —but he is expensive—you can't afford him."

"I cannot make cheese myself," pleaded Ursula, a little helplessly, for her. "I tried once, and nobody could eat it. It—it didn't stiffen."

But her stern adviser vouchsafed no responsive smile.

"It's a matter of life or death," he said; "the work that fellow does must be done by another man."

"But where would you find a better?"

"I can't find a better, but I can find a cheaper."

"Have you got him?"

"Yes; I mean myself. Stop a minute—let me explain. I told you I had always wanted to be a farmer" —his voice grew nervous again—"I'm sick of being a genteel sort of mannikin in a pot-hat. I'm especially sick of the post-office. I'm going to take that farm and work it."

"But, Mynheer Helmont, this sudden decision——"

"It isn't a sudden decision. It took twenty-four hours to come to, and it's twenty-four hours old already. I've announced it to my mother." He again made a pause, away at the farther, darkest end. "Oh, I dare say you don't like it," he burst out, "I didn't expect you would. But it's going to happen all the same. To have as my lady Baroness's close neighbour a farmer bearing her name——"

"I was not thinking of that," she interrupted him. "For, of course, a gentleman-farmer——"

But he would not allow her to proceed.

"A gentleman-gammon," he cried, still out of the distant darkness; "a common, common farmer. Nothing in all the world—not even drink—costs half as much as gentility. But, remember, if it isn't pleasant for you people, it's a hundred times worse for my mother and——" He broke off. "But she'll do it," he lamely concluded the sentence.

Ursula rose and came up the big room to look for him.

"Sit down, please," he said, hastily, "I haven't done. Please sit down till I've done. Women are such bad listeners!" She obeyed, knocking the chair against something which crashed to the floor. "I hope that isn't anything expensive!" exclaimed Theodore, emerging from his corner. His tone chid her as if she had been an awkward child.

"It didn't sound broken," replied Ursula, meekly, "but I suppose you object to my getting a light?"

For only answer he struck a match, revealing a *cloisonné* vase which lay in a pool of water and a tangle of white anemones upon an Oriental rug. The match flickered out.

"That'll keep," said Theodore, coolly. "I only want half a minute more. There is still one point, the most important. The three thousand florins we require next week will be found."

"But how?" Ursula's voice betrayed her.

"Oh, not picked up on the high road. When I say 'found,' of course I mean provided and paid for. *I* shall provide them. You can imagine that, poor as we are, we do not live on my salary only. As a matter of fact, I possess about twenty-seven thousand florins; I have looked so much into your private affairs that I suppose you have a right, if you care, to know something of mine. Three thousand, therefore, I will advance, if you can give me sufficient security."

"That is just what I cannot do."

"That remains to be seen. Freule Louisa mentioned that you still had a valuable diamond brooch."

Ursula was thankful he could not see the hot flare of her resentment.

"And do you think," she said, scornfully, "that I would not have sold *that?* But it isn't mine to sell. It is an heirloom. I must keep it like the rest."

"It is legally yours," he replied, "and, therefore, you must *not* keep it. Besides, I trust that you will be able to redeem it in the slow course of the years. All ladies like diamonds. I promise to take good care of yours. Bring the thing down before the carriage starts. And now, perhaps, I had better ring for somebody with a cloth."

"Stop!" she cried; he had lighted another match and was looking for the bell-rope. "Before you do that, I want to say——"

"Don't. I really do not think there is anything

more to be said just now." He had found the bell
and pulled it.

"But I do not want to do this. I do not want——"

"I know you don't. Did not I tell you so? However, permit me to say that I have as good a right to
interfere in this matter as you. I am quite as much
of a Helmont—even a good deal more." His voice
rolled out like the threat of a recoiling dog.

A female servant knocked and entered, letting in a
flood of light from the hall. She gazed with decorous
astonishment at the occupants of the room.

"Ursula," said Willie, coming in with the others,
"is it true that you have let the shooting?"

"No, that was not one of my crimes," replied Ursula
with a petulant laugh, "Otto did it immediately after
Gerard's departure." Then her voice softened. "I believe it was the greatest sacrifice he ever made. You
know he was such a splendid shot."

"He was," assented Willie, with that solemn admiration which no man can suppress.

"But, Ursula, I remember you used to say you hated
'splendid shots'?" suggested Helen, looking back over
the arm which still supported the Dowager. They were
passing in to dinner. Willie, glancing up, saw mischief
in his wife's blue eye.

"They are better than stabs," answered Ursula, and
from that moment it might be evident to any one that
these two women meant war. It would not, however,
be the feminine skirmishing of intrigue and innuendo,
for Helen, as we know, was reckless, and Ursula
blunt.

"I want to sit next to poor dear auntie," said Helen

as they took their places. "Mynheer van Helmont, I suppose *your* habitual seat is next to the lady of the house? Are you going to stay here long?"

"I have no habitual seat," replied Theodore awkwardly. "I leave to-night. I am only a three days' guest."

"Yes, no one of your name could be anything else at the Horst now. Not even the head of the house, away in Acheen." She smiled sweetly and turned to the Dowager.

Theodore was mortally afraid of this fine lady, all soft texture and vague perfume, like a rose. But he found conversation hardly easier with Ursula, in spite of the sullen admiration he unwillingly accorded her.

"Your mother will be glad to have you back," said Ursula.

"Yes, indeed," he replied fervently. "And I to go. —Back," he added, blushing.

"You know it was impossible," Helen's voice rang out again, "we are speaking of your Uncle Mopius, Ursula. They have had to withdraw his candidature. He is a very good sort of man—oh, very good—but he is not what Freule Louisa calls 'strong.' Papa tells me it is quite impossible, though I'm sure I worked hard for him—didn't I, Willie? Your uncle says it's all *your* doing, Ursula. He was very rude about you to Papa. I had to stop him, and remind him you were become my cousin by marriage."

"Indeed," replied Ursula.

"Would you like to hear what he said?"

"I cannot say I care."

"Well, as we are quite among ourselves, perhaps it

is better you should know. He said that your elevation had turned your head. You know, Ursula, he is
rather, rather—pardon me the word—vulgar!"

She had spoken French. The servant, by the side-
board, rattled his plates.

"And he said your political opinions were deplorable. What are your political opinions, Mynheer van
Helmont?"

"Deplorable," replied Theodore, with a ready
championship which astonished himself.

"Ah, you two are in close sympathy, I see. So
much the better." She dropped her voice. "But is it
not a strange thought to you, Mynheer van Helmont,
that this old place is now certain to pass, in due time,
to Ursula's children, whatever their name may happen
to be?"

"No," replied Theodore, "it's no business of mine."

"Ah!" she exclaimed, angrily. "The Baron van
Helmont thinks differently, no doubt. Why, if Ursula
has some seizure to-night, I suppose we shall soon see
a Lord Mopius of Horstwyk! Fie, Mynheer van Helmont, this poor creature at my side has more spirit
than you."

Ursula could not avoid hearing enough of this aside
to understand its meaning. She felt that everybody
had heard it. Passionate as she was, she fixed her
eyes on the table-cloth. She remained conscious that
Helen, that everybody, even while the talk went on,
was watching her. At last she lifted them—those steadfast brown eyes.

"It is six months to-day," she said, "exactly six

months. Only six months, since Otto and Baby died."
And she rose from table.

"Ursula, you have forgotten the dessert," cried Aunt
Louisa, lingering.

Ursula turned back.

"True," she said. "I beg everybody's pardon.
Won't you try some of Mamma's preserved orange-
leaves, Helen? You will find them as good as ever."

In the hall, just as the carriage had driven up which
was to convey the three visitors to the station, Ursula
appeared with a small parcel in her hand; she gave it
to Theodore, who buttoned it out of sight, without even
saying "Thanks."

"There is one thing still," she began hurriedly.
"You heard about the election. I had a letter yesterday from the Opposition Caucus, asking me if I wished
to put forward a candidate, or would accept one from
them. I have none. I have one. I mean, I had
thought, hearing what you said at dinner, that, if your
political opinions were theirs——"

"I have no political opinions," he answered, moving
away from the sheltering pillar to the light where the
others stood grouped.

She put out one hand. "I am sorry," she stammered, trembling from head to foot. "I had thought.
It is the one only thing I could have done to thank
you. To express my gratitude——"

"I want no thanks," he replied, literally shaking off
her hand. "Gratitude, pshaw! I told you a couple of

hours ago that I have as much right to do this as you have. I am not *all* peasant, Mevrouw. You remind me too frequently of that side." And he went and took up his own valise. "The servants forget these things," he said to Helen.

When they were all gone, Ursula crossed the cold emptiness of the hall and encountered Hephzibah. The maid shrank away. "Hephzibah, I want you to do me a favour," said the young Baroness; "would you take this letter, when you go to the Parsonage to-morrow with the Freule, and give it to a person who is staying at Klomp's? Please give it into her own hands. There is money in it."

"H'm," reflected Hephzibah, watching the tall figure in its slow ascent. "Money in it. Is there? And Why? Throw a barking dog a bone." She shook her head. "If I hear that noise upstairs again," she muttered, "I'll write to the Jonker, wife or not. But I've said that so often before! And if the Jonker's got a wife already, what business had he wearing Mevrouw's glove in his bosom and duelling? I saw him pick it up. It's a bad world, a bad world. But I'm a blessed body to feel how bad it is. I told cook about the groanings, though I didn't explain their reason, so she only said I ought to take medicine."

"Well, Willie, I've lost my wager," declared Helen, as soon as they were rid of the "post boy."

"I don't know about that, but pay up anyhow. You deserve to, Nellie, for your treatment of Ursula. Poor thing, she behaved very well, I thought. She's quite lost that magnificent rich complexion of hers. She looks sallow."

"Oh, that will come right when she marries little Theodore," replied Helen, with tranquil satisfaction. "The person I am sorry for is auntie. I'm sure I cried with her for nearly an hour."

———

## CHAPTER XLI.

### THUNDER IN THE TROPICS.

THE scene changes.

For one moment we look, with clearer eyes than the poor old Dowager's, across the cruel waste of waters into a very real dreamland, and we see Gerard, Baron van Helmont, after two years of weary waiting for glory, wearily waiting for glory still.

Gerard van Helmont stood before his hut in the compound of the little fort under his command, on the Acheen River. All round him trembled, with soft persistence, the thousand breathings of the tropic night.

An hour ago it had flung itself, the sudden blackness, down the slopes of the Barissan mountains, and away across the green islands of the Indian Ocean. It had fallen with the swiftness of a blow, wiping out all the luxuriance of dreamy glories that lay reposefully burning in endless variations of verdure under the moist veil of paludal heat. The wide sea of tropical foliage that laughed down the sides of the valley till within a few yards of the river-fort had sunk back from view like a swiftly receding tide, and a living silence now brooded over these jungles a-quiver with hate. The roar of the million frogs in the marshes had at last

ceased to beat against never-accustomed ears, and all
the other manifold murmurs and flutterings had died
down to one dully penetrative tone, whose ringing
music, in its rhythmical rise and fall, swelled upon the
ear of the listener like the pulse-beat of the world.
Now and then the sudden howlings of distant wild dogs
broke out hideously, or the clattering shriek of the
*tokkèh* resounded from the woods. And throughout the
long darkness came the swish of the turbid water
amongst its reeds and over-hanging branches, as it went
playing around the masses of logs and rotten refuse
over which it quarrels day and night, in slow pushings,
with the sea.

Nature under the equator knows not even the
semblance of rest. In northern countries she at least
appears to sleep; here she sits, through the cooler hours,
on her couch, listening.

Certainly there was no rest for Gerard van Helmont,
or for any Dutchman, at that time in Acheen; there
was only the tension of expectant inactivity amid all-
encompassing treachery, hundred-eyed, and hundred-
handed. Barbaric murder lurked behind every tree,
and behind every smiling face that bent in allegiance.
For if an Achinese stoop low before the Kafir it is with
the idea, in rising, of ripping him up.

Gerard in this small "Benting" had fifty men under
his orders, European and native fusiliers. His nearest
neighbours were established about half a mile off in a
similar entrenchment, a certain number of these permanent camps having been constructed to keep open
the way to the sea, for the invading force had gone up
the valley into the interior.

The lanterns along the outer side of the wall had been lighted; their yellow reflection created a circle of vaguely lessening defence. Across this, into the dark tangle beyond the clearing peered solitary sentinels by their guns. A sergeant tramped past. The night was starless and misty.

"Werda?" cried a sentry.

Something had moved, he thought, behind the glooming bushes. Something always seemed to be moving—creeping forward through the whispers of the forest, in the incessant alarm of guerilla night attack.

"Nonsense, it's too early," said the sergeant. "Besides, we're quite safe now, here in these pacified districts. Keep a good look out, all the same."

Gerard smiled, overhearing the concluding exhortation. He knew that they were not safe, no, not for one moment. The friendly villagers from the farther side of the marsh who had sold them victuals that morning might even now be meditating a raid, one of those terrible Achinese swoops and withdrawals, the hand-to-hand swarm up the battlements—Allah il Allah!—On!

He lighted a cigarette, and wondered how many he still had left. It was painfully lonely, and humdrum, and wearing. Danger becomes humdrum; death can become humdrum, they say. Occasionally he met his brother officer from the neighbouring fort. Otherwise not a white-faced Christian, except his own garrison, and the commissariat people from the camp, at long intervals, with stores.

He was thinking—no, not of home. Soldiers—thank God!—do not always think of home.

He was thinking of his men. One of them, an Am-

boinese, had got himself killed that morning through
sheer temerity and disobedience. There were a couple
of these insubordinates in the Benting who, wearying of
inaction, had broken out once before on the spree—
that is to say, on the hunt for a grinning, long-haired
devil with a klewang. He had punished them, of course,
but at daybreak this morning Adja had slipped away
alone, and had fallen into the hands of friendly Achinese.
Gerard knew what that meant. Death by the most
prolonged of cruelties, a slow chopping away of all
parts except such as keep life extant. He sighed as he
thought of the poor fellow's fate, and the inevitable re-
prisals, and all the official bother and blame.

And he reflected on certain instructions issued not
long ago. The army, whose women and children were
daily exposed to fiendish barbarities, had been reminded
that every Achinese was a man and a brother, and must
be treated as such. Kindness to prisoners (even if they
owned to having boiled your envoy); kindness to villagers
(even if they potted you as you passed their houses),
these were of the elements of Christian warfare. It was
quite true. And, moreover, the good people at home
that write, in their slippers, to the newspapers, never
pardoned an act of cruelty, unless practised by the foe.

"I must speak to the other fellow, I suppose," said
Gerard. "I wonder how he takes it. Sergeant, send
Popa along," and he passed into his hut, that the interview
might seem more imposing under the yellow glare of
the lamp. The hut certainly had nothing impressive
about it, with its bamboo walls and uneven furniture.
There was a small rug by the bed, a red blot on the
planks which alone distinguished this abode from the

mud-floored homes of the soldiery. And two or three of the articles scattered about bespoke the refinement of their owner.

Popa presented himself, a lithe little fellow, brown and fierce. He saluted.

"Popa, you know what has happened to Adja?"

"Tjingtjang, Lieutenant," replied Popa, saluting again. *

"You may be thankful that you didn't accompany him this time. If you had"—he paused, and looked at the man.

"Perhaps—forgive me, that I say it—we should not have been caught, Lieutenant."

"In that case your punishment would have awaited you here. You understand that *any* attempt at insubordination will henceforth be repressed with the utmost severity. I *will* not have it. You can go."

Popa saluted again, and tripped off. His heart was hot within him for the loss of his comrade.

"They call us 'tiger-faces,'" he reflected, "they will call us 'tiger-tails.'"

"A splendid fighter," said Gerard, aloud, "like so many of these Amboinese. And nothing to be gained but death or unrecorded glory. God forgive the worthies at home who care for no man's soul or body as long as consols remain at par. If some of us didn't love fighting for its own mad sake (which I certainly don't) where would their Excellencies' consols be?"

Then he lighted another cigarette, and once more told himself that really this time he must count his store. So he would, to-morrow.

* Achinese torture. The Dutch soldier says, "Lieutenant," etc.

He threw himself in his single rocking-chair and yawned. What should he do the live-long evening? What had he done through the creeping weeks and months? What could one do? It was the emptiness which tormented him—the not doing anything: he wanted to be with the invaders on ahead. He groaned over this misfortune for the five hundredth time. Otherwise, Acheen was not half a bad place—much more spacious and much more *mouvementé* than Holland. Of course it was always horribly hot, and here where he lay, by the marsh, it was even especially unhealthy. Everybody sickened. But then, on the other hand, there were no duns. Gerard looked down at his lean, yellow fingers. Yes, he had altered.

But what matter? Who cared? Only, he wished he had had something to show for it. He felt that the Home Government may send you to kill savages, but they ought to provide plenty of savages for you to kill.

In the military club at Kotta Radja he was popular. He would always be popular with brave men anywhere because of his unpretending unselfishness. And many of his comrades liked a fellow who was Baron van Helmont, you know, by George! and he never seems to remember, though, somehow, you never forget.

He devoutly wished himself in the club at this moment. They would be playing, and there would be unlimited tobacco.

"Werda?" He leaped to his feet. A swift brightness swept across the gloom outside. A signal rang clear. At his cabin door a sergeant met him.

"Friends, Lieutenant," said the man.

Under the protection of a suddenly uplifted fireball, half a dozen soldiers in dark uniform were seen approaching the Benting, whistling a signal as they came. Gerard recognised a party from the neighbouring fort, his companion in exile at their head. Greatly surprised, he went down to the gate.

"You, Streeling!" he cried. "What, in the name of mischief, brings you here? That light of yours will rouse the neighbourhood."

"Put it out, somebody," said the newcomer. "I only fired it as we emerged from the wood. I felt no desire to test your sentries, thanks."

"Well, what have you come for?"

"And why shouldn't I take my walks abroad in the cool of the evening? Isn't this the pacified zone?"

Gerard's brother-commander was a facetious little man, melancholy by nature, and with a melancholy history which he kept to himself.

"Let's go into your hut and I'll tell you," he said. "Have you anything left to drink?"

"Only brandy."

"Lucky fellow to have plenty of spirits still!" He settled himself, by right of sodality, in the rocking-chair, the proprietor of the shanty crouching on the bed.

"It's just this," began Streeling, with suppressed excitement. "Krayveld's turned up at my place from the ships with important despatches. The steam-launch can't get any further to-night, and he says they must be taken on to the front, in any case, at once. It appears they've big plans for to-morrow up yonder." He jerked his head in the direction of his hopes.

"Yes," said Gerard, and his downcast eyelids twitched.

"His orders are that one of us is to take them on by road, and that *he* is to remain in command for the man that goes. He doesn't know the road, you know —what there is of it, d—— it."

"Yes," replied Gerard, continuing the close study of his cigarette-point. *"Which* is to take them on?"

"There's the nuisance. The 'Vice' has left that to us to settle. Didn't know which had least fever, you know. But one of us may go."

"Yes," repeated Gerard, with a sigh, "I suppose it must be you."

"I suppose it must," admitted the little man, echoing the sigh, "I'm the oldest, you see. It's risky work. You're as likely as not to get hashed into mincemeat by some of those klewang-brutes. Save us from our friends, say I."

"True, I hadn't thought of the risk," replied Gerard, with much alacrity. "I'll go, if you like. In fact, you know, I think it had better be I."

"Why? Nonsense. You were awfully seedy when I was over here last week. And it strikes me you're looking pale to-day. The miasma 'll be murderous at this time of night round by the second swamp."

"Yes," said Gerard again, endeavouring to improve the lamplight. "How long is it—did you say—since your fever went?"

The other did not answer immediately, and in the silence that ensued, Gerard let fall one word from the tips of his lips:

"Humbug!"

"Humbug, am I? And what are you? Yah!"

The two men looked at each other.

"Well then, if it must be, it must be," said Streeling, submissively; "I don't want to spoil your chances, old man. Let's draw lots."

"You *are* the eldest," admitted Gerard. "Thanks."

"The eldest ought to remain in command," replied Streeling, with a grin. "But I'll tell you what. We'll sit by the doorway, and if the first man that passes is a native, it's yours. That'll give me the odds, for you've got more Europeans."

"Done," said Gerard, and they waited near the dark entry in silence, puffing.

Presently Popa came by.

"D—— my luck!" ejaculated the little officer with great energy, somewhere deep down in his throat. He got up. "Well, it's fairly earned and I wish you joy. I hope you'll have a chance to-morrow of getting near the blackguards. Meanwhile, I must make myself as comfortable as I can."

"Oh, as likely as not you'll see me back before breakfast to-morrow. However, if there's a fight on, of course I shall ask leave to stay."

"Of course. Well, here are the despatches. And— by Jove, Helmont, I beg your pardon—here are your letters that Krayveld brought up with him. I quite forgot, thinking of other things. Well, I wish you joy, that's all I can say."

"Thanks. I suppose I had better be getting ready."

"How many men will you take? Half a dozen?"

"A sergeant and six fusiliers. I shall let the men volunteer. But I want a couple of natives for the sake of their ears and eyes." Gerard went out and set to work at once, selecting the best men from among a

swarm of candidates.  Half an hour afterwards everything was ready; the eight dark figures filed through
the purposely darkened gateway: who could say what
eyes might be watching, alarmed by Streeling's sudden
blaze? Gerard came first with the sergeant, their loaded
revolvers in their hands.  Popa brought up the rear.

Gerard reflected that he owed his good fortune to
Popa's opportune appearance.  "Well, I'll take you,"
he said.  "You're in want of something to cheer you
up.  But none of your pranks, mind."

Popa saluted.

A clearing, as has been said, surrounded the Benting; immediately beyond that, however, the party
plunged into the forest and were obliged to advance
along the narrow path in single file.  They had about
two miles to go.

The night hung heavy in the enormous trees and
among the tangled masses of underwood.  Stars there
were none, and the air seemed to be full of grey float-
ings that veiled its usual transparency.  So much the
better.

It was very silent now.  The whole line of them
went creeping forwards, with eyes to right and left,
everywhere alert, every footstep hushed, as the dim
trunks loomed through the darkness in continuous
clumps.  It was the custom of the Achinese to lurk by
these pathways, day and night, waiting with infinite
patience for the rare chance of killing a single foe.  At
any moment their shriek might burst forth and their
scimitars might flash.  The air all around was full of
indistinct movement, soft and sultry under the palms
and waringin trees.

"'St! What was that?" They all stood as granite, finger on trigger. Only some faint breath high above them touching the never-silent tjimaras.

"Confound them tjimaras, sir," whispers the sergeant. "They're every bit as bad, sir, as women's tongues."

"'St! Forward." Every now and then Gerard halts and listens; his thoughts are of the precious packet sleeping on his breast.

In fact, it was madness, this night excursion along the most uncertain of footpaths. Why couldn't they send up their despatches earlier?

Krayveld had answered that they couldn't send them before they got them. Gerard shrugged his shoulders in the dark. Despatches *from* Government were hardly likely, he thought, to be worth a single soldier's life.

With a feeling of very real relief he reached the rice-fields beyond the wood. He stopped and counted his men. Rearguard there all right? Forward. Who's that making his poniard click?

Far in the distance, miles away, lay a couple of sleeping villages; those nearest had been razed to the ground, some brute was howling among the ruins. From the fort rang the beat of the hour, as struck by a sentry on a wooden block, breaking across the solitude with terrifying distinctness. Eleven.

Beyond the rice-fields, through the tall, still grass, and by the sickening marshes with their reeds and sleeping water-fowl, then up again into the great forest, darkling, dangerous. Into the depths of the forest, deeper, deeper.

"Hist!" In a moment the men had formed round their leader, for the noise of crackling branches resounded in every ear. Again.

The enemy was upon them!

"Kalong. Kalong," said one of the Amboinese.

"It's the big bats, sir, out feeding," echoed the sergeant.

"I know," replied Gerard. "What's all this row about? Single file. We shall have to be doubly careful." And on they went, with that occasional breaking of twigs around them that was infinitely worse than the silence had been. It would now prove impossible immediately to distinguish an approaching assassin. The darkness seemed to thicken, as with a flood of ink.

At last they once more stood outside the jungle. Before them, with an open space intervening, lay the camp, black against the darkness of the plain. All around stretched the rapid ruin of a roughly widened clearing; the smell of roots and rotting plants and freshly-hewn logs was almost insupportable. It would have signalled the camp from afar. Everyone who has slept in these clearings knows the odour. From time to time a rocket went up, in silence, piloting the patrols.

"Halt!" said Gerard. "What's wrong behind?"

"Rear man missing, sir."

He turned sharply. "Impossible!" No one ventured to contradict him, but their silence did not alter the fact that Popa had dropped away.

"We must go back," said Gerard. "He must have fallen. How did you not notice?"

"Please, Lieutenant, it was the crackling. I thought it was the Kalongs."

They retraced their steps in glum anxiety, and searched back into the forest for nearly half a mile. At last Gerard dared go no farther; already his military conscience pricked him. The military conscience almost always pricks.

"I must take on the despatches," he said. "After that, we can see. I don't understand at all. He can't have fallen. You, Drok, surely we have gone far enough?"

"We have gone too far, Lieutenant," replied the man in an awe-struck whisper. "I saw him farther on than this."

"Very well; it can't be helped. Forward." In grave procession the little party reached the camp.

Having delivered up his despatches, Helmont asked first for leave to stay and see to-morrow's operations, and secondly for a search-party to hunt up his missing man. It cannot be said that the Colonel jumped at the latter proposal.

The next day was to be an important one, and he wanted every soul that could to get a decent sleep.

"Depend upon it," he said, "the fellow has been cut down by a marauder. They always cut down the last of the troop."

"Yes, but I should like to find that marauder," replied Gerard, "or the corpse. May I go back with my own men?"

"Oh, certainly," said the commanding officer, a little testily. "You may go back all the way, if you like. Good-night."

So the little troop slipped away from the encampment and back into the jungle again. They all considered it hard lines, but entirely unavoidable. And they peered the more closely into the dark.

Presently one of the native soldiers stopped on a slope and pointed to the bush close behind him. None of the Europeans could distinguish anything.

"Man gone down here," he said; "there's a track." He knelt and began cautiously feeling along the ground. "Lieutenant, there's a man gone down here," he repeated; "gone into the Aleh-Aleh (the long grass); you could see, if it wasn't so black."

A path of any kind there certainly was not; still, Gerard consented to reconnoitre a short distance, cautiously following the trail.

It turned abruptly, and, after a few steps which rendered them clear of the trees, the little party stood enclosed in tall green spikes on every hand.

"'Tis along here to the right," persisted the fusilier. Here, at least, the dark sky hung free above them, and the air was fresher than in the wood. Gerard hesitated. "We shall lose ourselves," he said. But even as he spoke, a faint purl of human voices reached them, evidently coming from some distance farther on down below. For a moment they crouched, with straining ears. Then "Forward," said their leader, and they slunk through the labyrinth, with constant precaution lest any weapon should catch, pausing to hearken, seeking the sound.

Their pulses quickened as they realized that it was drawing nearer. After a slow descent, which seemed well-nigh endless, they could even distinguish a flow of sound in suppressed but eager torrent. It was im-

possible to distinguish words, yet, suddenly, each man's
heart asked the self-same, silent question. Why were
these Achinese marauders, with whom they were on the
point of colliding, conversing in *Malay?* The voice
ceased.

The Aleh-Aleh broke off unexpectedly on the ridge
of a steep incline. Gerard, slipping forward, sprang
back under shelter not a moment too soon. In the
sudden opening he had descried above them, a little
to the right as the fusilier had foretold, a dozen of the
enemy grouped on a narrow, bamboo-protected ledge
round a tiny, low-burning lamp. Cautiously he now
peeped forth, and by the feeble flicker, recognised the
wretched Popa, bound and stripped to the waist, in the
centre of the group.

"There," he said, pointing. "Forward." Slipping
and crawling along the edge so as to keep clear of the
swish of the grass, the men followed him up. Under
them the abyss fell straight.

On the skirts of the little plateau they stopped.
They could now plainly perceive that Popa had a gap-
ing klewang-wound across his shoulder. What feeble
light there was had been turned full upon the prisoner,
the wild forms of his captors sinking away into the
darkness. They have been arguing with him, reflected
Gerard, trying to induce him, by the usual horrible
threats, to desert. Judging by the man's countenance,
they had now accorded him time to consider.

Even while his comrades stood watching, waiting—
to shoot were to imperil the central figure—the allotted
moments must have run themselves out. One of the
Achinese sprang to his feet, his big gold button twinkling,

and with a hideous flash of his scimitar across the dilating stare of the soldiery, he swept off one of the prisoner's ears. Another started up with a similar movement, but before he could fling himself forward, a shrill chorus of shrieks overflowed on all sides. Somehow, he can never tell how, Gerard was up, on the ledge, in the midst of them; Popa's assailant had fallen, shot through the breast, a dozen distorted, yelling faces were seething around the drawn sword of the "Wolanda."

Thirty seconds, swift, interminable, an unbroken clash of steel through the smoke and crash of the bullets—thirty seconds intervened before his soldiers, getting up to him, plunged fiercely forward, with bayonet and poniard, into the indistinguishable mass. The little lamp had immediately rolled over; the solemn darkness shook with a turmoil of oaths and outcries rising high above the clang of the fighting and the thud of the fallen. In a moment it was all over. Yet the trembling air still seemed to listen among the sudden silence of the tall tjimara trees.

A heavy groan shuddered slowly forth. Then another. And again another, in a different voice.

Gerard struck a match and lighted a pocket-lantern. Of his seven men three, including Popa, still stood upright; a fourth rose, stumbling, from the dark confusion on the ground. Of the three remaining two were already dead (one decapitated) and the third lay unconscious. Not one of the Achinese was able to continue the fray.

"Hurry up," said Gerard, cutting Popa's bonds. "No, I'm not wounded; it's nothing but a scratch.

We're quite near the camp; the least hurt must help the others."

The tom-tom, the enemy's well-known alarm, came thumping down the valley, re-echoed on every side from twenty watchful hiding places.

"Hurry up for your lives!" cried Gerard. In shame-faced silence Popa pointed to an easier track. Slowly and laboriously the two badly wounded were passed down by the others; the trail was followed back again; the footpath was reached. Near the entrance to the wood a patrol met them, sent out on the report of the firing.

"And you, Popa, speak," said Gerard after the tension was over.

"It is my crime, Lieutenant; the fault be on my head. I observed the trail as we went by; my thoughts were heavy for the murdered Adja. I wandered down it a few steps in my curiosity, knowing I could soon rejoin you. Suddenly one struck at me from the darkness, through the grass."

"And why did they not come after us?" questioned Gerard.

"You were gone on, up above; the grass is high. There were two of them only; I was alone, marauding."

"You shall be shot to-morrow," said Gerard.

"Lieutenant, it is right."

But on the morrow nobody had any time to think of shooting Popa. At a very early hour, in the dewy silence of sunrise, the gates of the fortified camp were thrown back, and the stream of soldiers, solemnly emerging, went curling down into the ricefields, with a long glitter of guns. All eyes were fixed on the farther frontier of forest, where stretched, half-hidden, the low, sullen line of the enemy's defence. A couple of advance-forts whose small cannon were proving especially trouble-some had been marked out for the morning's attack. Of late these operations had been greatly restricted, and the men now sent out accepted gratefully a possi-bility of painless death. For the shadow of cholera lay lurid upon the camp.

Gerard was indeed in luck, as Streeling had said, after all these wistfully patient months. He had taken a sick man's place and was acting as a (mounted) captain.

In the slow splendour of the burning daybreak, across that vast expanse of increasing sun, the "right half of the seventeenth battalion," separating from the main body, advanced with half a company of sappers, under cover of artillery, against the fortifications of Lariboe. They were barely within range when the enemy opened fire from his lilas or little cannon, almost immediately backing up the discharge with the flat bang of numerous blunderbusses, and the rarer whistle of the breechloader. The roar of his resistance now became continuous, and soon his entrenchments ran like a torrent of flame under rapidly thickening clouds.

At a distance of some two hundred and fifty paces the troops halted, momentarily, to send back a volley in reply. Then on they went again, silently filling up the gaps in their ranks, while, after the custom of Eastern warfare, a hailstorm of curses and abusive epithets now mingled with the deadlier missiles that poured into their midst. At fifty paces the order was given to charge.

The men, rushing forward to their special point of attack, found themselves arrested by an outer hedge of thick bamboo bushes, with a broad border of bamboo spikes. Once close up against this position, they were somewhat more sheltered from the fire of the central line, and, moreover, protected by the artillery behind them; but the garrison of the fort did not leave them one moment unharassed. They were now compelled to unsheathe their knives, and, with the aid of the sappers, they began calmly carving a passage through the dense obstruction of the bamboos.

A few terrible minutes elapsed. Some of the soldiers, cut by the spikes, flung themselves in furious effort against this living wall; others recoiled for a moment, disheartened by the groans of the wounded around them, feeling hopelessly arrested between advance and retreat. Then, as death still continued to blaze down upon them, amid the taunts of the enemy, they rushed bravely to their task again, cheered by their officers, who well knew the strain of such an obstinate impediment. Every moment of delay was calamitous. Through an opening the fort became visible, lying well back behind a field, its ramparts vaguely crowded with brightly turbaned heads. And halfway between hedge and fort rose insolently the banner of Acheen's Sultan, with its crescent and klewangs, over a stuffed doll, intended for a caricature of the idolised Dutch General, ignominiously hanging by the feet.

Not one man who was there but will remember with what a fury of reprisal this childish insult filled our breasts. Amid shouts of execration, the attack on the breach was renewed; but at that moment, above the hacking and swearing, a dark mass, rushing swiftly from the background, rose mighty in mid-air, and at one leap—grown historic—Helmont's horse cleared spikes, soldiers and bamboos, and landed serenely on the farther side. Then, galloping up to the derisive effigy, Helmont rapidly cut it loose, bringing down the enemy's flag along with it, and, flinging the colours of Acheen across his revolver, he fired through them five swift barrels at the clustering turbans which were concentrating their aim on this unexpected target. Then, holding the image superbly aloft, he began backing his horse—all in one exquisite instant of time—and fell heavily, horse, rider, and effigy rolling together amid a sudden rush of blood. Before and behind rose a mingling yell as of wild beasts wounded. A little brown Amboinese, his clothes and limbs torn and ensanguined, ran forward, having fought his way first through the aperture, and flung himself as a screen across the prostrate officer. Only a moment longer and the whole lot of them, with faces distorted and uniforms disordered, came pouring over the field under a fierce increase of projectiles. They swept upwards in the madness of the storm, the brief pandemonium of shouts, shrieks, and imprecations, the whirlwind of firing and fighting, in a mystery of dust and smoke. And a cheer, leaping high above that hell, leaping high with a human note of gladness, announced that the fort had been carried, that victory was won. Up with our own orange rag on the summit! Hark to the shrill blare of the bugle! Hurrah!

They disengaged Helmont from his dying charger and carried him away to the ambulance. In undressing him, cutting loose the clothes, the doctor came on his parcel of letters, and, a moment afterwards, on an old brown glove. The left hand still firmly clutched the hideously grinning doll. Popa would permit no one to force the fingers asunder—Popa, who, in spite of his shoulder-wound, had obtained leave that morning to get himself killed by the enemy if he could, and who certainly had done his best. The doctor gently put aside the relic and the opened letters. Gerard had still read them the night before. There had been one more, which he had read twice over, and had then burnt carefully and ground to dust.

"Helmont," cried the purple Colonel, hurriedly, stooping low by the young man's unconscious ear. "Can't you understand what I'm saying? I've only a moment. It's the Military Cross. Gentlemen, surely that should call him to life again. Helmont, I swear, by the Heavens above us, it's bound to be the Military Cross!"

The Dowager looked up from her placid embroidery and smiled to Plush. Beyond the great grey window the sleepy twilight was softly sinking back into an unbroken veil of mist. "What a dull drab day it has been," said the Dowager. "I wonder——" But she left her sentence unfinished. And the folds of the curtain hung dense. For an Angel of Mercy has drawn it across our horizon.

---

## CHAPTER XLII.

### THE FINGER OF SCORN.

IT was quite true, that the days at the Horst were
drab-coloured. They seemed to be that even all through
the long and brilliant summer, and their darkening could
hardly be called perceptible when the northern sun
sank from sight for seven slow months. Time appeared
to lower over the house with the dumb threat of an
approaching thunderstorm. And some people are fretful
before a thunderstorm; and some hold their breaths.

The Bois-le-Duc Helmonts were settled at the Home
Farm. The tranquil mother had said: Oh, yes; she still
knew how to milk cows; it would really be rather
amusing! And she had spread her fat hands on her
ample lap and smiled her good-natured smile. But
Theodore had frowned: "Leave the cow-milking," he
had said, bitterly, "to the Baroness Ursula." As soon
as he got away from Ursula he felt that he hated her.

His temper did not improve during the first year of
his new occupation. Work as he would—night and
day—he could not make up for initial mistakes, nor
could he victoriously combat increasing agricultural de-
pression. The dispossessed farm-steward successfully
harassed him on every hand. If Otto, the lord of the
manor, had made himself unpopular by putting down
abuses, what must be the fate of this stranger with his

perky, boyish face? The whole neighbourhood, for miles round, was full of people with grievances, some deep down, of Otto's inflicting, others freshly bleeding under Ursula's hand. And a low tide of resentment was secretly swelling under smooth water against My Lady Nobody.

Ugly stories began to be told about her, diligently propagated by Meerman, the discarded agent. As if all her administrative sins were not sufficient, accusations had lately cropped up which appealed far more vividly to the popular imagination. Substantial house-wives whispered behind her back, "Fie! Fie!" and young fellows winked to each other, grinning. No one knew whence these stories had suddenly sprung, but everybody had heard them. A patient inquirer might, perhaps, have traced their origin to Klomp's cottage in the wood.

When they first reached the ear of the village con-stable, that worthy portentously shook his head. It was in the tavern parlour of Horstwyk, where the lesser notables sat nightly, pipe in hand, waiting for each other to speak. The village constable was a great man, chiefly because he managed to keep clear of animosities, and his opinion carried weight. Every man present, leering up at him in the peculiar, deliberate peasant way, felt that he knew more than he deemed it wise to acknow-ledge, and they all approved his prudence. But nothing could more resistlessly have condemned the Lady of the Manor. The Law—mysterious Weigher of all men in secret balances—*knew*.

"There's something written up against her," they

reflected, awe-struck. Juffers, the constable, merely
said:

"The Lady Baroness is a very charitable lady. I
wish you all good-night."

He shook his head to himself all the way home, and
in passing a particular spot, by a great elm-tree, on the
road near the Manor House, he flashed his dark lantern
across the ground, as if struck by a sudden doubt.

Just then—some two years after Otto's death—there
were plenty of rumours afloat to interest the village
cronies. Quite recently, lazy, good-for-nothing Pietje
Klomp had come to grief, "as everybody had always
expected she would," in the usual "good-for-nothing"
manner. Strangely enough, her equally lazy and worthless father had driven her forth from under his roof
with unexpected energy—an abundance of oaths and
blows—when, confident in his oft-proven affection, she
ventured to confess her now hopeless disgrace. After
half a night of hail and snow in the wood, she had
crept back to obtain admittance from the pitiful Mietje,
but next morning her inflexible parent had once more
turned her adrift. She had watched for an opportunity
while he dozed, and then quietly slipped to her accustomed seat. During several days this singular duel
had lasted, and ultimately, of course, the woman's persistence had triumphed. Klomp only ejected the girl
when he had to get up, anyhow. As long, therefore, as
he remained on his bench by the stove she was safe.
And Mietje, tearfully exerting herself, took care to
anticipate all her father's few wishes—for coffee, fuel,
last week's newspaper, *et cetera*—and to keep him "im-
mobilised" during a great part of the day. He was not

unwilling, provided he could scowl · at Pietje in the pauses of his almost continuous snore.

Ursula, of course, heard from Freule Louisa what Freule Louisa had heard from her maid. So Ursula called to see the criminal. She had compromised with the ladies of her household, and only went to visit such patients as the doctor had certified free from any risk of infection. The village, knowing this, wrote her down a coward.

"May I come in?" asked Ursula at Klomp's door.

No answer, for the door was locked; Klomp would not stir to open it, and Pietje dared not pass near her father. She cowered in her corner, stiller than any scratchy mouse.

Ursula rattled the lock in vain. Then she peeped through the window, darkening its dirt, and saw Pietje's woeful eyes staring out of the gloom from the floor. With the resolute movement she herself delighted in she thrust up the low window from outside and stepped over the sill.

"Would you shut it, please, m'm, now you're *in*," said Klomp's sleepy voice.

Ursula sat down in the middle of the room, facing Pietje's dark corner.

"I've come to see *you*," she said, very severely.

She could not help herself. She knew that it was every right-minded woman's duty under these circumstances to be very, very severe.

Pietje moved a little uneasily, but did not rise. So, without delay, Ursula began her lecture. It was very conscientious and rather long, and all quite true and exceedingly severe. After the opening sentences Pietje's head bent low, and, about midway, she began to cry. She had not cried much during the scenes with her father, and tears now seemed to come to her as a pleasurable relief. Entering into the spirit of the thing, she cried so very loud that Ursula's lecture had to come to an abrupt conclusion, tailless, like a Manx cat. In how far Pietje calculated on this result none but she may presume to decide.

"So, of course, you must go to a reformatory," said Ursula, firmly. "I am willing to help you on condition that you take *my* advice."

"Don't want to go to no performatory," sobbed Pietje, with vague perplexities concerning circuses and ballet girls. "Father 'll keep me if I says I'm sorry."

A grunt from the other end of the room.

"Pietje, you have behaved very badly," continued Ursula. "It seems to me that you hardly understand the wickedness of your act. You only regret its unpleasant results. No, Pietje, you are"—she felt it her positive, painful duty to speak plainly—"a very wicked, guilty, evil-hearted girl."

"Dear me, Mevrouw," growled a voice half choked against a sleeve, "can't you leave the poor creature in peace?"

"No, Klomp," replied Ursula, "'tis my duty to help you both. I understand and appreciate your righteous anger, but, fortunately, *I* can provide Pietje with a home. It is only natural you should not wish her to remain near Mietje."

At this very moment Mietje came downstairs.

"Father, here's your li—yes, sister's going to stay with me," she said.

"Get you upstairs again," shouted Klomp, with a big oath, "and don't come down till I call you." He sat up, his listless face full of fire. "Now, Mevrouw," he said, "you just kindly go back to the Manor House, please. That's where you belong—*now*—and thank your stars for it. And leave poor people like us to settle our troubles between us. Pietje's a poor, ignorant girl, and she ain't got the wit to go hunting for a husband—least of all in the papers. She just took the first villain that came fooling her way."

"But, Klomp, I had understood——" began Ursula, rising with dignity.

"No, you hadn't, m'm: there's just the mistake. You hadn't understood nothing, begging your pardon. Nor, in fact, you needn't. There isn't anything to understand."

He actually got up, and, shuffling across to the door, he opened it. There could be no mistaking his exceptional earnestness now.

"Well," said Ursula, gently, preparing to depart, "when you want me, when Pietje wants me, send up to the Manor House, and I will do whatever I can."

He bolted the door behind her.

"Father——" began Pietje, timidly.

"Hold your tongue," he broke in. "I don't want to know you're there." And he threw himself down violently on his bench.

Ursula had nearly reached home before the meaning of Klomp's attack recoiled upon her brain. "Looking for a husband in the papers." Suddenly she understood. It was the old story of the trysting-place cropping up again. Not for nothing had Adeline stayed with the Klomps! Her brow mantled, and with quite unusual *hauteur* she acknowledged the salute of two passing labourers.

The men looked at each other.

"Stuck up, ain't she?"

"Yes"—with immediate oblivion of all former graciousness—"so she allus was."

The old Baroness received her daughter-in-law in a tremble of pink-spotted excitement. There were letters from Acheen—exceedingly important letters! Ursula must sit down at once and listen. Gerard had been in action. Gerard had done something wonderfully brave. He had been just a little bit wounded in doing it—oh, nothing, the merest scratch; but it happened to be the right hand, so a comrade wrote for him. He was going to be rewarded in some magnificent manner—made a colonel?—and the deed had been so very brave, he would probably soon be sent home again. *That* was the Dowager's reward.

"Sent home," repeated Ursula, motionless in her chair. "Mamma, did you say he was wounded?"

"Oh, the merest scratch," replied the Dowager, testily. "He says so himself. Ursula, you always try to make people nervous. Gerard never lied to me. And you see he is coming back. If he were really hurt he would never undertake so long a journey. I remember my poor dear husband"—she always avoided, if possible, saying "papa" to Ursula—"once cut his hand with a breadknife so badly that he couldn't use it for nearly a month."

"Oh, yes," admitted Ursula, hastily. "Yes—yes, I dare say it is nothing. I am glad, mamma, I am glad. I am proud of him."

"You!" replied the old Baroness, quite rudely, in a tone altogether strange. "What is he to you? When he comes back, Ursula, he will take away the Horst."

"I dare him to do it," said Ursula, fiercely. She drew herself up, looking down on the poor little heap of ruffles by the writing table. Some moments elapsed before she spoke again. "I found the letter you were looking for, mamma," she said, and her voice had grown quite gentle, "it is one from the late Prince Henry to papa."

"Thank you, Ursula. I am afraid I was rude to you just now. I have no wish to be rude to you, nor to anyone. It is not in my nature to be rude. But this news from Acheen has excited me. I am not as young as I was"—she peered across, with a quick glance of anxiety, at her daughter-in-law—"yet, I am thankful to reflect that Gerard, when he comes, will find me but very little changed."

The Freule Louisa came in. "Have you heard?" she asked. "Now, that's the kind of thing I like, and I never expected it of Gerard. I always thought Gerard was a bit of a coward, a curled darling of the drawing-room, like Plush. Didn't you, Ursula?"

"No, indeed," replied Ursula.

Freule Louisa giggled suddenly. "Well, I daresay
*f*ou knew better," she said. "Only I hope he won't
come back too soon."

"Why? What?" exclaimed the Dowager. Ursula
had left the room.

"Because Tryphena has just sent him out a large
box of Javanese tracts to get distributed among the
enemy. We feel that the Achinese should not be killed
but Christianised. Ursula's father behaved very badly
about the tracts. He said that the only way to get
them 'sent on' would be for the soldiers to wrap their
bullets in them. Scandalous, for a Christian minister,
and so I told Josine."

"Louisa——"

"And he says besides that the Achinese don't know
the language."

"Louisa——"

"As if they couldn't learn. I daresay there is'nt
much difference."

"Louisa, when Gerard comes he will send Ursula
back to her father."

"I doubt it. You know. *I* have always said——"

"Don't say it again; it sounds like—like blas-
phemy."

The Dowager seemed for the moment to recover all
her intellectual force.

"He will take back the Horst, do you hear? They
dare not refuse it him after what he has done. And
he will marry money. Then nothing will be left me to
do after I have seen him except to finish my Memoir

before I depart in peace. I should like to tell Theodore that the Memoir was finished."

"If he is going to prove so strong a man," replied Aunt Louisa, "I think I shall leave him what little money I possess. But what is that? A mere drop in the ocean. I am a poor woman, Cécile, as you know."

———

# CHAPTER XLIII.

## ARRESTED.

THAT evening some household duty called Ursula into the unused upstairs corridor which, as a rule, she avoided. And as she passed the "Death-rooms," she very nearly came into collision with Hephzibah, issuing from them, eyelids downcast.

Ursula felt that the woman had been watching her as usual. And although, as a rule, she resisted the feeling, to-day, by a sudden impulse, she turned like a dog at bay.

"If it makes you uncomfortable why do you come here at all?" she said.

"Why do you?" retorted the woman, adding— "Mevrouw."

"I never do, I was only passing."

"Ah, you *daren't*. But I must. I can't help myself. I can't rest downstairs. I seem to hear it calling to me all the time. Mevrouw, it *drags* me up. There's guilt in this house. It won't sleep."

Ursula leant up against the wall and closed her eyes.

"Have you anything you wish to say to me, Hephzibah?" she replied, "if so, say it."

The woman hesitated.

"No, I've nothing to say to you," she began, slowly.

"I suppose it's true, Mevrouw, that the Jonker is coming home?"

"Of course it's true."

Hephzibah began moving away.

"If you go in there, Mevrouw," she said, "perhaps you'll hear it to-night. It's groaning and gasping worse than ever to-night."

She ran down the long passage.

"Oh, Lord! oh, Lord, have mercy!" she murmured. "I've done what I could to make amends. I thought, after what I'd done, I should never hear it again. Oh, Lord, I'm not a bad woman. There's those sit in high places is a great deal worse than me."

"The creature is crazy," said Ursula, aloud, as she pushed open the door of the antechamber.

In the inner-room all was dark and still. Ursula shut herself in, and sank down by the bed.

"Otto, I have done my best," she said.

An immense weight of guilt lay upon her. Gerard was grievously wounded, was dying; perhaps already dead. Who could tell what was happening out yonder, in the fatal sunblaze? Before a message could be flashed across the waters his body would already lie rotting in the red-hot ground. And his soul, for all she knew, might be standing, even now, by her side.

"Gerard, I have done it for the best," she whispered.

But the words brought her no relief. She knew that, if this man died, his life would be required at her hands. And if he returned alive, yet broken in health, mutilated, crushed, she would have to confront him ever after, reading in every furrow of his forehead the charge against herself.

"I have done right," she gasped. "I could not do otherwise. I have done right."

And her thoughts went back to Otto, dying here, gasping out with every successive stifle his last, his only appeal. For a long time she knelt there, her face upon her hands.

"If only someone would answer!" she thought. "If only one of them would speak!"

The place was very silent. She could hear the dog Monk sniffing and vaguely whining beyond the outer door.

"If only Otto would answer me! If only he would release me! What am I that I must bear this weight single-handed? If only I knew. If only I knew."

A great agony fell upon her, such as was strange to her strong and steadfast nature. She wrung her hands and, prostrate against the oaken, empty bedstead, in impotent protest, she moaned softly through the darkness.

Suddenly someone—something—struck her through the darkness, heavily; she fell back, losing consciousness, across the floor.

When she opened her eyes they rested on Hephzibah. The waiting-woman knelt, with a crazed expression on her white face, peering close down upon Ursula, by the faint glimmer of a night-lamp on the floor. Ursula shuddered and dropped her eyes again.

"Not dead!" exclaimed Hephzibah, in a distinctly disappointed tone.

This touch of involuntary humour restored the invalid. She tried to sit up, and lifted one hand to her hair, which seemed to have grown oppressively warm and unsettled. She brought away her fingers covered with blood.

"I am bleeding still," she said. "What has happened, Hephzibah? Help me, please."

The woman pointed impressively to a clumsy carved ornament lying near her, which had fallen from amongst several others placed on the rickety canopy of the bed.

"*That* struck you," she said. "I thought it had killed you. 'Judgment is mine,' saith the Lord."

Ursula staggered to her feet. She became conscious of the great dog standing close beside her—attentive, benevolent. His deep eyes met hers; they were overflowing with sympathy. Steadily gazing, he wagged his tail.

"Help me to my room," commanded Ursula. "There is no necessity for saying anything more. Get me some water." She gave her orders calmly, and the woman obeyed them. "Leave me," said Ursula at last, lying back on a sofa with a bandage over her brow.

As soon as she was alone she got up, still dizzy, and rang the bell.

"The brougham," she said to the man.

He hesitated, in doubt if he could possibly have heard aright.

"The brougham," she repeated. "Tell Piet to get it ready as soon as possible. I am going far."

"Your nobleness is not hurt?" he stammered.

"No, no. Be quick." She hastily found a hat and mantle—she had recently laid aside her mourning—and then waited till the carriage was announced.

"To the notary," she said.   "Tell Mevrouw that I shall not be back till late."

Mynheer Noks lived some way out, on the farther side of Horstwyk.   The coachman, unaccustomed to any sudden orders, whipped up his horse in surly surprise, and reflected on the chances of meeting the steam-tram.

His mistress did not think of the steam-tram to-day, often as she recalled, in passing it, her wild drive with Otto, and Beauty's cruel death.   To-day she sat motionless in the little close carriage, watching the lamps go flashing across the roadside trees in a weary monotony of change.

"*If* it had killed me!" that was all her thought. She had never realised till this moment the possibility of immediate death.   There would always be time, she had reasoned, for final arrangements, deathbed scenes. People did not die without an illness, however sudden. Besides, when she had risen from the long prostration of her early widowhood, "God has not permitted me to die," she had said.   "He knew I had a mission to fulfil."

And now—supposing she had never regained consciousness?

She saw the lights of Horstwyk pass by, and wondered if she should never reach the notary's, and reproached herself for her foolishness.

"The notary is in?" she asked eagerly, at his door.

Yes, the notary was in.   He was entertaining some friends at dinner.   Ursula drew back.   "Show me into an office, or some such place," she said.   The notary, convivial in dress and appearance, came to her in a little chilly back room, full of inkstains and dusty deeds.

"Nothing is wrong, I hope," he began; then, noticing the queer bandage under Ursula's dark red bonnet, "You have had an accident?"

"No," replied Ursula. "Mynheer Noks, I am sorry to disturb you just now, but I can't wait. If I were to die to-night, who would be my heir?"

"That depends upon whether you have made a will," replied the notary.

"I have not made a will."

"In that case your father is your natural heir."

"So I thought. Then, notary, I must request you —I am very sorry to trouble you—but I must request you to make my will to-night."

"My dear lady, certainly. I presume you have brought your written instructions? Leave them with me, and to-morrow I will bring up a draft which we can talk over together." Ursula stopped him by a gesture.

"I must have the document signed and sealed," she said, "with its full legal value, to-night."

The notary stared at her; then he looked ruefully down at his resplendent, though already much crumpled, dress-shirt.

"I can't help it," continued Ursula, desperately. "It will only take you a moment——"

"Only a moment! Dear madam, documents of such importance——"

"Yes, only a moment. Just two sentences. That is all."

The notary sat down with a sigh, and drew forward
a sheet of paper. "You wish to say?" he asked, and
shivered—twice. The first shiver was real, the second
ostentatious.

The second caused Ursula to disbelieve both.

"Only this: if I die without other arrangements——"

"Pardon me. I must already interrupt you. You
cannot die 'with other arrangements' (the expression is
exceedingly faulty) if you make a will."

"I can alter it, surely!" exclaimed Ursula.

"Only by another will." The notary sighed and
looked at the clock. Quarter-past ten.

"Very well. I wish everything I possess to pass
unconditionally to my brother-in-law, the Baron van
Helmont."

The notary gave a visible start, and pricked his pen
into the great sheet of paper. He nodded his head
with complacent approval.

"Should he be dead," continued Ursula, "I wish it
to belong to his cousin, the Jonker Theodore. That
is all."

"Quite so," said the notary. "Quite right. And
now, Mevrouw, I have only one objection."

"No objection," interrupted Ursula, vehemently,
"There is none. Surely you have understood me?"

"I have understood you, but the objection remains.
The thing can't be done. That is all."

Ursula started up.

"Can't be done!" she cried. "I am the best judge,
Mynheer Noks, of what I choose to do with my own.
I understand your being vexed at my disturbing your
party; but if you refuse to draw up my will as I desire,

I shall drive on till the horse drops, in search of an-other attorney." She trembled from head to foot.

But the lawyer was also exceedingly angry. He had always, since Otto's death, disliked and distrusted "My Lady."

"You may drive to Drum if you wish to," he replied, "but you won't find a lawyer who can alter the law. No, Mevrouw, nor can I, even though you disturb my party to get it done. Be sure that *I'd* draw up a deed of gift, if you chose, this minute; but the law's stronger than you or I. And as long as your father lives he must come into half of your property."

"My father!" repeated Ursula. "Do you mean that I cannot disinherit him?"

"You cannot. If you happen to die before him, half of your possessions *must* pass to him. That is the law of the land. And, as I remarked, the law is stronger than you or I."

"It is stronger than justice," said Ursula.

The notary shrugged his shoulders.

"The case is altogether exceptional," he answered. Again he shivered, and looked at the clock. "So I suppose we may as well leave the will-making to a more convenient occasion," he added, half rising.

"No," replied Ursula, with an imperious movement; "make it at once, if you please, just as I said. Never mind it's being illegal. You will be law, and my father justice."

"It is exceedingly incorrect," said the notary.

"A great race like that of the van Helmonts cannot let itself be tied down by every paltry police regulation," replied Ursula, proudly. How often had she said so to herself, remembering her first experience of Gerard's *hauteur* at the railway station, hammering the thought firmly into her "bourgeois" heart. The high-born are a law unto themselves. So Gerard had understood— so Otto, and so she herself.

"Write it down," she said, "and leave the rest to us."

"Now at once?"

She clenched her hands to avoid stamping forth her impatience.

"Now at once," she said.

"But there must be witnesses, Mevrouw."

"Must there? Well, there are the servants, if some-one can hold the horse, and——" She stopped.

"Witnesses," she repeated. "You mean people who must learn what I have just told you? Oh, but that is infamous! No, no! Do you hear? I will not have it. I don't care for your infamous laws. What I have said is between you and me. As long as I live no 'wit-nesses' shall know it."

"You wish to make a secret will," replied the lawyer, coldly. "Well, there is no objection to that. I will write it out for you, and you can copy and seal it. Then I draw up a deed of deposit, and the witnesses only witness that deed. But all this will take time. My guests will be thinking of departing. My wife——"

"Draw up a form," exclaimed Ursula; "I will copy it to-night. My father and Gerard will respect my plainly stated wishes, even if——something were to happen to-night."

Her voice dropped.

The notary glanced sideways, as he wrote, at the

tall figure pacing restlessly to and fro. She was not natural, not herself; and herself, in his eyes, was strange enough for anything. That bandage! How had she come by so sudden a wound? What was the meaning of this unseemly hurry? He wondered uneasily whether this strange woman was minded to make away with herself. He resolved to do what he could to prevent it— a Christian duty, if rather an unwilling one.

"Here is the paper," he said, rising. "Nothing more can, with decency, be done to-night. It has, you will understand, not the slightest legal value."

"Give it me," she replied; "I shall expect you to-morrow morning with your clerks. Thank you; I am sorry I was obliged to disturb you, Mynheer Noks. Can I pass out unobserved?"

He unlocked the office entrance for her, holding up the oil-lamp. Under the little portico she looked back.

"I do believe," she said, "you think I am going to kill myself."

"Mevrouw!" he stammered, horrified, over the wine-stain on his shirt-front, "Mevrouw!"

"Set your mind at rest, my good notary. Only fools think they can kill themselves. God has not made life quite so easy as that."

The carriage-lights came twisting round to the little side-gate. As the footman held open the door there was a glitter of polished glass and a cosy vision of shaded silk.

"Come to-morrow morning early," said Ursula, with her foot on the step, "and you shall have one of my poor father-in-law's regalias."

As soon as she knew herself to be out of sight she

pulled the checkstring and ordered the coachman to drive to the Parsonage.

"There goes eleven o'clock," said Piet to his companion. "One would think there was truth in what people say."

"What do people say?" asked the footman.

"Why, that Mevrouw likes being out by herself of nights. At the tavern they were calling her 'nightbird.'"

"I know what they *used* to call her," grinned the fresh-faced young footman. "It used to be Baroness Nobody."

"Oh, everyone knows that. But hold your tongue. The Jonker Gerard never would allow a whisper on the box. He seemed to hear you in the middle of the night."

"The Jonker Gerard was a real gentleman," replied the footman, crossing his arms.

Ursula, as the carriage neared her old home, looked out anxiously, seeking for the light above the hall-door. It was gone; yet she knew her father to be in the habit of sitting up late. She lifted the carriage-clock to the ray from one of the lanterns: a quarter-past eleven.

"Let me out," she said, "I will go round to the back."

For a moment she stood, in the chill night, by the study window, listening. She knew perfectly well that she was acting foolishly; but that seemed no reason for leaving off.

"I must do it to-night," she said, "I cannot sleep until it is done."

She knocked at the window, timidly, terrified by the

prospect of meeting with no response. The soughing of the trees struck cold upon her heart.

"Father!" she cried, with a sudden note of pain. "Father! Father!"

Somebody moved inside, and soon the heavy shutters, falling back, revealed the Dominé's mildly astonished face against the large French window.

Ursula brushed past him and threw herself into the faded old leather chair. She looked up into his questioning eyes for one long moment, then, as the *home-feel* of it all came over her—the room, the books, the loving countenance—she dropped forward on her hands, and broke into convulsive weeping.

"Don't be frightened," she stammered between her sobs. "Nothing has happened. It's only—only——" She wept on silently. Presently she dried her eyes. "It's only—nothing," she said, smiling. "I am stupid. I have come to you for courage, Captain, as when I was a little girl."

The Dominé laid his single hand upon his daughter's head, and under his gaze she found it very difficult to keep to her brave resolve.

"No, no, you must scold me," she said. "That is not the way."

"You do the scolding yourself, child. It is only fair that one of us should attempt the comforting. Have you hurt your forehead?"

"Yes," replied Ursula, quickly. "It is not mnch, but it has upset me. It has upset me, you see."

"Ursula, Ursula, when a woman like you finds cause for tears, a bodily pain comes almost like a diversion. Dear child, I know your path is far from smooth. Some-

times I wonder whether we did right. It seems to me
as if, with you, it would have been 'No crown, no
cross.'"

"You ought to be proud of my career," said Ursula,
still resolutely smiling.

"And I know, the home-cross is the worst cross,"
continued the Dominé, as his eyes involuntarily wandered
to a simpering portrait of Josine upon his writing-table.
"Attack is not so hard, as all young soldiers soon find
out. It is the standing, patient, under fire."

"You pity me. You encourage me," said Ursula,
with sudden vehemency. "You think I am not to
blame. But if I *were* to blame for my misfortunes? If
I were wrong? If I had brought them on myself?" She
looked up anxiously.

"I should pity you all the more."

"Father"—Ursula rose—"do you think I could ever
become a criminal?"

"Let him that standeth," replied the Dominé, "take
heed lest he fall."

"And if he be fallen already?"

"'There is no better posture for prayer."

The little room, so warm, so *anheimelnd*, grew very
still. At that moment, perhaps, Ursula would have confessed everything.

But before she could utter another word, the door
was thrown violently open, and Miss Mopius, in a red
flannel bedgown and nightcap, rushed over the threshold
with a recklessness which entangled her in the Dominé's
paper-basket and precipitated her, a brilliant bundle of
colour, on the hearthrug.

"I wish you would knock!" cried the Dominé,

irrational from sheer annoyance. Ursula had started back into the shade, and her aunt did not at first perceive her.

"Roderigue," gasped Miss Mopius, "there are thieves in the house!"

Burglary was Miss Mopius's most persistent bugbear.

"What? Again?" said the Dominé.

"Hush. Not so loud. This time I distinctly heard them."

"You always do," interrupted the Dominé, who was an angel, but angry.

"At the window just under me, as I awoke from a restless sleep, I heard them, Roderigue. And I *saw* them. I saw two figures stealthily creeping. 'Ah!'" Miss Mopius, who had hissed out all this from the landing, now clutched her brother-in-law's arm. "We shall be murdered," she sobbed. "Shut the door, Roderigue; lock it. I don't know how I ever managed to summon up courage to come down."

She gave a shrill scream as something moved behind her. Ursula stepped forward.

"Fear sees every danger double," said the Dominé, with a smile to his daughter. "Go upstairs again, Josine, and take some of your Lob."

"Ursula!" cried Miss Mopius, in a fury, "Ursula, if I die, my blood will be on your head. I was ill enough, Heaven knows, this evening, and now I shall have a sleepless night." She put her hand to her side. "Ah!" she said, "Ah!" Her face was deadly pale. "Is it not enough that I devote my whole life to your poor old father, while you—live in luxury and pomp."

"I am very sorry," answered Ursula, lamely. "You have dropped all the Sympathetico on the carpet."

It was too true, and this misfortune annihilated Josine. In her hand she held the bottle from which the stopper had escaped as she fell.

"I had forgotten it," she said. "I had to take some before venturing down. Now I shan't get a wink of sleep. But I shouldn't have got that anyhow." She shuffled towards the door. "Roderigue, would you mind watching me up the stairs? I certainly saw two men. But, of course, it is very dark. Is Ursula going to stay all night?" Upstairs, at her bedroom-door, she turned. "Nothing wrong, I suppose, at the Horst?"

"No," called back the Dominé from the hall.

"Of course not—only mad pranks. Ursula's behaviour is criminal."

The Dominé's thoughts lingered over this last word as he returned to his daughter. "She did not even observe your bandage!" he said.

"The room is dark," replied Ursula. "I am going now, but I just wanted to ask you this. I came to ask it. By the bye, Captain, did you know that, if I were to die, you would succeed to the Horst and the Manor of Horstwyk?"

"Yes, I knew," replied the Dominé, gravely. "But you are young, and I am old."

"Captain, dear, if ever you own the Horst, I want you to give it to Gerard."

"Yes," replied the Dominé, more gravely still.

"You will, won't you?"

"Let me ask you another question. Why don't *you* give it to Gerard, then?"

She faced him. "Because I can't," she said. "Don't ask me, father. It isn't mine to give."

"Ursula, that would be exactly my standpoint. Property is never ours; we are God's stewards. And if I became owner of this great estate—God forbid, child, God forbid!—I should hardly deem it right to disannul my responsibilites by abandoning them to another man."

"You think the property is better in other hands?" cried Ursula, eagerly.

"I do not wish to say that of Gerard," replied the Dominé, gently. "Responsibility changes character: even the reckless Alcibiades felt as much. Still, I cannot help observing, Ursula, in what a marvellous, I might well say miraculous, manner, the estate has passed away from Gerard, to fall into your hands. Surely, if ever man can trace Divine interference, it is here. No, Ursula, inexplicable as the course of events would be to me, I see God's action in them too plainly to venture on resistance. Never should I *dare,* child, to return the estate to Gerard. God, in prolonging your child's frail life for those few minutes, *God himself took it from him.*"

Ursula fell back to the door. "And afterwards?" she stammered. "Afterwards?"

"The afterwards is God's. It is only when every soldier plays general, that God's war goes wrong. But, dear girl, you are young; I am old; we are all, young and old, in His hands."

"Let me go away, father," gasped Ursula, putting out her hands, as if to keep him from her. "It is near midnight. I must go home. The servants won't understand."

He led her to the carriage; out into the night wind again.

"Obey orders," he said, softly. "It's so magnificently simple—like Balaclava. Says the private: The general *may* be wrong, but I, if I obey, *must* be right. And our General cannot be wrong." He leant over the door of the brougham in closing it. "Be of good courage," he whispered. "I have overcome the world."

She caught at his hand and kissed it in the presence of her sleepily staring footman. Then she sank back among the cushions as the brougham rolled away.

"Divine interference," she murmured. "Divine interference. Oh, my God! my God!"

The Dominé stood watching her away into the darkness.

"Ursula and Gerard!" he reflected. "Had Gerard but acted differently. How I wish it could have been. For to human perceptions the estate seems rightfully his. I trust I have entirely forgiven Otto the wrong he did my child!"

He had done so, fully; but a doubt of the fulness was one of his most constant troubles.

## CHAPTER XLIV.

### AFRAID.

"Ursula, you look ghastly," said Tante Louisa at breakfast next morning, "and the whole house is full of your gaddings about."

"Ursula," said the Dowager, spilling her egg, "have I told you that Gerard is coming back?"

"Yes, she knows," interposed the Freule, hastily. "I can assure you, Ursula, that the servants disapprove."

"The servants!" echoed Ursula, with such immeasurable scorn of the speaker, that the latter could not but feel somewhat ashamed.

"No one can afford to brave his servants' opinion," the Freule rejoined, with asperity. "No, not the bravest. Even Cæsar said he was glad to feel sure that all the servants thought well of Copernica. You will find out your mistake too late, if once the servants are against you."

"Everybody is against me," replied Ursula, bitterly.

"Now, Ursula, how unjust that is! I am sure, not to speak of myself, your dear mother here has always shown you the greatest consideration."

"Oh, certainly, and my father too!" exclaimed Ursula. "I was not thinking of them. And the villagers. And the people at the Hemel. They all love me too."

"It is for the Helmonts' sake, then, mumbled the Dowager. "They all love all the Helmonts."

"They don't love you, and you know it," said Freule van Borck, incisively. "As for me, of course I admire those who dare to confront popular hate. "Drive over the dogs!" That would be my theory. I envy the woman who had the opportunity of saying it. All I advise is—take care."

"I do," replied Ursula, "of them all, as much as my limited means allow. And this is the way they repay me."

"Ursula, my dear, your charities are all wrong. To give with as much discrimination as you do, you ought to be able to give much more. Only the very rich can afford to give judiciously."

"Aunt Louisa, I believe that is very true," replied Ursula, gravely.

"Of course it is. There are lessons, child, which only a gradual tradition ultimately develops. I am a Radical, of course. That is to say, I am an Imperialist. I believe in the Napoleons of history. But, genius apart, it takes half a dozen fathers and sons before you produce enough collective wisdom to float a family. And I have always declared you were a remarkable woman, Ursula; but I should hardly say of you, as your father-in-law once said of some celebrated artist: 'Heredity? Nonsense. Why, Genius is a whole genealogy.'"

"Did Theodore say that?" cried the Dowager. "Now, I did not remember. But he was always scattering witty things, in bushels, like pearls before swine."

"Thank you," said Louisa, who had not learnt in the least to bear with her sister's infirmity.

"I don't mean . . . Louisa, you must write that down for me. There is nothing that distresses me more than the thought how imcomplete my work will be at the best."

"Mynheer van Helmont is asking to see the young Mevrouw," interposed a servant. Ursula rose hastily.

"Take my warning to heart," Aunt Louisa called after her—"about the servants."

"I am not afraid of servants," replied Ursula, disappearing through the door.

"Again!" said the Baroness. "He comes here constantly and at all hours. It is not yet half-past nine. Louisa, when he marries Ursula, we can go and live on the farm. Ce sera le comble."

"I tell you," replied Louisa, coolly, "that Gerard is going to marry Ursula, and then all will come right."

"And I tell you," echoed the Dowager, with an old woman's insistence, "that Gerard is going to marry Helen, sooner or later. I have always known it."

"Helen? Helen? Why, she's married already. Really, Cécile, I believe you are going crazy?"

"I know, I know," replied the Dowager, in great confusion. "But her husband might die. Otto died."

"Pooh!" said Tante Louisa, departing.

The Dowager also beat a hurried retreat. She sat down in her boudoir, and gathered poor grumpy rheumatic old Plush on to her lap.

"They'll find me out," she reflected. "If only I could hold on till Gerard comes." And her chin shook.

"You are come so early," said Ursula to Theodore, "that I suppose your news is especially disagreeable."

"If so, it meets with a fitting welcome," replied her visitor. "But you have guessed right. Ursula, you remember my telling you that the Hemel cottages by the Mill, the worst on the property, must come down, and you said they couldn't?"

"You said they couldn't," interrupted Ursula. "Who was to pay for rebuilding them?"

"Well, whoever said it said wrong. They could. They have come down of themselves."

"What?"

"One of the middle walls has given way during the night, and the three cottages are a wreck."

"Oh, is anyone hurt?" Ursula clenched her hands.

"Only you," answered Helmont, with a sneer, not at her. "All the whole filthy rabble are encamped outside among their household goods, swearing at you."

Ursula sat silent for a moment. "They never paid any rent," she said at last.

"No, of course not."

"That is something to be grateful for. Theodore, I cannot help it. You know I cannot help it. Nor could Otto. How could we make good, in our poverty, the result of half a century's profusion and neglect?"

"I did not say you could help it. And now we shall have the inspector, and the hovels will have to be put up again somehow. But how?"

"How?" repeated Ursula, vaguely. "Never mind. Wait a little. We shall see."

"Wait!" exclaimed Theodore. "Twenty-four hours! Have you no more diamonds?"

"No. Theodore, I am beginning to feel that I can fight no longer. I owe it to you that you should receive the first warning. I am going to give up."

He turned on her hotly. "What, frightened already?" he cried.

"Frightened?" she repeated, growing pale. "Why frightened?" A sudden light seemed to strike her. "Oh, you mean because of what they say against me in the village. What do they say against me in the village, Theodoré?"

"If you know, I needn't tell you," replied Theodore, pale also under his ruddy glow, unconsciously wondering how much had reached her.

"They say that I used dishonourable means to secure my husband. There is not a word of truth in it, Theodore."

"I know that," he answered, much relieved. "If I didn't know that, I should long ago——" He checked himself, as much from pride as from any gentler feeling.

"Have given it up," she quietly concluded his sentence. "You are right. I have been making up my mind. I, too, give over."

"Mynheer Noks is asking to see Mevrouw," said the man-servant, once more disturbing her, in the same careless, impersonal voice.

Theodore started at the name. "Do nothing in a hurry," he pleaded—"nothing to-day. As a personal favour to myself. I have a right to ask that. The villagers will say you are afraid."

"I promise," she answered, "for to-day. I have no right to refuse you. But I am not afraid of villagers."

A moment later she stood opposite the notary.

"I have brought the deed of deposit, Mevrouw," said that functionary. "And my witnesses are waiting in the hall. Have you the document ready?"

"No," replied Ursula. "My good Notary, I owe you most ample apology, but I cannot help myself. I have been compelled to abandon the idea of making a will."

The notary stared at her for a moment, too angry to speak. He was a rough man by nature, as she had seen, but not devoid of intelligence. At last he burst out, "Then go and—— see '*Rigoletto*,' Mevrouw, next time you visit at Drum."

Ursula had never been to the opera in her life, Mynheer Mopius's one attempt to take her having failed.

"I do not understand," she said, "but I see you are angry. It is very natural. All I can say is, that I ask your forgiveness. I did not know, when I came to your house last night, that I could not leave my money away from my father."

"But you knew when you left," said the lawyer, surlily.

"True, but I had not had time to reflect. I see now that I must leave things as they are."

"I, too, have had time to reflect, and I have come

exactly to the opposite conclusion. You will probably survive the Dominé; you say that you do not intend to marry again; then the best thing you can do is to draw up a will as you intended."

Ursula looked down at the carpet pattern.

"I am an old friend of the Helmont family," continued Mynheer Noks. "I do not deny, Mevrouw, that I was sorry to see this manor pass out of their hands. I should be still more sorry, and so would everyone, to find the Mopius family ruling here." He hesitated; then, with an effort: "Mevrouw," he said, "you are, perhaps, the best judge of your own conduct, but, after your visit last night, you will pardon my calling it strange. I don't know whether you came of your own free choice. I don't know what tragedy is being played here. I don't want to know. But something is happening: I can see that"—almost involuntarily he pointed to Ursula's wounded forehead—"All I say is, be careful. You acquired all this property by the merest accident. If anyone could have proved that Mynheer Otto lived half an hour longer—there would be no question of any will of yours."

"What do you mean?" exclaimed Ursula. "Do you dare to accuse me——"

"I accuse nobody. I only say be careful. There are strange stories floating in the air, and your strange conduct can only augment them. It only wants an unscrupulous lawyer——"

· "I am not afraid of lawyers," said Ursula, standing calm and queenly. "I have humbly begged your forgiveness, Mynheer Noks; I can do no more. This interview is at an end."

She swept to the window, looking out on the lawn, the near cottages, the far-spreading trees.

"I am afraid of myself," she whispered.

Half an hour later the post brought her a letter from Uncle Mopius.

It was a complaining letter, full of the writer's continual ill-health and all his sufferings and disappointments; but it had an unexpected wind-up.

"This year, once in a way," wrote Jacóbus, "I am going to make you a birthday present that you may be able to keep up the honour of the family in the face of those beggarly Helmonts, who, I hear, are abusing you everywhere. I hope you will use it for *display*. Show the naked braggarts that a wealthy burgher is a better man than they."

The envelope contained a cheque for two thousand florins.

Ursula stood holding it contemplatively on the palm of her outstretched hand.

"He is wrong about the date," she said to herself. "My birthday is next month, not that anyone except father cares. But I will keep the money; it will do to rebuild the cottages."

She wondered if Harriet knew of the gift; she fancied not. In reality it was entirely due to Harriet's influence.

Ursula stood by the writing-table on which lay her dead aunt's faded bit of beadwork: "No Cross, no Crown." She recalled her father's inversion of the words.

"Uncle Mopius has mistaken the date," she said aloud, "and to-day, of all days in the year, he sends this money. I accept the omen. I will not confess at this moment; I will not give up. No one shall say that my motive was either fear or despair. I will fight them all."

## CHAPTER XLV.

### THE HOME-COMING OF THE HERO.

THE rebuilding of the cottages was undertaken without delay, and, chiefly to comply with Mynheer Mopius's injunction an entertainment was organised by Ursula in honour of her birthday. It was a feast of the usual kind, in the village schoolroom, with dissolving views, and still more rapidly dissolving cakes. The whole village criticised the various good things provided, especially the patently didactic slides, and went home replete and grumbling. Furthermore, last year's potato-crop having failed, the village demanded provisions. These also Ursula distributed, especially in the Hemel, as far as the two thousand florins could possibly be made to stretch. Even elasticity has natural limits, and presently dissatisfaction rumbled forth again.

That spring, however, remains memorable in the annals of the Hemel. In April its oldest inhabitant died. He had been breaking up all through the winter, and his gradual decline had been watched by every man, woman, and child in the place: for, firstly, he was the only one among them who could be described as "pretty well off"; secondly, he was a childish bachelor; and thirdly, every household in the hamlet laid claim to some form of connection with "Uncle

Methuselah," as they called him, though nobody wished him that patriarch's tale of years.

Uncle Methuselah having died intestate on the seventh day of April, every able-bodied adult in the Hemel, not to mention the children, stood outside Notary Noks's little office-door on the morning of the eighth. There was much jostling and jesting, also some affectation of sorrow by those who considered that laughs should be taken in disproof of relationship.

The raggedest of the ragged troop, fat Vrouw Punter, had actually concealed an onion under her tattered shawl. Her face was so resolutely jovial that she fancied the lachrymose vegetable might prove useful in her interview with the man of law, for she had heard, and devoutly believed, that, if you but held such a thing in your hand, at an emergency, your eyes were certain to overflow. Most of the others poured forth rivers *ad libitum,* scorning artificial assistance.

But Notary Noks put a stop to that. "Come up in succession," he said, "and those who feel bad take a turn outside."

A list was made out of some seventy claimants, and then a period of darkest anxiety and suspicion began for the Hemel. Every day, as it slowly wore itself out, deepened the agonising conviction that "the judges" were cutting their slices off the communal cake. "Humpy Jack," who could fluently read words of three syllables, gave voice to the general sentiment. "A legacy in the lawyers' hands," he said, "is just like a lump of ice on a red-hot stove."

Pessimists shook their heads and expressed an opinion that "nobody would get nothing."

In a fortnight the excitement reached fever-heat. Meanwhile, numerous members of the community regularly visited—and called upon—Ursula.

At last, on a beautiful spring day, full of promise and hope, all the heirs, or their legal representatives, obeyed a summons to fetch each man his share. Not a soul but was amazed by the vagaries of "the judges," and annoyed by their rapacity. The people who received a couple of hundred florins were almost as angry as those who stared down on half a dozen silver pieces in a grimy palm. Yet, surely, the queer fractions and subdivisions should have convinced the unconvincible.

But after the return of the anxiously expected gold-seekers, a general appeasement settled upon the whole clan. Then followed a brief period of frizzling and frying, of dancing and shouting, and the children's cheeks were shiny and the parents' breath was strong. And the voices of the singer and the swearer were abundantly heard in the land. Then the flame burnt low, like a dying "Catherine-wheel," and fell away. Seven days after the visit to "the judges" not a penny of Uncle Methuselah's inheritance was left in the Hemel.

On the eighth day several woe-begone faces appeared at the kitchen entrance of the Horst. Not one of these faces, according to information freely vouchsafed, belonged to "a cousin" of the patriarch.

Horstwyk, as always, pulled up its collective nose. "Can anything good come out of the Hemel?" it asked. Besides, Horstwyk had other matters to interest it. Scandal about Ursula had become more general than ever, and to this was soon added the all-engrossing topic of "the Baron's" return. He came back as soon as the chill Dutch summer could feebly be counted on to cherish this hero-son of the soil; he came back, enfolded in wraps and coverings, with the imprint of wearying pain on his white but unchangeably hand-some face.

"Your rooms are quite ready at the Manor House," said Ursula, having gone with the Dowager to greet him on his arrival in Amsterdam. The Dowager could only sit silent with her hand in his; it had been her intention to ask him if really he had been wounded, but she had got sufficient answer before the question could be put.

"Thank you," said Gerard, "I am going to stay a few days with the Trossarts, and I shall be glad to come and see you from Drum. I am thinking of settling down for the present at the Hague."

Ursula bit her underlip. The Dowager's pale eyes flashed fire. "For the present." Of course. The best legal advice, she supposed, could be obtained at the Hague.

"Gerard," she said, and her eyes grew soft again as she filled them with his presence, "what is the use of letters that only tell half the truth?"

"It is a fair average," he answered, gaily. "Why, even before the introduction of the penny post man had discovered that the object of speech is to dis-semble. A dumb man with expressive eyes would tell all his secrets. And there has been since the creation of the world no greater multiplier of falsehood than the penny post."

"A man who daren't answer straight is bound to take refuge in nonsense," replied the Dowager, feeling quite young and clever again. "I wasn't speaking of the penny post. What you say there is so like your father, Gerard. Don't you remember how he used to declare that the breeding of centuries, after having come triumphant out of the French Revolution, had been killed in fifty years' time by the railway and the penny post? I have got that down in the Memoir. You remind me so much of your father, Gerard. I must show you what I have written since you went away."

And then they began talking of many tender memories, and Ursula left them alone.

Gerard had resolved from the first to avoid anything that could have the appearance of a home-coming to Horstwyk. This sentiment Ursula, of course, understood. But there are no more powerless creatures in the world than its rulers, big or little. It was a case of the driver driven. For the population of the whole neighbourhood made up its heavy mind to do honour to "the Hero," as everybody seemed agreed to call him. It was an excellent opportunity of protesting against Ursula's government, of glorifying the *ancien régime* and of saluting the national flag; also it gave a great many nonentities a notable chance of displaying their importance: there would be speeches, and favours, and, best of all, widespread good cheer. Once a committee had been formed and subscriptions gathered, both Gerard and Ursula saw that resistance would be vain. So they gave in, separately and simultaneously, each with the best possible grace, and the Lady of the Manor promised flowers and a collation, and invited the gentry for several miles round. Also she drove with the Dowager to inspect the triumphal arches in course of erection at the distant limit of the Commune, on Horstwyk village-square, at the Manor House gates.

The appointed day dawned white with early heat, rippling over as the sun rose higher into the colour-glories of triumphant June. The splendour of the cloudless morning lay almost like an oppression upon the drowsy pastures and the dusty roads. The washed and smartened crowds by the park gates and near the church shone visibly with heat and happiness. As always at the beginning of every public holiday, "the temper of the crowd was excellent": the local reporter of the *Drum Gazette* remembered that stereotyped phrase without requiring to make a note of it.

The Manor House carriage with Ursula inside met the train at the market-town station, and, by an irony of fate, she had to drive along the highway seated next to her brother-in-law. It was still stranger, per-haps, that this should be the single occasion on which she appeared since her widowhood, before all the countryside, in the *rôle* of Lady of the Manor. The "county families"—her cousins by marriage—gathered around her with abundance of malevolent curiosity.

Gerard was very silent and reserved; she saw how distasteful the whole ceremony was to him. He still looked ill, in dark clothing, with his military cross on his breast.

At the first triumphal arch, where a white stone marked the extreme limit of Horstwyk, the simple reception commenced. It had been distinctly arranged that only the returning soldier was to be honoured as such. The Burgomaster's welcoming speech, therefore, was all glory and gunpowder, and could hurt no one, not even Ursula, though she might have drawn her own conclusions, had that been necessary, from the silence which had attended her solitary drive to the station. Loud cries of "Long live the Baron!" now resounded on all sides; they · broke out afresh as the carriage halted by the church, where the school children sang a couple of patriotic anthems, and the Dominé, wearing his Cross of the Legion of Honour, held a second discourse. The village band having played a military march, the carriage drove off to the Horst. It was unattended, a sore point with the tenantry, whose proposal to get up a mounted guard of honour had been met by Gerard's unhesitating rebuff.

Everybody he cared about (and a good many other people) had assembled to welcome him on the Manor House lawn. The Van Trossarts were there, and the Van Troyens; and Helen, a fond, though fitful, mother, had brought her baby girl. A big luncheon was served in the house for the guests, and another outside for the members of the committee and the numerous village notables. Ursula sat calculating the cost all through her father's toast, which was necessarily rather a repetition of his speech, a glorification of bravery, secular and religious. Nobody could doubt that Gerard was utterly miserable.

Nor could anyone ignore the delight of the Dowager. She stood by her son's side, bowed yet beaming, all through the sweltry afternoon. It was her feast day.

She drank in with eagerly upturned countenance the unceasing flow of banal compliments, seeming to derive some personal satisfaction from the clumsy praises of the peasantry. For, after luncheon, while the children's sports were in progress, the returned warrior endured a congratulatory *levée.* Farmer after farmer came up, red-hot with clumsy good feeling; farmer after farmer remarked:

"Now, Jonker, you've kept up the honour of Horstwyk, say."

Gerard, rousing himself, found a kind word of recognition and interest for each. Ursula, as she watched him from afar, saw on the altered features the old smile.

Once she drew near to him suddenly. "How much you must have suffered!" she said. "I had no idea—I——"

He looked at her gravely.

"Not as much as you," he answered. "I would not have exchanged my fight for yours."

"Gerard, you do not mean that," she said, quickly, avoiding his gaze. "Now that you see the old place again, after all these months, you are glad it is still there, still—ours. You would not willingly now have lost a rood of it. Say so—say so, *now.*"

Her voice grew desperately pleading.

Gerard waited long before he answered. "I am glad it is yours," he said at last, "as you seem to care. I should not care for it to be mine."

She sprang back as if he had stung her. For the rest of the time she remained with Theodore, trying to believe that she did not observe the "county people's"

impertinences. She felt Helen's eyes upon her constantly, and was surprised by their benignity. That
woman must be a worse woman than Helen van Troyen
who can receive, immutable, a little child from God.

All through the sultry splendour of that long-drawn
summer day the peasantry enjoyed themselves in their
own peculiar manner. Towards five o'clock a slate-
coloured bank of cloud began slowly to border the far
horizon, as if rising to meet the yet lofty sun. One
carriage after another emerged from the stables, and
the local grandees drove away. · Then the people
gathered for a final cheer, before melting in groups
towards their respective neighbourhoods to finish the
evening, many of them—alas—in drink.

"Hurrah," cried the burgomaster, "for the hero of
Acheen! Hurrah!"

"And now," said Gerard's clear tones in the ensuing silence, "a cheer for the giver of this whole entertainment, the Lady of the Manor! Hurrah!"

It was a mistake, but Gerard knew nothing of
Ursula's unpopularity. His chivalrous impulse met with
but feeble response. A strident voice—one of those
voices you hear above the crowd—even cried out,
though hesitatingly, "Down with all thieves!" A murmur of approbation, from the immediate surrounders,
saluted the words. Ursula overheard them and, looking
up, saw a pair of villainous eyes fixed, evilly, on hers.
"Who is that man? Do you know?" she said, turning
to Theodore.

"That man," he answered, with studied carelessness.
"Oh, nobody. A writer that the notary has lately
taken on. His name is Skiff."

"Stay to dinner," said Ursula. "We shall be quite a small party. Immediately afterwards Gerard goes back to Drum with the Van Trossarts. I want you to see them to the station."

"Very well. There is a thunderstorm coming up."

"Is there? I don't mind thunderstorms. But this one is several hours off. You will be able to get back in time."

\*     \*     \*     \*     \*

It was about ten o'clock. The great curtain of deepening blue had crept steadily upwards, sweeping its broad rim, like a mass of cotton-wool, across sun and sky, and gradually mingling with night in one unbroken heaviness. The black weight now lay low on the thick, expectant air. The summer evening was pitchy dark, and threatening.

Inside the Manor House everything was once more quiet, with the numbness that follows on a long day's fatigue. A light glimmered here and there in the big, dim building. In the basement the servants were busy, washing up. From time to time a distant yell of drunken merry-making or sheer animal excitement came faintly ringing through the solemn denseness of the trees.

Ursula sat alone in her room, thinking of many things, especially of Gerard's reply to her question regarding the Horst. On her side that question had assumed the importance of a supreme appeal. How coldly he had pushed it aside.

"I know not what to do," she reflected. "I cannot advance or retreat. Merciful Heaven, how he has suffered! And the suffering has taught him nothing."

The noise from the village beat vaguely against her ear. It was growing louder, coming nearer, but she did not remark it. She looked up as from a trance, when Hephzibah broke, unannounced, into the room.

"Mevrouw, they are coming!" shrieked the waiting-woman, her white face still whiter from terror. "Save yourself! Escape by the terrace!"

"Silence. Keep calm," answered Ursula, long ago accustomed to recognise the poor creature's insanity. "If you can calm yourself, tell me what is wrong."

"There's no time," burst out Hephzibah, "for calmness. They are coming—the people, up the avenue! They swear they will murder you, or burn down the castle! Save yourself! Save yourself! Down by the stables."

Ursula, hearkening, distinguished indeed the fierce roar of an approaching mob.

"Hush," she said, white to the lips. "Go upstairs to Freule Louisa. Tell her to reassure the Baroness. Nothing will happen—do you hear me?—if you all keep calm," she spoke slowly and impressively. "But if there is to be shrieking and screaming, I cannot answer for the consequences."

Then, brushing past the momentarily paralysed servant, she went out into the entrance hall. Its white pillars shone dimly in the insufficient lamplight, half hidden behind gay patches of flowers. The house had not been decorated for the occasion, but the stands had been refilled and freshened up, and a floral "Hail to the Hero!" of the head gardener's fabrication, still hung unfaded over the great dining-room door.

The loud menace of the swiftly approaching danger

rolled up with increasing distinctness under the lowering heavens. Ursula could plainly distinguish enthusiasm for the rightful Van Helmont and denunciation of the usurper. "After all, they are right," she thought, bitterly; "they little know how right." Somehow, the reflection seemed to bring her assurance. She now remembered, without bitterness, all the manifold charities which the usurper, unlike the rightful lords, had constantly dispensed, as bread from her own mouth, to both deserving and undeserving poor.

She went out on to the wide steps and stood waiting: the hot air struck her pallid face, and the clouds seemed to sink yet lower.

In another moment the cries all around her struck a yet crueller blow. A dark mass, yelling and drunken, was surging vaguely across the blackness of the lawn —the lowest rabble of the purlieus of Horstwyk, and all the aristocracy of the Hemel.

"Down with the usurper!" "Down with the tyrant!" "We won't have any thieves in Horstwyk!" "Long live the hero of Acheen!" "Down with the parson's daughter!" And, cruellest of all, "Down with the light o' love!"

For one instant, as those mad words reached her, Ursula shrank back, and a torrent of crimson swept over her cheeks. Juffers, the constable, had supplemented Adeline's stories, telling how, even in her early widowhood, Mevrouw had despised all decorum.

At sight of the single, light-robed figure standing there in the dull radiance from the hall, the shrieking, struggling conglomeration swerved back. There came a lull: then the wild shouts went up anew.

"As no Helmont's to have it, let's burn down the house!" cried a dominating twang which Ursula recognised. A yell of approval swelled high around the words. The logic of this tribute to the family immediately enchanted everyone; and all the half-grown boys and raw youths in the horde howled with delight at the prospect of so grand a conflagration. The tumult for some time, however, rendered action of any kind impossible. Then followed the inevitable ebb.

"There is no necessity for burning anything," said Ursula, in far-reaching tones; "the house is full of defenceless women. I am here. What do you want?"

Another roar answered her, and, with re-echoing cries of "Burn it!" the mob swayed forward to the steps.

Suddenly the fierce note of fury changed to a shrill surprise. Ursula felt a hand upon her arm. Removing her eyes for the first time from the turmoil in front of her, she saw the little Dowager standing by her side.

"Go in, mamma, go in," she whispered, hurriedly. But the little Dowager did not move the hand.

"Hurrah for the old Baroness!" screamed a drink-sodden voice. The response was lost in an uproar of terror as the darkness momentarily vanished, and the whole scene—the massive building, the soaring beeches, the upturned distorted faces, the two figures on the threshold—all stood out white for one brilliant instant before the opening heavens crashed down the full weight of their pent-up derision in torrents of mingling rain and thunder on the wasps' nest beneath them which men call the world.

Mechanically the two women fell back under shelter.

The rush of water poured past them like a falling curtain amid the tumult of the elements. The startled and blinded crowd, as flash followed flash, sought an insecure refuge under the great trees of the park, still restrained by that pair of locked and steadfast women from roughly invading "the House." The whole place was wrapped as in a whirlpool of contending fire and water. Vaguely the half-sobered drunkard realised that the young Baroness stood inviolable, girdled by God.

House and park were black and still in a widespread drip and shine of water, when Theodore van Helmont, drenched to the skin, sprang from his flecked and foaming steed and rang softly at a side-door. He ran to the corridor where Ursula met him, lamp in hand.

"That I should have been too late!" he gasped. "Oh, God forgive me, Ursula, that I should have been too late!" The tears sprang forward as he looked at her, and rained down his cheeks.

"Don't," she said. "You hurt me." She had never seen a man shed tears before. "Of course you were too late. How could you help it?"

He mastered himself with an effort. "How pale you are!" he said.

"Well, of course, it is hardly a pleasant experience. It was my own fault for encouraging conviviality. It is over now, Theodore. Be comforted; you could have done nothing had you been here."

"I could at least have died first," he muttered. And he went away without saying good-night.

When Hephzibah had carried the alarm to Freule Louisa, the latter had run screaming to the Dowager.

"And where is Ursula?" the old lady had asked, gasping and trembling.

"Ursula has gone out to meet them, like the mad creature she is. Dear Heaven, we shall all be murdered! Come away with me, Cécile, come away! We can get out at the back and take refuge at the gardener's. Come immediately—come away!"

The Dowager rose, tottering, from her easy chair.

"I am going to Ursula," she said.

"To Ursula? Oh, mercy! Cécile, have you turned crazy too? Let her get herself killed if she wants to; what business is it of yours? Oh, Heaven, I'm so frightened, I daren't stay a second longer. Come with me! You, surely, don't care so remarkably for Ursula?"

"That may be," replied the Dowager, with one foot already on the stair; "but I am going to her now."

## CHAPTER XLVI.

### THE FATAL KNIFE.

MYNHEER MOPIUS was slowly dying. He amused himself with playing the part and schooling Harriet, little realising that her willingness to accept the fiction found its source in her certitude of the fact.

"Harriet has become quite docile," reflected Jacóbus; "she will make an excellent wife for my old age. I had always a gift for managing women. Look at Sarah, my first, whose character was fundamentally selfish. Love, based upon obedience, that is the secret of wedded bliss. But it would never do to let the women know it. When a woman knows a secret there's no secret left to know."

Mynheer Mopius spent much of his time in bed, especially the daytime. At night he would gasp for breath and have to be helped to an easy chair, and Harriet nursed him, carefully balancing her strength.

"Two invalids are no use to anyone," she said, when stipulating for repose in an adjoining apartment.

"My first wife——," began Mopius, but Harriet stopped him.

"That subject's tabooed," she said. "Why, Jacóbus, it is months since you mentioned her. Your first wife died. What would you do if, at this moment, I were to die?"

"Marry again," replied Jacóbus, coughing against his pillows, and looking exceedingly yellow and bilious, and unwholesome.

"It takes two to do that," said Harriet, colouring, as she spoke, under the reproach of her own acceptance.

"Does it?" answered Mopius, clinking his medicine-bottles.

"Jacóbus, we have never quarrelled. Don't let us begin now. There is only one question I should like to ask you without requiring an answer. How many people did you propose to when left a widower before you got down to me?" She left the room abruptly, and in the passage she struck her white hand across her face.

Not very hard.

Jacóbus sat up and adjusted his nightcap. "Ah, you see, she ran away," he said. "A year ago she'd have braved it out. I shall still make something of Harriet."

She came back presently with a bundle of papers. It was part of her daily task to read aloud all the official documents connected with the government of Drum, which were sent to the caged Town Councillor. Jacóbus fretted incessantly at the thought how everything was going wrong.

"The people in the streets look just as usual," said Harriet; but that consideration afforded her husband no comfort. She yawned patiently over endless statistics regarding gas and drains. It was her ignorance which caused her to wonder whether the town would not have been governed far better without a council, and especially without an official printing-press.

"It is time for my medicine," said Mopius, who, by saying this five minutes too early, constantly succeeded in suggesting an omission on Harriet's part. "Well, what says the Burgomaster concerning the market dues? He is a fool, that Burgomaster. And so are the aldermen. Heigho! I wonder what will become of this poor town when I am gone? It is strange how greatly I have attached myself to it. Almost as much as if it had been my birthplace. But I had always 'une nature attachante.' It is a great mistake."

"Not necessarily," said Harriet.

"Yes, yes. Life is too short: here to-day, gone to-morrow. Ah, well! Is that idiot going. to lower the rent for market stands?"

"I don't know," said Harriet, wearily, turning over her pile of documents; "I'll read you the whole lot; you can see for yourself." And she did read, monotonously, for an hour and a half, Mopius following everything with eager interest, interrupting, gesticulating, nodding approval or, more frequently, dissent.

"Right, right," said Jacóbus, in high good humour over somebody's opposition to the powers that be in Drum. "Give it them well. I never approved of knuckling under to grandees. You gain nothing but kicks by bowing to 'My Lord.' Ah, they'll miss me when I'm dead, Harriet, and so will you."

"Yes, I shall miss you," replied his wife. "Dear me, Jacóbus, what shall I do with my time all day?"

"First you will cry," said Jacóbus, with ghastly enjoyment of a far-off possibility; "and then you will get tired of crying." He waited a little ruefully for a disclaimer. "And then you will begin to enjoy your money."

"By the bye, that is a subject we have never spoken about since the marriage settlement," said Harriet, holding one of the stiff yellow papers against her check. "At least, *I* have never spoken about it. Of course, you tell me twenty times in a week that you will leave me a lot of money; but that counts for nothing. I believe you used to say the same thing to Ursula. Seriously, Jacóbus, have you ever made a will?"

"I have," said Jacóbus, enjoying his importance.

"I thought people who had been notaries always died intestate. If you had died intestate, Jacóbus, I suppose Ursula would have had all your money?"

"Ursula and that foolish Josine. Ursula, Baroness van Helmont of Horstwyk and the Horst. This conversation appears to me unpleasing, Harriet."

"Unavoidable conversations almost always arc." Harriet's face was entirely hid by the "Report on Sewage." "Has this will of yours really appointed me your heir?"

Mynheer Mopius fell back and gasped. "Can you not wait a little longer?" he said—"a very little longer?"

"Jacóbus, I am only repeating what you have told me over and over again. I want to know, if you please, whether you have really left your whole fortune to me."

She drew near to the bed.

Mynheer Mopius sat up again, and looked askance at his wife anxiously. "I'm getting better," he said. "I feel a great deal better to-day."

"I'm so glad. You look better. And now, Jacóbus, answer my question, on your honour."

"Harriet, I do believe you want me to die. I don't think I shall last much longer; still, don't reckon too much on my speedy demise. I heard the other day of a man who was buried and resuscitated, and lived forty years afterwards."

"Nonsense," replied Harriet, unsympathetically. "If you were buried, I should hardly be asking about your will. Now, tell me."

"What if I don't?"

Harriet shrugged her handsome shoulders. "I suppose the truth is you have left me nothing," she said, walking away, "and you don't want to avow your life-long lies. One can never trust your boastings. Perhaps there isn't so much to leave."

"You will be a rich woman, Harriet," answered Mynheer Mopius, solemnly, "a very rich woman. Yes, I have left you all, on condition that you never marry again."

"A foolish condition," said Harriet, once more applying the Report. "Should the question present itself, I would certainly not be influenced by considerations of that kind."

"Hum!" said Jacóbus. "Well, now I have told you. So let's talk of something else. I wish you would give me my jelly."

She got it for him. "And if I marry, everything goes to Ursula, I suppose," she persisted. "Well, so much the better for Ursula."

A sudden jealousy flashed into his orange-green eyes. "I believe, if I died, you would marry the doctor," he said.

Her face flushed protest; her heart thumped assent.

"You have no right to say that, or anything like it, she cried. "I have been a faithful wife to you, Jacóbus. Keep your dirty money."

Her rising violence always cowed him. "Tut, tut," he said, "so I shall. For many a long year, perhaps. And after that you may have it.",

"Not on those conditions." She turned away from him altogether. "Make your will over again," she said. "Do you hear me? And leave your money to Ursula, whose, in fact, it is by right. I am content with my settlement, as I told you at the time. You will remember that I told you to leave your money to Ursula. Money, with me, is not the one thing worth living for and talking about. But I wanted, in honesty, to warn you. You had better send for the lawyer to-night."

"What nonsense!" he cried, angrily. "To hear you talk, one would think I hadn't a week left to live. Is that what the doctor thinks, pray? The wish is father to the thought."

Harriet controlled herself, forcibly. She came close to the bed. "You needn't make it to-night," she said, softly. "But you had better make it soon."

About a fortnight later Mynheer Jacóbus Mopius was buried with all the pomp he had himself prescribed. All his virtues and dignities were engraved upon his tombstone, so that his first wife's adjoining one looked very bare by comparison. His last words had been, in a tremulous, squeaky sing-song:—

"If thy dear hand but lift the fatal kni-i-fe,
I smile, I faint, and bid sweet death 'All hail!'"

## CHAPTER XLVII.

### TRIUMPHANT.

THE day after the attack on the Manor House Ursula came down to breakfast as usual.

"Has Monk not been found yet?" she asked.

In the servant's face she read disaster. She had not missed any of the menials in the hour of danger, presuming them to be hidden away under bedsteads upstairs, but she had been astonished by the prolonged absence of the dog.

"Yes, Monk had been found," said the servant, uneasily.

She cast a quick glance at his shifty eyes, then, without further question, she went down to the basement, straight to the mat where the St. Bernard slept. Monk was lying there, in a great huddled mass of brown and white wool, motionless. Before she had come near she knew he was dead. She stood for a moment by his side. Already the limbs were stiffened, the eyes rolled back. She understood that he had been decoyed the day before, and poisoned.

She knelt down and kissed the soft, white head.

"I used to think I was alone," she said as she rose. A maid came towards her.

"Yes, it's a pity, Mevrouw, is it not?" said the maid.

"The old Mevrouw sent me to ask you to go to her, in her boudoir."

Ursula obeyed the summons. As she entered, the Dowager rose to meet her.

"My dear," said the old lady, trembling very much, "you saved the house last night. I'm afraid I have not always been fair to you. I am old, Ursula; you must forgive an old woman's prejudices. But you are worthy to be a Van Helmont. Your father-in-law would have appreciated your conduct, my dear."

Henceforth, there was one recent event, on which the Dowager's mind remained perfectly clear. Its fierce terror seemed to have burnt it in. Much that had happened since the old Baron's death was a blank or a muddle, but she was always ready to talk of the attack. And she spoke, therefore, with far greater kindness of the heroine.

"Yes, Ursula is strong," assented Tante Louisa.

Presently came the tidings of Uncle Mopius's death, and very soon after that, a letter from Harriet. She told Ursula quite frankly that she intended to marry again, as soon as her period of mourning was over, so that there would be no use in first pretending to ignore the fact. "Therefore," she wrote, "I can only lay claim to the ten thousand* a year of my marriage settlements, and, barring a handsome legacy to Josine, you are your uncle's heiress."

Ursula dropped the letter on her writing-table and sat thinking, till disturbed by one of Theodore's frequent

* £830.

business calls. These unavoidable discussions were rarely agreeable.

"First, I can tell you," he began, "that Juffers has been dismissed."

"Good," replied Ursula. "That is only right. It would be foolish to pity him."

"Secondly, nothing will result, I fear, from the judicial inquiry as regards either the attack on the house or the murder of the dog."

"That, too, is natural. It was a drunken outburst. Still, somebody must have been the deliberate instigator, or the dog would not have lost his life. I am sorry they can't find out who did that."

"I think I know. That new clerk of Noks's has some grudge against you. Would you like Monk's murderer punished, Ursula?"

A responsive flame shot into her eyes. They met Theodore's.

"Oh, no," she said, quickly. "No, no. Leave the man alone, Theodore."

"Thirdly—the usual worries. The old refrain, 'Money! money!' Money wanted for the expenses of Gerard's reception. Money wanted for the completion of the cottages. Money wanted for a new roof on the Red-dyke Farm. If only we had more money, Ursula, all would be well. As it is——"

She interrupted him. "There is money," she said. "I am a rich woman, Theodore."

He smiled an annoyed little smile. "Very funny," he said, "if only——"

"It is quite true."

"Oh," he exclaimed, suddenly understanding. "Has that precious uncle of yours disinherited his wife?"

She coloured angrily. "My uncle's wife is quite able to manage her own affairs," she said. "Be thankful, you, that henceforth there will be money enough and to spare."

"How much do you think?" he questioned, with a man's curiosity to know the figure.

"Some twenty-five to thirty thousand florins a year, Theodore. We shall be able to carry out all your improvements—all Otto's improvements—all that he used to say he would do if he could—all he could have done if he had married his cousin Helen. And I shall have a chance of trying my charity schemes. We must build an Institute. You must help me, Theodore; there will be heaps to do. We must do it all—all!" She spoke hurriedly, feverishly, as one who crushes down a tumult in his heart.

Theodore stood looking at her, his face puckered and puzzled. "All the fun of the thing is gone," he said.

"The fun?"

"Yes, the fun. Can't you understand? I can't explain. There's nothing more for to-day. Good-morning."

"Theodore, I wonder whether thirty thousand florins will suffice to purchase their affection?" She paused. "Their armed neutrality," she slowly said.

But when left alone her manner changed. She sank down by the window—looking out, looking out. The other day in her supreme appeal she would have aban-

doned everything to Gerard on his coming home; she
had hoped against hope. And what had been his reply?
"I am glad you have it, if you like it. I would not have
exchanged my struggle for yours." The words came to
her now with superficial meaning; long afterwards she
learnt to fathom their sorrowful compassion.

"It is God's doing," she pleaded, still gazing away
upon the landscape, "God's answer. He confided these
hundreds of human beings to my care, and now gives
me the means to help them. I dare not abandon them
to Gerard—to ruin. Right is an abstract idea. It were
wrong to do right."

The next two days brought Ursula a strange medley
of emotions. Gerard had telegraphed immediately after
the riot, offering his services; but she begged him not
to come over just yet. She dreaded all contact with
him. She dreaded his pale face.

He, on his part, gladly held aloof. He was looking
for a small house at the Hague, where he expected his
mother to come and live with him. The Dowager meanwhile waited patiently. Gerard had only been back a
fortnight. To her it seemed one brief yesterday.

Meanwhile the news of Ursula's accession to wealth
filled the province. In one moment the tide turned
completely, and the waters of adulation came running
from all sides to her feet. Tenants and tradespeople
vied with each other in denouncing those who had
wronged her. Demands for improvements and repairs
poured in hourly; petitioners of all kinds jostled accre-
dited beggars on the Manor House steps. A rumour
had gone forth that the young Baroness really intended

to spend her wealth on the property, and when early requests received a hearing, and vague projects got bruited, then enthusiasm knew no bounds. Not more than a week after the attack on the Manor House Ursula was compelled to exert herself, amid a storm of delation, to prevent both a criminal trial and a lynching of scapegoats by lesser offenders. She would have extended small mercy to the poisoner of her dog had not a story recently reached her ears, after going the round of the neighbourhood, to the effect that the notary's new clerk had been found one evening, not far from his home, lying in the road unconscious, with the coat thrashed off his back.

Ursula, a little dazed amid this sudden revulsion, could even smile at the faces that beamed upon her and serenely decline the honours of a swift counter-demonstration after the manner of Gerard's reception. She could make every excuse for the fawning of those whose daily bread lies in a master's hand, but what hurt her to the quick was the sudden melting of the "cousins," who poured down upon her like icicles suddenly struck by the beams of a belated sun. They could not understand her shivering in the bath of their con-gratulatory condolence. Ursula pushed the Barons and Baronesses aside.

But the rush of popularity was pleasing, even when correctly estimated; the importance was pleasing; and the possibility of fulfilment—the sudden nearness of life-long ideals—was most pleasing of all. It was all so sudden, so unexpected. Ursula, triumphant, gasped for breath.

\*        \*        \*        \*        \*

One morning, three days after the news reached her, Ursula rang the bell and sent for Tante Louisa's maid.

"Hephzibah," she said, "if you are so wretched in this house—and your face proves it—why do you remain?"

Hephzibah began to whimper.

"Klomp won't have me," she said; "not unless I bring him enough money to support me. He can't but just support himself, he says. And Pietje and her child would have to be boarded out."

"You shall have the money. You can go and tell him so—that is settled."

But Hephzibah lingered with her apron to her face.

"Forgive me, Mevrouw," she said; "I never meant no harm to you—but we're all poor, guilty sinners; and that woman Skiff, the insolent liar, pretending to be wife to honest folks, and then bringing along another husband of her own!"

"You have done me no wrong that I know of," replied Ursula, calmly; "but I see you are uncomfortable here, and I am willing to help you. Do you hear your foolish voices still?"

Hephzibah shuddered; then she said, enigmatically,

"No, I don't. Not *after*—— Nevertheless, repentance comes too late. I'm not as bad as other people,·but I'm doomed to be unhappy; privileged, I should say."

"You can go," said Ursula.

Hephzibah turned by the door.

"Why don't you marry the Jonker?" she began, suddenly; "I know he loves you. He loved you when he didn't ought to, and I know he loves you still."·

"Peace, woman!" exclaimed Ursula, rising fiercely. "The Jonker does not love me, nor I him. Go you, and marry your clod."

A few hours later, as Ursula was sitting alone, thinking—— "Why," asks Freule Louisa, "does Ursula always sit thinking, since her inheritance came? Is she counting up her money? Oh, fie!"——as Ursula sat alone thinking, a stone flew suddenly through her open window, alighting almost at her feet. It had a paper attached to it, and the paper bore these words:

"Beware of Adeline Skiff and her husband. They will work your downfall, if they can."

She turned the paper over and over. She had no doubt that it came from Hephzibah, whom she—and the world generally—believed to be mildly crazy. She knew that Hephzibah had suspicions regarding many things, but she also had always known these to be harmless. Nobody would attach any importance to Hephzibah's mutterings.

Ursula smiled sadly.

The paper lay in her lap. And now, unexpectedly, as she gazed down, a great fear fell upon her, she could not have told whence. For the first time she was frightened, afraid of a secret enemy, afraid of discovery, exposure. Who was this man Skiff, the notary's clerk? What did he know? What could he do? She started up.

To be forced, against her own will, to surrender! To be compelled to do what she would so gladly have done of her own accord, if she had but known how! She set her teeth tight.

An hour later, in the early fall of the slow August evening, Ursula knocked at Skiff's humble door. Adeline opened it, and immediately tossed her head. "And what may you please to want of me?" she asked.

"I wish to speak to your husband," replied Ursula.

"Find him, then," said Adeline, and banged the door.

The insult did Ursula good in this hour of universal adulation. It braced her.

She took a few steps down the lonely lane, reflectively, and then remembered the public-house at the end. She wondered she had not thought of it before. She called to a child at play, gave it a penny, and bade it tell Skiff he was wanted at home immediately.

"Wanted at home, you hear," she cried after it, as she hastily retreated.

The urchin scampered off and burst into the bar-room. "My lady Baroness wants Mynheer Skiff," he screamed. "She's waiting in the middle of the road."

This bombshell, at least, had its desired effect, which a quieter summons from Adeline might easily have missed. Amid general, but silent, astonishment, and much arching of eyebrows, Skiff started up and stumbled out.

"I wonder he ain't afraid of another beating," said one of the topers.

"He gets drunk so as not to be afraid," replied another.

Ursula's heart almost failed her when she saw the miserable little creature come lurching down the lane. Oh, the humiliation of condescending to such a low hound as this! At this moment, standing awaiting his approach, she touched the lowest depth in all her long descent of suffering.

17*

She had not made up her mind what to do. She had no plan. Only she was resolved, in accordance with her character, immediately to face uncertainty.

He slouched up and jerked his hat, "And what can I do for you, ma'am?" he said.

She sickened at his manner, feeling as if a snail were creeping across her hand. "Answer a simple question," she replied. "What do you want of me?"

He swayed to and fro, passing his hand across his eyes. "I'm a poor man," he said, "a very poor man. A little money never comes amiss."

"Money?" she echoed. "What should I give you money for? Drink? You will get no blackmail out of me!" Her gorge rose; she felt her pulse grow steady again.

"Now, ma'am, best be civil," remonstrated Skiff, with tipsy ferocity. "Blackmail isn't the word, yet there's stories enough about you to make a little hush-money worth your while. You'd better pay up, my lady; you'd better pay up!"

"Threats! And to me?" exclaimed Ursula, scornfully. But at this moment the cottage door was thrown open and Adeline came running out.

"Don't let her off too easy!" cried Adeline. "Skiff, you fool, how much did you say? It shall be five thousand florins, if it's a penny, my lady. Or we'll show you up, Baroness Helmont of the Horst!"

With Gerard's return, Adeline had grown utterly reckless in her fierce hatred of Ursula.

"I am glad you speak so plainly," said Ursula, coldly. "In this manner you will certainly never get a penny out of *me*."

For only answer Adeline poured out a flood of accusation, sprinkled with foul language, from which Ursula gathered for the first time, what tales had been circulated against her in the village.

She stood frozen to marble—to marble splashed with mud that no current of years would ever again remove. "That is all?" she said at length, when Adeline paused for breath.

"All!" shrieked the woman. "Skiff, d'ye hear my lady? She don't think it's enough! I wonder what your two lovers 'll say, Madam, Theodore and Gerard!"

"Hold your tongue," growled the man, shamefacedly, "or I'll make you. She has such a temper, my lady, she goes off her head at times. I hope your nobleness 'll forgive her and remember I'm a poor man."

Ursula had understood, as the torrent swept down upon her, that these people knew nothing—absolutely nothing. They could not hurt her, except by such vague slander as any man may speak. Her secret was still her own, entirely her own, shared by none but a half-crazy creature, whose tardy story, if told, would never carry conviction. And now her set face grew gentle, and the flood-gates of her charity opened.

"I will arrange for your emigrating to Canada," she said, "if you promise to sign the Pledge."

"Oh, I'll sign it, and willingly," answered Skiff. "If I may make so bold, how much would you make it, My Lady?"

"That will depend on many things," replied Ursula, and turned to go. "I will have no money wasted."

Adeline stood in the path, looking as if she would fain have struck her successful rival.

Ursula paused.

"You poor thing," she said, "I cannot understand what you have against me. I am in no way responsible for your ruin. Believe me, I did all in my power to persuade Baron van Helmont to make you his wife."

No other words the Baroness could have uttered would have enraged Adeline more than these. The woman stood foaming at the mouth, with the hysterical passion of her class.

"You! You!" she sobbed out. "*He asked* me to marry him, do you hear, like the true-hearted gentleman he was! And I threw him over for Skiff! What I said later was a lie, as you know, but I'd have kept up the game if the child hadn't died, as it did last year, more's the 'pity! And I *could* have been Baroness van Helmont, if I'd chosen, so there. You can take my leavings, madam."

Ursula came a step closer; her face seemed to alter suddenly. "Answer before God," she said, "did Gerard van Helmont offer you marriage before your child was born?"

"Yes, I tell you, yes!" laughed back Adeline impudently. "There, you didn't expect that, did you? There's pleasant news for My Lady so proud! Take Miss Adeline's leavings, do!"

The man, who had stood watching them, stumbled forward.

"Go in, d'ye hear?" he said, roughly, "or I'll give

you another taste of yesterday's dinner." He turned to Ursula with a leer he intended for a smile. "You must forgive her, Mevrouw," he said, bowing. "She's a bit fantastical, as I said, but I know how to manage her. I hope that Mevrouw will kindly remember the arrangement she has just made with myself."

## CHAPTER XLVIII.

### A WIFE FOR GERARD.

URSULA walked back through the darkening fields. She knew herself now to be safe, yet she hung as one trembling in the recoil from the flash across a sudden abyss. *Supposing* she had discovered that these horrible creatures held her in their power? Would she have flung herself down into degradation unspeakable? She hoped not; she trusted not. Yet the oppression of wrong-doing was upon her, the fatal closing of successive links, the terror of the "might have been."

Then every other reflection died away, and one thought only spread large, in falling shadows across the clear blue sky.

How greatly had she wronged Gerard through all the silent years! It was but a single point—this question of Adeline's ruin: it was "no business of Ursula's" —oh, pure sisters of the impure!—yet how deeply had it influenced her womanly heart in all her thoughts of him! She could understand, in her own pride, his haughty shrinking from self-assertion before the bar of her complacency. How many err as he! How few make good their error! She saw things more calmly now than in that ignorant girlhood which seemed to lie so far behind her. Her thoughts dwelt sweetly on the companion of her childhood; his happy, noisy youth, his early manhood, now so steadfast in its slow endurance. And her strong eyes grew dim beneath the dying day.

On the steps of the Manor House a gay party were assembled, laughing and talking, in a bouquet of bright dresses. Helen van Troyen ran forward to meet her.

"We have been waiting to see you," she cried. "I have brought Toddlums—the baby—and also someone I knew would interest you all, Gerard's Colonel from Acheen."

"How delighted Mamma will have been!" said Ursula, a little hypocritically, as she advanced to be introduced to a tall gentleman, all brick-dust and moustache.

"Colonel Vuurmont's descriptions of Gerard's bravery are too charmingly thrilling," said Helen. "Dear Gerard! And so romantic! Tell Mevrouw van Helmont, Colonel, about that bit of brown glove."

"Mevrouw, Mevrouw, that is a kind of a sort of a secret," expostulated the Colonel, looking slightly bored.

"A secret! when half a dozen men saw it produced, and all Kotta Radja knew, and teased him about it afterwards. Nonsense. Ursula, you must know that when Gerard was so terribly wounded—terribly wounded, it appears, and in four different places—they found an old brown kid glove on his breast. Isn't that delicious? I had *hoped* the glove was mine, but Gerard says it wasn't. There, Nurse has let Toddlums upset herself again. Come, Ursula, I can't bear to hear the child scream like that."

The two men remained on the steps. "You must

know, Van Troyen," said the Colonel, "that Helmont maintains there is no love story connected with that glove at all; only it would be a pity to spoil your wife's amusement. He says that the glove saved his life in a duel, through his adversary slipping on it, and that he wore it as a kind of talisman."

"I certainly remember about a duel," replied Willie, "with a foreign officer, who had said, I believe, that Dutch soldiers were wanting in courage."

"Helmont was just the right man to say that to," remarked the Colonel, quietly.

"Ursula, I have got a wife for Gerard at last," said Helen, fondling her baby. "On the whole, I think, she is suitable, though it has cost me a lot of trouble to admit it. But I am growing old, and have a baby, and one learns to see things differently. I have talked to him about it all, and I think he understands."

"Really!" replied Ursula, much interested in Toddlums.

"But men are so contrary! He pretends that he is going to live in the Hague with his mother, and never marry. Gerard never marry? 'Ah, quel dommage d'un si bel homme!' I have explained all about it to aunt. She is rather exacting, but, on the whole, I believe she agrees with me."

"Has this young lady means of her own?" asked Ursula.

"Fie! what a question! The very last I should have expected from you! Yes, the lady has means of her own. She has recently come into a fortune. They will be able to live in some style, as the Baron and Baroness van Helmont should."

"And you think Gerard consents?"

"Oh, yes, I feel sure he will. To begin with, he says he won't, which is always a very good sign. And then there are others. I suppose you have no idea who the lady is?"

Helen looked up sharply, with petulant goodwill, into Ursula's grave face.

"I! No; how should I tell? Do I know her?"

"Oh, yes, better than I ever did. But, really, we must be going; we have missed our train as it is. I was so anxious to tell you about this coming marriage of Gerard's, and to express my admiration of your bravery last week, that, for the first time since her birth, I have neglected Toddlums. Colonel Vuurmont admires you awfully, Ursula. He says he wishes he had had you out in Acheen."

"He had Gerard," replied Ursula, simply.

That evening the young Baroness's "family circle" gathered, as usual, round the shaded lamp. Ursula tried hard to bestow due attention on Tante Louisa's prattle; the Dowager had sunk to sleep over a bundle of letters which she had been laboriously sorting, first according to their writers, and then all over again, according to their dates.

The month's *Victory* lay spread out before Tante Louisa, who was holding forth in Batavo-Carlylese.

"Napoleon was the world's ruler by right of power," said Louisa. "Kings are they who can rule. A hereditary King is a puppet."

"But the other day you sang the praises of heredity," suggested Ursula, politely.

"Did I?  Well, that also was consistent.  We praise things for the good in them; we blame for the bad. There is nothing so consistent as inconsistency."

A tap at the terrace-window awoke the Dowager. The Dominé stood outside with Josine.  Ursula started up in delight, for her father's visits were of the rarest.

The Freule immediately took possession of the pastor, while Josine considerately settled down by the Dowager to tell her of recent successes gained by Sympathetico in arresting mental decline.

"I disagree utterly," broke out the Dominé, as soon as he had heard a few words of Louisa's jargon.  "The world is not ruled by human strength (forsooth!), but by the Power of God.  In big things and little, it is we who make trouble by not marching straight. If only we would do the moment's duty, leaving the responsibility to the Commander-in-Chief!  "To do a great right, do a little wrong!" exclaimed the Dominé, spluttering in his energy.  "It is the worst lie ever invented! It is the curse of a little evil conscientiously done, that wrong must breed wrong for ever.  Satan himself is nearer than a Jesuit to the kingdom of God!"

Suddenly Ursula looked up from her work.  "Is that not putting it rather strongly, papa?" she said.

"It is the simplest of Christ's teachings," cried the excited Dominé.  "It is the deepest conviction of my heart.  Never was good got out of a false start!  To deny that is the confusion of all distinctions, the death of all discipline.  Ursula, would you make of the Lord's army a company of free-shooters?  Right is right; wrong is wrong; shout it out upon the house-tops!  If you don't know, for the moment, *what* is right, ask God to help you. *When* you know, do it. That is all philosophy, and all religion. Sufficient for the day is the duty thereof!"

He had got up pacing the room with rapid stride, and waving his empty sleeve.

"I'm excited, ladies," he said, wiping his forehead. "This afternoon I heard the dying confession of a man who has ruined his whole life and his brother's, by a generous lie told in his youth. It is not to remain a secret; I will tell the story to you some day. Well, Mevrouw, that is a pretty child of Helen van Troyen's!"

"Captain, listen." Ursula followed her father out on to the terrace after he had taken leave. "Do you really mean it all?"

He did not ask what she alluded to, but answered straight: "From the bottom of my heart. You know I mean it. Remember our talk about Gerard. And you, too, mean it. Did you not go down last week, like a soldier's daughter, to face the mob!"

"Papa——," began Ursula.

"Why are the Helmonts going away?" asked Josine's voice behind her. "I shall miss Theodore's mother very much. She is a good, plain, sensible body, and not above taking judicious advice."

"Going away? How do you mean?" asked Ursula.

"Yes, going away. Don't you know? How odd. She told me that Theodore had come in this afternoon after having met the Van Troyens, and had said in his disagreeable way (though she didn't call it that, but I think him very disagreeable), 'Mother, our work here is done; we are going back to Bois-le-Duc.' She couldn't get anything more out of him. He went away and banged the door. So selfish."

"Josine!" called the Dominé on ahead.

"Coming! coming, Roderigue. How odd, Ursula, that you didn't know that."

Ursula stood looking after her father's vanished figure. "To-morrow I shall tell him," she said.


## CHAPTER XLIX.

### FACE TO FACE WITH HERSELF.

SHE stood on the terrace, amid the gloom of the placid, moonless night. The great house gleamed dully white behind her, and the wealth of foliage that embowered it stretched in black masses beyond.

"It is the end," she said, clutching at the flimsy folds about her throat. "What a pitiful little end it is."

Fronting the facts calmly, as was her manner, she knew everything she had striven for to be now fully in her power. At last every enemy was silenced, every danger averted; with the money just inherited she could begin her great work of regenerative charity; in fulfilling her dead husband's ideals she could accomplish her own.

Had she desired greatness for herself, now was the moment to grasp it firmly as it lay in her hand. "No, I have not desired it for myself," she said aloud.

She had done her evil deed for Otto's sake, for the sake of all these Helmonts. She had done it, with the desperate self-persuasion that the wrong she was committing was better than all right. She had taught herself fiercely to believe it so, strengthened again and again in the teeth of growing conviction, by Gerard's recklessness, by Otto's dying entreaty, by her own invigorating failures, dangers, sudden deliverances. She had struggled to believe that God Himself was helping her in this self-appointed mission — the saving of Horstwyk and all its dependencies under her righteous rule.

She knew now that the truth was otherwise. She had known it long, with a gathering clearness that broke in sunlight through the fogs of her own calling up; but now, in the sudden hush of the contest, the falling away of all adverse winds to dead calm, she saw God's reality of right as she had not beheld it before. Right is right. Little wrongs do not bring forth great blessings. Her father, in his simplicity, spoke true.

She herself—what had she called up in the hearts of these people around her, by the sense of the great wrong done to Gerard, but a foolish, fruitless hate, to be bought off now by the vilest of all persuaders—gold? She loathed—suddenly—this filthy popularity she had thought pleasant for the moment. Better, a thousand times better, the frank rebellion against her stern and sterile righteousness, better than *this*. And for her own heart—she knew that her sin had brought her own heart no profit. Far from it. With loathing she remembered Hephzibah and Adeline and Skiff, and all the possibilities of shame. Oh, her father was right, a thousand times. The outcome of evil is evil, the outcome of sin is sin.

She had been resolved ever since the day of Gerard's return to Horstwyk, though she was not aware of her own resolve, to give up the Manor to its rightful lord. Resolved to do it, come what may, leaving the further development of events to Him whose the end will most certainly be, if only the beginning be His.

She would have done it at all costs, but now God, in His mercy, made the duty yet plainer. The moment was come to which she had ever looked forward, when the Manor would be safe in Gerard's hands. He was about to unite himself in marriage to some wealthy woman. He would be able, as Helen had unwittingly pointed out, to fulfil the duties of his position.

So far, so good. She could reason calmly; she could even face the shame of her confession. She could see herself pointed at, hooted by all. She would be punished, she supposed, when the crime got abroad. Even if the Van Helmonts were merciful—as why should they be?—Government punished such criminals as she. She would be sentenced, in open court, to a long period of solitary confinement or of penal servitude, she did not know which, as a common convict. That was inevitable. She stopped for one moment in her rapid walk along the terrace. Pooh, she had judged that issue so many times already! When a citizen commits a crime, the State must attempt to check him. The State punishes crime, and God punishes sin. The two have but little in common. So far, so good.

But now! now! She pressed both hands to her forehead, staring out wildly into the darkness. She loved Gerard. She knew that she loved him. She loved him since his return; but Adeline's confession had opened the floodgates of her heart's admiration for the man she had wronged. She was one of those women who fancy there can be no love without respect; she had taught her own, soul that early lesson. But now she knew that she loved him. She had honoured Otto and dutifully admired him, but this— now at last she recognised it—was love. She loved his manliness, his uprightness, his chivalry; the pale face she herself had discoloured, the form she had wounded, the glory her guilt had called forth. Ay, she even loved the memory of youthful errors, courageously atoned for.

God punishes sin. Perhaps, if she had let all things take their natural course, Gerard might in due time have made her his wife. However that might be, now, at any rate, nothing need have kept them apart. For she knew that Gerard also loved her, in spite of this unwilling marriage to which his womankind were pressing him. And between her and him arose up, for all eternity, the shadow of her crime. She herself must speak the word, crushing down his righteous love into a pool of scorn. .

She sank by the parapet, with her face on the stone, and then nothing disturbed the breathless silence, but one sudden, suddenly arrested moan.

When Ursula came down next morning, there were circles under her eyes. Yet she had slept peacefully enough towards dawn. It must have been the merest accident that Aunt Louisa noticed,—for the first time, she declared,—some faint suggestion of grey about her niece's brown ripple of hair.

"I am going to town on business," said Ursula, "so I shall want the carriage, if you please."

"Dear me, how annoying!" exclaimed Tante Louisa. "I had been wanting to drive across to Mevrouw Noks, and arrange about Tryphena. You're sure you couldn't select another day?"

"Quite sure," answered Ursula, cutting bread. "It is business which can't be put off."

"Well, that's very provoking. But, if you're going to town, you must bring me some floss-silk from the Berlin-woolshop."

"I am going to the Hague," answered Ursula.

"The Hague? Oh, you're sure to be able to match it there. I must give you a bit to take with you." Tante Louisa felt aggrieved, for did she not pay her "pension"?

Ursula, alone in her compartment between Horstwyk and Drum, could not but reflect on her first railway journey with Gerard. "The great of this earth are above the common law." She smiled bitterly at the thought of the error. There may be two social laws for high and humble; there may be even two civic laws for rich and poor—there are no two laws of right and wrong with the Judge of all the Earth.

But at Drum acquaintances got in, and she had to talk of the weather. She said it was very fine, though a little too warm. It was a pity, she said, that the days were growing so short already.

Arrived at the Hague, she thought she had better begin by hunting for Aunt Louisa's silk. She tried

several shops without success.    At last she found herself compelled regretfully to desist.

She hailed a passing tramcar which took her to
Gerard's lodgings.   As she lifted an unfaltering hand
to the bell, the door was suddenly drawn back, and
Gerard himself appeared, coming out.   Both of them
started aside for the moment.

"You here?" exclaimed the Baron.    "We very
nearly missed each other.   I had no idea you were
coming."

"Nor had I," she replied, "till I came.   I want to
speak to you, Gerard."

"Yes," he assented, without inviting her to enter.
"Can I walk on with you?   I am due at the Ministry
in half an hour.   You have connections, if I remember
right, in the Hague?"

"I was coming to you," she answered.   "Let me
go into your room for a moment.   I shall not keep
you."

Reluctantly he led the way.

The thud of the closing door crashed down upon
her heart; in the sudden stillness and shutting-out she
realised that the crisis was come: her courage sank.
And, while leaning against some unnoticed support, she
was angry with the pride within her which could not as
much as ask for a glass of water.   The room swam past
her eyes in a swift recognition of many familiar objects
—mementoes of her child-life with the owner—amongst
a recent glitter of gaudy trophies and gleaming swords.
As he threw back his coat she noticed, with dull indifference, that he was dressed for some Ministerial mid-
day reception.   Somehow, she connected this fact with

his life in society, his search for a suitable wife. She
sank into a large armchair, shielding her brow for one
instant with both hands.

Gerard waited, standing by his writing-table. The
room seemed very subdued after the glare of the noisy
street.

Presently she lifted her still, white face—as a vessel
might right herself, suddenly becalmed.

"Gerard," she said, "I have come to tell you something I have long been wanting to tell you; but I didn't
tell you, and that makes it all the worse. I have
wronged you very cruelly."

She rose and remained standing, before his stern
attitude grown suddenly rigid, his crossed arms and
relentlessly downcast gaze.

"I am not come to ask forgiveness," she went on,
hurriedly. "I am come to make confession and then
to leave you. There is nothing to be done but to confess. Gerard, when Otto died, and Baby, it all depended,
you remember, upon the question who died first. I said
that it was Otto who died, and I inherited the property
from Baby."

She paused with a gasp. He neither spoke nor
moved.

"It was Baby who died before Otto, Gerard, and
you were Otto's heir."

A faint flush crept over Gerard's firm-set cheeks.
It was the only proof that he had understood.

"That is all I have to say," she went on, in the
silence closing round her. "But I wanted to say it to
you first before repeating it to strangers."

Then, suddenly, amid that deepening stillness, she

felt that she must get away, must escape, and she hurried towards the door.

"Ursula!" said Gerard's voice behind her, quite gently.

She turned; he had lifted his eyes, and his steadfast gaze met hers.

"Have you really nothing to say?" he continued. "No explanation? No extenuation of such conduct? *No* excuse?"

She drew herself up. "What would be the use of all that?" she answered, coldly. "Who listens to a criminal's perversions? I have told you now, and you know."

"I knew before," he said.

When the words had struck her ear, an instant of expectation intervened. Then she caught at the wall beside her, saw him, as she did so, check a futile impulse to spring forward, and once more stood outwardly calm.

"I learnt the news some weeks ago," he continued. "On the night before the battle, as it happened. I got a letter from—someone who knew."

"From Hephzibah," said Ursula. "But then—when you came back—why——"

"When I came back I told her to await my good pleasure. I myself was waiting for this moment, Ursula. God only knows *how* I have waited for it, hoped for it——" He broke off.

"Then be thankful it has come," she answered, in the bitterness of her righteous abandonment.

"Yes, it has come. And now there is nothing else to say."

"No, there is nothing else to say."

She fancied she caught a strange flicker in his firmly fixed eyes.

"And of what use will the Manor House be to a poor beggar like myself?" he went on. "You had much better have kept it, you, who are rich."

She flushed scarlet under the taunt.

"May I go?" she asked, almost meekly, under the pain at her heart. "You will do what you like with the Manor. Perhaps you will sell it. Though Helen Van Troyen tells me you are going to marry a rich wife of her choosing—and your own."

"Did Helen Van Troyen tell you that?" he asked, uncrossing his arms, and the brightness of his nature seemed to come flowing back from all sides.

"Yes, but do not be afraid. She mentioned no names. Besides, it is no business of mine. I do not know whom she means."

"I am sorry it is no business of yours," replied Gerard, coming boldly forward, "for, Ursula, she means yourself."

"She—she——" stammered Ursula.

"And so do I." Very quietly he put his arm around her, and drew down the tired head upon his breast. "We have both of us suffered quite enough," he said.

The tears came swelling across her eyes.

"Through my fault," she whispered—"my fault."

"Let *me* find the criminal's extenuations, Ursula. Do you really think, you poor, noble creature, that I do not understand?"

"I must confess to my father," she continued in the

same tremulous whisper.    "To my father, and the world."

"To your father, if you will.    But the world has not been injured by anything you have done, and you owe it no reparation.    It is not our function to supply the world with the empty scandals it delights in.    Suffering is a holy but a very awful thing.    We will have no more superfluous suffering, Ursula."

"It shall all be as you wish," she humbly answered, her head at rest upon his shoulder.    She closed her eyes.    "Gerard, I am not afraid of them.    I was never afraid of them.    But from the very first, I think, I was afraid of God."

"God be thanked for it," said Gerard, softly.    And a flood of sunlight, falling leisurely around them, lighted into sudden brilliance the cross upon his breast.

**THE END.**

www.ingramcontent.com/pod-product-compliance
Lightning Source LLC
Chambersburg PA
CBHW060610030726
47498CB00005B/1617